POSITIONED
TO DIE

Denise Osborne

BERKLEY PRIME CRIME, NEW YORK

POSITIONED TO DIE

A Berkley Prime Crime Book / published by arrangement with the author

PRINTING HISTORY
Berkley Prime Crime mass-market edition / July 2002

Copyright © 2002 by Denise Osborne.
Cover art by Yan Nascimbine.
Cover design by Pamela Jaber.

Visit our website at
www.penguinputnam.com

ISBN: 0-425-18547-8

Berkley Prime Crime Books are published
by The Berkley Publishing Group,
a division of Penguin Putnam Inc.,
375 Hudson Street, New York, New York 10014.
The name BERKLEY PRIME CRIME and the BERKLEY PRIME CRIME
design are trademarks belonging to Penguin Putnam Inc.

PRINTED IN THE UNITED STATES OF AMERICA

10 9 8 7 6 5 4 3 2 1

Feng Shui Mysteries by Denise Osborne

A DEADLY ARRANGEMENT
POSITIONED TO DIE

Acknowledgments

⊛

The author wishes to thank the following feng shui practitioners for their continual inspiration and both direct and indirect influence on the material herein: Professor Lin Yun, feng shui master and spiritual leader of the Black Sect Tantric Buddhist Feng Shui School; Cathleen Rickard, owner/practitioner, Feng Shui Wisdom; Madhu Brodkey, owner/consultant, Feng Shui Reflections; and Nancy SantoPietro, consultant/educator and author of *Feng Shui: Harmony by Design*.

For support and encouragement during the process of writing this book, special thanks to my parents, Alberta and Harrison Barker, and to my sister, Diane Barker.

The author is deeply grateful to agent Don Gastwirth for his dedication and belief in the work, and Berkley editor Samantha Mandor for fine-tuning the Feng Shui Mysteries. Many thanks to the staff at Berkley Prime Crime for making the author's work look good. Special thanks to Tom Colgan.

For support, laughs, high spirits, and additional material, the author is grateful to Signe Nelson, Dana Richmond,

Lorraine Kessler, Dolores Osborne, Phillip Osborne, Steve Osborne, Judy Osborne, Beverly Hogg, Marilyn and Mike Fitzgerald, Harriett Manclark, Kathryn and Tony Gualtieri, Dianne Day, Mara Wallis, Richard Recker, Cinnamon Stillwell, Charlotte Morrison, Kevin Bransfield, Sue Marshall, and the great ladies of the Capitola Women of Mystery book club.

Without the computer skills and patience of Chris Osborne, the author would still be using stone tablets, nor would the Feng Shui Mysteries have a fine home on the web at www.deniseosbornemysteries.com.

While the book is a work of fiction and all characters creations of an active imagination, all material concerning the practice of feng shui is, to the best of the author's knowledge, factual.

Feng shui. *This is an ancient Chinese system for arranging rooms by placing mirrors, screens, fountains, and furniture to balance the forces of yin and yang and maximize harmony with nature. Western companies such as Chase Manhattan, Citibank, and Morgan Guaranty Trust and innumerable organizations in the East employ feng shui consultants to create brain-nourishing environments.*

—Michael Gelb
How To Think Like Leonardo da Vinci

Feng shui helps us to understand that our homes are direct extensions of ourselves; they are mirrors reflecting who we are.

—Gina Lazenby
The Feng Shui House Book

THE BAGUA

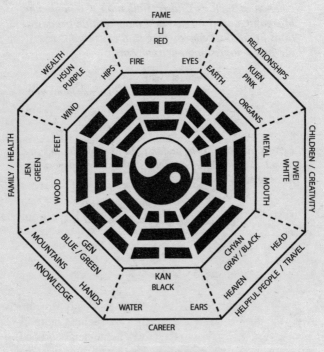

FAME
LI
RED
FIRE   EYES

RELATIONSHIPS
KUEN
PINK
ORGANS

WEALTH
HSUN
PURPLE
WIND
HIPS
EARTH

METAL

CHILDREN / CREATIVITY
DWEI
WHITE
MOUTH

FAMILY / HEALTH
JEN
GREEN
FEET
WOOD

GEN
BLUE / GREEN

CHYAN
GRAY / BLACK

HEAD

HELPFUL PEOPLE / TRAVEL

MOUNTAINS

KAN
BLACK

HEAVEN

KNOWLEDGE
HANDS
WATER   EARS

CAREER

← THE MOUTH OF CH'I →

Prologue

"THE murder house," Kayla Rudd announced grimly. She and her passenger, Salome Waterhouse, exchanged glances, then Kayla switched off the red '84 Chrysler. After a couple of ticks and pings, the engine went dead quiet. Outside, silence spread like a swiftly growing vine, a living thing that had already suffocated the neighborhood and now threatened the unwelcome visitors.

Kayla sniffled and gurgled. On the way over, while turning up the air-conditioning, she'd complained of allergies that left her hating spring. Tuning out Kayla's swampy breathing, Salome stared out the window concentrating on the house, composing a description beyond "murder house."

From the outside, the two-story clapboard structure with the peeling paint and weedy yard seemed more innocent than guilty, kin to the others in the neighborhood, all of them victims of neglect. There was, however, one distinguishing characteristic that none of the other houses could boast: a neat, white-and-blue FOR SALE sign.

The bunch of keys with a metal nameplate—Kayla's

Keys—clattered and jangled from ignition to shoulder bag, there to join notebooks, a clipboard, a packet of tissues, and other paraphernalia carried by the reporter/ real estate agent/wife of the chief of police/mother of two teenage boys. According to Kayla, most locals were "multitaskers." That was the way in small towns.

"Now, you said you just want to walk around outside first? Take pictures?"

"Yes, thanks." Salome pulled a pen and notebook and a small camera from her own purse and slipped them into the pockets of her uniform. The full-length, long-sleeved black garment with a stiff Chinese collar had silk frogs securing the tight bodice and gave her the appearance of a priest, of someone engaged in spiritual pursuits. Kayla said she'd heard about feng shui both through newspaper and real estate work, even acknowledging that it was known in the West as the Chinese art of placement. But Salome was her first practitioner and she wasn't quite certain how to maintain control—control being central to the life of a multitasker.

"Might want to put on sunglasses, too," Kayla said. Her own had been on since they left the offices of the *Willard Beacon*/Rudd Realty, maybe worn in the hope that no one would recognize her as she chauffeured this middle-aged stranger dressed in black through town. Of course, given her allergies, the sunglasses could simply be protecting her eyes. "Glare off the water'll blind you."

"Water?"

" 'Dillo creek out back. That's short for armadillo. Texas's state critter."

"Ah."

"What's yours?" Kayla asked, curiosity sounding genuine.

"A bear. A California golden bear."

"Really? You'd think it would be a sea lion or something."

Salome started to roll up the window wondering what Washington, D.C., her second home and destination, would have as a state "critter" if the District ever did receive statehood and the residents their long-overdue representation. Would a politician qualify as a "critter"? There were certainly enough species and phylums and whatnot from which to choose.

"Leave the window down. Car'll get too hot."

"What about our purses?"

"No one'll bother 'em."

Salome looked over at Kayla. "Two murders were committed in that house."

"Yeah, by a drifter. I know most people around here and everybody sure as hell knows me." Sweat beaded her upper lip and forehead, threatening the beige-pink foundation.

"Well, if you don't mind, I'd rather leave my purse in the trunk."

"Fine!" From the yawning mouth of her shoulder bag, Kayla plucked a tape recorder that resembled a small silvery-coated tooth, grabbed the keys, and turned on the ignition. Then she reached across Salome's lap to open the glove box and pressed a button inside. Salome heard a hollow snap as the trunk's hood was released. Kayla gave Salome a stiff smile, the kind that basically polite people muster when they feel they've been insulted, and one that accessorized Kayla's exaggerated movements.

With a loud rattle the keys went back in the bag.

Outside the car, Kayla stayed by the door to smooth her pale-blue shirtwaist dress, pat her short blonde hair, and blot her makeup in the side view mirror, studiously ignoring the trunk while Salome secured her purse inside.

On this drab street, the red car stood out like an apple in a slagheap. Salome looked around, seeing movement behind curtains in the neighboring houses. The yards and porches were devoid of toys or bikes or any evidence of children. Several houses sported old-fashioned porch swings; others had plastic chairs, some white, some green.

"And no one saw anything?"

"That's right," Kayla said.

"No one heard anything?"

"Right again."

"On a warm fall evening. *Two* warm fall evenings."

"Uh-huh."

Then, with her attention fully on the murder house, Salome moved to the cracked sidewalk. Kayla joined her as she faced the house and began jotting notes.

Kayla pointed at the notebook. "That Chinese?"

"Gregg shorthand."

"Um."

After a moment, Salome exchanged the notebook for the camera. She snapped pictures of the bowed and cracked walkway bisecting the yard currently green with abundant spring weeds but probably parched and bristly in summer, the lopsided steps leading to the porch, the torn and rusty screen door, and the grimy front windows. The exterior was weathered to a dull gray with leprous patches of chalky-looking paint. Kayla's wheezing provided a somewhat annoying but, given the state of the house, appropriate sound track.

Salome would have preferred to be on her own but could hardly expect to be given a key and allowed to poke around someone's private residence. Thanks to Jack Genet, Salome's brother-in-law, Kayla Rudd had agreed to accommodate such an unusual request—even though Salome wasn't even interested in buying. While continuing to snap pictures, her thoughts jumped to the previous night. . . .

". . . shit fire, Willie," Jack Genet had blurted at the dinner table after Salome mentioned her latest project. "Get on the horn to Clyde and Kayla."

Never without her cell phone, Salome's sister, Willow, took the tiny device out of the breast pocket of her denim work shirt. "What's the number?" Willow leaned across the table and said to Salome, "Clyde's chief of police."

"Here, give me that." Jack plucked the phone from his wife's hand. Then he leaned back in his chair like the proud and arrogant but still charming rancher he was and talked to Willard's top law-enforcement officer, punctuating sentences with winks at Salome.

"Hey, look, my sister-in-law's visitin' from Cali-for-niay. She's what they call a feng shui practitioner."

Wink.

Salome winked back, pleased that he'd pronounced it correctly. *Fung shway.*

"Has to do with moving furniture around to make ever'body content and happy."

Wink.

Out of the corner of his mouth, Jack whispered, "Clyde says it sounds a helluva lot safer than charge cards."

Salome smiled. She figured Clyde was always agreeable whenever Jack called. "Anyway, ol' buddy, she's studyin' houses where murders been done. Seeing if there's something that brings out the meanness in people; makes 'em want to haul off and kill somebody."

Wink. More like a twitch now.

"Yeah, I know it's a great idea. 'S why I called you. Figured Kayla'd want to do a story for the *Beacon.* She could take her on over to the Twomey place. I understand Dwayne's outta town but Kayla's got permission to go in and show the house, right?" A beat. "Good. How's tomorra mornin' sound?"

Apparently it sounded good. " 'Preciate it, Clyde. Her name's Sally Waterhouse."

Salome's smile disappeared.

"We'll drop her off at Kayla's office at ten." He paused. "No, Willie and me got business in Houston so Sally'll be on her own. Tell Kayla to treat her right, hear? That's ten sharp. Lunch'll be on me at the club."

Jack passed the phone to Willow, his eyes on Salome, and dropped the good old boy banter. "The God-fearin' folk hereabouts wouldn't take kindly to a person whose namesake had John the Baptist decapitated. Know what I'm sayin . . . Sally?"

Salome lowered the camera and looked at Kayla, thinking she'd best do something to release the tension. "May I let you in on a little secret?"

Kayla appeared surprised.

"You see, this is new to me—not feng shui, of course, I've been involved with it for over a decade, the past six years as a professional. What I'm talking about is studying houses in which murder has been committed." She nodded at the house ahead of them.

Pleased to be included in the confidence, Kayla smiled and said, "I was wondering how you got involved in such a, well, unusual pursuit. I thought feng shui was only about moving furniture and that kind of thing."

"Believe me, there's much more to it. But anyway, last year there was a murder on a property I own in California. I became involved with the investigation," she said, not adding that her involvement included being a suspect. "And before I got into feng shui, I worked for a mystery writer researching crime, murder in particular." Here again she left out a pertinent detail: that she'd also been married to the author.

"Anyway, it started me wondering if so-called murder houses had anything in common; and if I found similarities maybe I could do something—come up with a feng shui cure—to prevent future acts of violence. You understand?"

"Uh, sure."

"I realize you were roped into this and I want you to know I appreciate your help."

"Oh, no problem," Kayla said. "Certainly breaks up the routine. You just do whatever you have to. I'll try not to get in the way or interrupt too much, but you do realize I want to write a story. I've been kind of wondering how to go about things myself; what sort of questions to ask and all. If I seem a little hesitant, it's just that I've never been around anyone, uh, quite like you."

"Why don't we just play it by ear—help each other."

"Sounds good to me," Kayla said. "So where to?"

"Let's head around back," Salome said. "Would you mind filling me in on a few more details? How about the victims?"

As they moved toward the shade at the side of the house, Kayla began.

"First one was a woman in her late twenties. Hadn't been in town long and worked as a waitress." She stopped for a moment, putting her thoughts in order.

"Just a couple weeks after her death, a male this time was murdered. Some folks thought he might have killed the woman. He was a musician. About Dwayne's age—mid-thirties. Played guitar at one of the bars where the young people hang out. His alibi checked out though. He'd been living at the motel, which, I'm sorry to say, is a real dump. He didn't mind moving into a room where someone died."

"So this was a boardinghouse?"

"Just the downstairs. Dwayne Twomey owns the place and lives upstairs. He's gone to Galveston looking for a boat to buy. Can't say I blame him for wanting to sell the place and move on."

"What's he like? How long has he owned the house?"

"Oh gosh, Dwayne moved back to town when his parents died, what? Ten years ago? They left him the house and a little money. He spruced up the place—though you wouldn't believe it now. Couple years ago, he had the interior remodeled and fitted out so he could rent rooms. He's single and young for this neighborhood. His tenants don't stay long. But, of course, they're mainly students from the junior college."

When they reached the back, Salome stopped. "Good heavens! What happened here?"

"Kids. Sometimes they have a little too much beer and come down here to make trouble."

Salome frowned at the forlorn sight: boarded windows looking like sightless eyes, the broken glass below like frozen tears. Past the house, the hard scrabble ground, dotted here and there by old tree stumps, extended for about twenty feet to a muddy creek. Kayla had been right about needing sunglasses. Sunlight flared off the surface of the water.

"In feng shui, water represents money and opportunity," Salome said, looking at the sluggish stream. "For the record, the simplest translation of feng shui is wind and water. There's a more elaborate, poetic version that includes the relationship of wind and water. Anyway, this creek hardly looks up to its potential."

Kayla put her hands on her hips and shook her head. "And it's not likely to, either. Quite a while back, during a drought, the water was diverted onto your brother-in-law's land."

"Was that about the time this area started deteriorating?"

Kayla's mouth dropped open. "I could sure check. But

I bet that's right. Now, isn't that something!"

"And the trees?"

"Nothing feng shui about that. Trees were cut down a long time ago for firewood. Gets cold in the winter around here. Thank God it's not for long, though."

"Remove those stumps and you could have a nice garden back here," Salome observed and started snapping pictures again, finishing up at a patch of freshly turned soil sporting about a dozen sprouts at the upper right-hand corner of the property. "Those tomato plants seem to be doing well."

"Dwayne manages to grow a decent crop every year. Shares with the neighbors. Say, mention of a garden would be a good selling point."

Salome jotted notes of her impressions.

They started back, now around the other side of the house. From a neighbor's open window she could faintly hear a country-and-western tune, which brought some relief to the stifling silence.

"Your husband was in charge of the investigation?"

"Oh, yeah." She switched off the tape recorder momentarily. "Just between you and me? He didn't like it one bit. Clyde's *father* was police chief last time there was a murder in Willard. And to have *two* within a couple weeks of each other . . ."

"And in the same house," Salome added. "What about Dwayne?"

"What about him?"

"Was he a suspect?"

"Heavens, no! He's a lamb."

"Where was he?"

"Both times he was in bed asleep. Can you imagine? Something like that going on? Gives me the creeps just thinking about it."

"It didn't bother him to stay in the house?"

Kayla was taken aback. "Well, he is trying to sell. Thing is, he couldn't afford to go anyplace else. The house is all he's got."

"Does he work?"

"Sure. Does odd jobs. Helps people in the neighborhood. They surely don't want him to go."

Once they stood at the front door, Kayla brightened. "Well, here we are."

The screen door shrieked on rusty hinges as she pulled it open to lean against her back as she inserted the key in the front door. Salome noted that the etched oval of glass above the knob could do with a cleaning. There was also a mail slot that needed polishing.

"Now, Dwayne's real proud of his entry. So, you just wait a sec. I don't want to be showing the house on completely false pretenses. Thing is, I'll have to tell him you were looking for a place here in Willard. My story'll be a feature on feng shui and you being Willow's sister and all . . ." She trailed off as she stepped inside, easing the screen door behind her.

Salome called out, "Just so you're not startled or anything, I'll be coming in with my eyes closed. And I need a minute to clear my mind. Okay?" Salome dropped the notebook and pen in her pocket. She held her hands at waist level, palms up, the left above the right, the thumbs barely touching and, in a low voice began to chant, *"Om ma ni pad me om . . ."*

"Whenever you're ready," Kayla said.

At the conclusion of the ninth repetition, Salome stepped inside. She closed the door behind her.

Kayla gave her an odd look while carrying a stack of mail to a long table in the foyer. Then she began murmuring into the tape recorder.

By keeping her eyes closed, Salome could better "see" or interpret the energy inside. From her solar plexus on up, she registered erratic, abrupt, and jagged vibrations. At floor level it was as if she'd entered a void. She wondered vaguely if the all the energy on the first floor had clung to the second murder victim as he was carried from the house. She opened her eyes. "Jesus," she whispered.

"What's the matter?" Kayla sputtered, her voice pitched with alarm.

Salome held up her hand for silence, then took a deep breath to steady herself. She looked around the shadowy foyer.

"Uh, light's burned out." Kayla pointed to a switch by the door then looked up at a naked bulb in the ceiling.

Salome turned and opened the front door, which brought in some light and fresh air. She retrieved the notebook and pen and made a sketch of the area.

Like arms embracing the wide foyer, two curved iron staircases lead to the second-floor landing. Behind the landing was a stark, dingy wall, and in the middle there was a narrow door and nothing else, not even a picture or a plant.

Straight ahead a hallway extended all the way to the back door. From where she stood, Salome could see chinks of light shooting between the narrow boards nailed to the window in the back door.

"You might want to record this," Salome said and moved further into the room. "On the most fundamental level, feng shui practitioners are concerned with the manipulation of energy, which we call *ch'i*." She stopped and spelled the word. "The front door is known as the mouth of ch'i. The idea is to have the ch'i gently meander through the house. But here, the ch'i rushes from the front door and, unobstructed, right down the hall and out the back. If I were here for a consultation, I'd suggest hanging a faceted crystal in the hallway." In this house, she mused, that would amount to putting a Band-Aid on a gunshot wound.

Then she indicated both staircases. "Stairs have special problems. Let's just say good ch'i must be coaxed upward. Something has to attract it. You with me?"

"Sure. Ch'i."

"Now, a split staircase works well in a large public building as it's able to accommodate more people than just a single set of stairs would do."

"Dwayne's so proud of these stairs. When he put them in, I guess he thought they gave the place class, if you know what I mean."

"Yes, a split staircase can look elegant. Notice the open spaces between the risers. Even if the ch'i reaches the stairs, it can escape through those spaces. Plants will help if they're placed beneath the stairs. Their lively energy will float upward."

"So how do you attract the ch'i?" Kayla asked, her eyes full of interest.

"First, give the stairs a good scrubbing," she said. "Place a potted plant at the base of each staircase. Plants both attract and enliven ch'i. Install a light on each wall facing the landing to illuminate the stairs and coax the ch'i up to the second floor. Hang mirrors opposite the light. The mirrors will reflect the light and give the illusion of greater, less-confining space, which in turn will lift the ch'i. As is, both stairways are murky and the energy stagnant." She turned to Kayla. "While we're on the subject, can you show me the upstairs?"

"Sure, I've got the key."

Kayla walked gingerly up the stairs as if concerned about stepping on ch'i. Following behind her, Salome wondered if she should mention *sha*—bad ch'i—a killing, destructive energy that most commonly accumulated around clutter and in dirty and dimly lit areas of a residence. The house had already revealed disturbing elements, and barely into the tour, Kayla was exhibiting signs of unease. Salome decided to be silent until she could point out a positive aspect.

Inside Dwayne Twomey's apartment they were met by another long hall, both walls covered in mirrored tiles. Straight ahead was the living room with a picture window, still intact, and a bookshelf beneath it. Once out of the hallway, they moved to the right a few paces, then entered the kitchen. There was a gas stove, then a small counter, and then a new refrigerator pressed in the apartment's top right corner. Salome opened the refrigerator. The interior was clean and smelled fresh. Dwayne Twomey wasn't the sort of bachelor who let anything that wasn't already green become so and he stocked expensive gourmet condiments. In the freezer, costly cuts of meat were neatly labeled in plastic bags.

The gas stove had four burners and a clean oven and broiler. Pots and pans were neatly stacked in the lower cupboards, canned goods, spices, and dishes in the upper cupboards. Salome pulled out a large dinner plate with red chilies on a blue background. Turning it over, she noted that it had been made in Mexico.

"Nice to see a bachelor with a real set of dishes, not just the odd plastic plate. I've got one client," she added with a smile, "who eats off his old Boy Scout kit. You'd never guess where he lives."

"In a teepee?"

"Penthouse apartment overlooking San Francisco Bay."

"You never know about people, do you?"

"Amen to that." Salome leaned against the stove and faced Kayla.

"In feng shui, the stove symbolizes prosperity. It needs to be kept spotless and the more burners, the better. I always suggest that a client hang a mirror behind the stove as it figuratively doubles the number of burners; hence increasing prosperity."

A porcelain sink was positioned beneath a window with a yellow curtain covered in baby chicks, material more appropriate in a nursery. Nonetheless, it added a cheery detail to the kitchen, so far the most pleasant room she'd seen.

Across from the kitchen was a bathroom with a claw-foot tub and makeshift shower, all surrounded by a clean, opaque plastic shower curtain. The door opened onto the toilet. Both the lid and seat were up. Salome squelched the urge to lower them.

"One way to prevent finances from draining away is always keep the toilet seat and lid down."

"I bet you rarely see *that*," Kayla remarked. "Especially in a bachelor's apartment." Then she added, "Hell, I live with three men."

"Money is the magic word, Kayla. You'd be surprised how quickly men can be trained when money's part of the equation."

The living room was furnished with a shabby couch and two faded overstuffed chairs. The TV was set up in the top left corner. A metal TV tray leaned against the wall underneath a print of a fishing scene. The books in the bookshelf were paperback novels; a couple, she noted, were in Spanish.

The bedroom was off the living room to the left of the hall. Like the rest of the apartment, it was clean enough (though hardly up to Salome's standards) and neat, the furnishings old and worn.

"At least Dwayne didn't have to buy furniture," Kayla said brightly. "All of this belonged to his parents."

"Really? Keep in mind, there is what we call ancestor ch'i, the energy from the past. Sometimes it's better to get rid of a hand-me-down, especially if it belonged to someone you didn't get along with. As an example, another client of mine had difficult relationships with men. She had a gorgeous bedroom suite she'd inherited from her grandparents. While talking to her, I learned that she'd hated her grandfather as he used to beat her grandmother. Over the years, that negative energy accumulated and, on a subconscious level, she picked up on it when she was in the bed. After our consultation, she sold the bedroom suite. Almost immediately, she met a really nice guy and they've been together over two years now.

"Same thing applies to buying secondhand. Best thing to do is really clean an item and make any small repairs before you put it in your house."

"And I'm a garage sale junkie!"

Salome now had to squelch another urge, this one to snoop in the tall chest of drawers, under the twin bed, and in the nightstand.

"Mind if I look in the closet?"

"Gosh, Sally, I don't know—"

"A prospective buyer would want to know the amount of closet space available."

"Well, since you put it that way," she said with a nervous laugh.

Dwayne Twomey's wardrobe was as tepid as his quarters but did reveal that he was a big man and one who kept his clothes in good order.

"Dwayne always dresses nicely," Kayla remarked.

Salome glanced down at the shoes with run-down soles. "Looks like you could sail the ocean blue in one of those. What is he, about six-four? Weighs maybe two-fifty?"

"You're a regular Sherlock Holmes, aren't you?" Kayla said slowly, now actually looking spooked.

On the way out, Salome stopped and picked up one of

about a half dozen framed photographs from the top of the chest of drawers. It featured an older couple sitting on what looked like the living room sofa but in a different room.

"Dwayne's parents?"

"Yes."

"How did they die?"

Kayla cleared her throat. "They were attacked while on a vacation with Dwayne in Mexico. Dwayne managed to escape, but Ruth and J. T. were dragged off. Never seen again."

Then Kayla literally bolted out of the apartment.

THERE WERE TWO APARTMENTS ON THE first floor, one on each side of the hall. The tenants, Kayla said, shared the bath and the kitchen, both of which were located at the back of the house; the kitchen in the far right corner, the bathroom in the far left, the back door between the two.

Both apartments were painted white. The apartment on the left—as one entered the house and just below Dwayne's own bedroom—had a bricked-in fireplace and two rooms separated by a cheap plasterboard partition that didn't fully reach the ceiling. More of the same mirrored tiles used in Twomey's hallway had been affixed to the lower half of the partition, suggesting he'd run out of tiles before he ran out of space to cover. The apartment on the right hadn't been sectioned and consisted of one long room. In both apartments, a single window provided minor variations of the same view of the neighboring houses.

"Another item of note," Salome said, "the doors to each of these apartments open on the foot of the bed. This is bad feng shui. You see, to the Chinese, this symbolizes death as when a person dies, they leave the house feet first."

By the stricken look on Kayla's face, Salome wondered if there was a bed in Kayla's house positioned thusly.

Salome snapped more pictures. One thing did stand out. The bed in the left apartment was made whereas the bed in the right consisted of a naked mattress on a set of springs. The dust beneath the unmade bed was thick as a carpet, indicating that the room hadn't been used in some time.

They returned to the foyer. "So, it was determined that a stranger murdered both victims?"

"That's right. Dwayne's just not the killing type. Lot of people around here depend on him. He runs their errands." Then she added with a laugh, "Cuts the grass for those who've got some. Like I said, he does odd jobs."

"Where were the bodies found?"

"In bed. Heads bashed in, probably with a baseball bat. The killer took it with him."

"You mean, it hasn't been found."

"No, I mean just what I said. The killer took it with him."

"And both were murdered in the apartment on the left," Salome commented more than asked.

Kayla licked her lips. "Uh, yeah, the one on the left."

"Frankly, Kayla, the whole house would benefit from a good professional cleaning. The way it looks now, I think the only sort of buyer you'll get is someone who just wants the land and would simply tear down the house."

"Then we shouldn't waste money on cleaning." Kayla checked her watch. "If that doesn't beat all—we've been here almost an hour already! You hungry?"

"I suppose I could eat. Will Jack's club be open?"

"That would be the Petroleum Club," Kayla said with certain disdain possibly birthed in envy. "Even here in Willard we got one. Though it hardly compares to what you'll find in Houston. But yeah, we can have a cup of coffee 'til they start serving." She hesitated, then added softly, "Let's just get out of here."

Once outside, Kayla perked. Even her hair seemed to regain its bounce.

"The murders aside, is there something else about the house that upsets you?" Salome asked.

Kayla rubbed the back of her neck. "Oh, I don't know." She looked around the forlorn neighborhood. "Back in the fifties when I was growin' up, this was the best part of town. At Halloween my dad used to drive us kids over to trick or treat." She nodded toward the houses. "Always handed out the best candy. We'd come over at Christmas, too, to see the lights.

"Thing is, in small towns, neighborhoods like this suffer a slow death. Now, if this was Houston, the whole place woulda been torn down and you'd be seeing all new houses."

Salome did some simple math. "Was Dwayne a late-life baby?"

"Why, yes. I believe Ruth was in her forties when she had him."

"I would like copies of the news stories about the murders. There'll be details that can help as I put together the case study."

"No problem. I wrote them after all."

LATER THAT AFTERNOON, KAYLA DROPPED her off at Willow and Jack's. His new Mercedes was parked on the curved drive in front of the ranch-style house indicating they'd returned from Houston.

"This has been great," Kayla said, the sweet scent of bourbon on her breath more than likely responsible for the declaration. Lunch had more than made up for the unpleasant tour of the Twomey house. "Now when you're all done, you be sure and email me a report, hear?" She waved her hand out the window. "Just don't mention anything that might embarrass Clyde."

Clutching the file of news clippings, Salome watched Kayla's car disappear in a cloud of Texas dust, considering a title for the case study. Until something else came to mind, she'd stick with Kayla's reference. After all, it was appropriate. *The Murder House.*

Chapter 1

☯

Georgetown, Washington, D.C.

SALOME Waterhouse gripped the metal shaft of the umbrella, the vivid-yellow canopy sheltering her from the rain but not from the torrent of feelings unleashed by both what she saw and what she *didn't* see at the end of the cul-de-sac.

At the moment, her umbrella provided the only bright spot on the street. The antique Federalist houses, old elm trees, uneven brick paving, and parked cars simply blended into the drab gray day as if they were distorted elements in a smeared watercolor.

She turned and spit—a feng shui trick to relieve tension—wondering who could have done such a thing, though the answer was obvious. The new tenant. Better to ask *why* they'd chosen to rip out the late Isabelle Malabar's prize rosebushes. But even that interrogatory had a clear answer: parking for the maroon Jaguar S-type sedan. No, what she really wanted to know was *what sort of person* would destroy a garden of beautiful, aromatic roses just so they could park their car off the street.

The air reeked of the acrid, oily smell of asphalt, suggesting the work—no, the crime—had been carried out recently, probably within the last few days. Rose petals provided additional evidence. Some were huddled in corners next to the stoops of the nearby houses, some floated in the rain-filled gutters, and still others not yet washed away were crushed on the sidewalk, their deep-red color leaving the impression of bloodstains.

Certainly Georgetown had a chronic parking problem. Some residents converted their carriage houses, old servants' quarters, or all or part of their basements into garages, which, if they didn't keep for themselves, they rented out. A few iconoclasts proudly disdained car ownership altogether. Most residents though, rich and semi-rich alike, parked on the street. Along with her neighbors, Salome had been renting a space in Isabelle's carriage house since she'd moved into the Close.

She became aware of music filtering from a partially opened second-story window of the manor house and recognized "O Fortuna" from Orloff's *Carmina Burana*. For an instant she thought it was being played for her benefit. Indeed, the music provided an ominous accompaniment to the feelings of foreboding that began when she exited the taxi not five minutes ago. Maybe someone in the house had watched as she dropped off her bags then quickly covered the thirty yards between their respective houses. If that someone had been Isabelle, she would have come outside and, with clippers in hand, cut a homecoming bouquet for Salome.

But Isabelle had been dead nearly six months now, passing on last October, just before Salome left for her winter home on the central coast of California. Isabelle's will must have sped through probate. Most likely a relative had inherited the property, though certainly not Isabelle's love for roses. These old houses were usually passed down from one generation to the other. Then again, maybe the house had been sold, the new owner having no connection to Isabelle whatsoever.

For a few minutes Salome tried to recall relatives of Isabelle she'd met during the six years they'd been neighbors. Her thoughts were interrupted by footsteps coming up behind her.

Salome spun around.

"Salome! Welcome home!"

"Fee!" Pleasure replaced distress as she greeted her next-door neighbor, Fiona Cockburn. "You're looking well," Salome declared, raising the umbrella. Fiona ducked underneath, closing her own smaller version.

"Had my walk for the day," Fiona announced with the pride of someone who hates exercise. Coils of artificially enhanced black hair sprang from beneath a head-hugging watch cap that matched Fiona's navy pea coat. Add the Doc Martens and jeans and she looked like an older student or a small but feisty longshoreman. In fact, she was a documentary filmmaker.

"What took you so long? I was beginning to think you weren't coming back."

Salome told her how she stayed on to run Otter Haven, the twelve-acre seaside resort that had been in the Waterhouse family for nearly a century, while her parents, who owned and managed the resort, recuperated from the flu. "Then I paid Willow a visit."

Fiona often joined the sisters for a meal when Willow—either on her own or with Jack—visited Washington. Willow and Fiona were the same age, a year younger than Salome, and got along well. "Has she finally dumped that redneck? What's his name, Jack?"

Fiona and Jack Genet weren't exactly soul mates. On

the way to the airport, Jack had said, "Oh yeah, and give your squirrelly neighbor a kick in the butt for me."

Instead of passing along Jack's message, Salome said, "Twenty-five years and they're still in love. Death'll be the only thing to separate those two."

"And how are you doing?"

Salome shrugged. "Oh, I'm okay. A least I was until I saw this."

Both women fell silent. Salome now realized the music had stopped. She had a creepy sensation she'd imagined the sound.

"Did you hear music just a minute ago?"

"Sure," Fiona said and motioned to the small headphones around her neck. Against the dark coat, Salome hadn't noticed them. "Bob Dylan. 'Rainy Day Women.' The anthem of my youth."

"So what happened here?"

Fiona sighed. Her eyes were the color of, and at the moment, the consistency of flint. She was just over five feet tall, and from a distance looked more like a child than a middle-aged woman. Despite their dissimilar ethnic backgrounds, an odd resemblance existed between the two. Salome's Japanese features, inherited from her Nisei mother, were mirrored in Fiona's eyes and high cheekbones, though Fiona's mother had been Czechoslovakian. Both women's fathers were of Anglo descent, a bloodline responsible for their similar rosy coloring.

"It's funny," Fiona went on, "until it was torn out, I never realized the garden was so small. It must have only been about ten feet by ten feet. But with all the color and fragrance it just seemed to fill the end of the cul-de-sac."

A wet gust suddenly shot down the street, buffeting the two women. Fiona turned around as if confronting a corporeal being. "Hey!" she scolded. Then she turned to Salome.

"What the hell are we doing standing out here in the rain? Come in for a drink and I'll fill you in on what's been happening."

Fiona's Federalist house was catty-corner to Malabar Manor, a ten-yard dash from where they'd been standing. Just as Fiona unlocked her glossy-black door adorned by a polished-brass lion's-head knocker, Salome glanced back. A Chinese man who looked to be in his early twenties, wearing a suit and topcoat and shielded from the downpour by a hulking black umbrella, hurried out of the house and opened the rear passenger door of the sleek Jaguar. A moment later, a tailer man in a beige trench coat, his hands shoved deep in the pockets, his head down, slipped into the car before she had a chance to get a good look at him. The man in the topcoat shut the door and moved around to the driver's side.

Fiona settled Salome in the sitting room, where a bay window offered a strategic view of the front and east side of the manor house, insisting that she didn't need Salome's help preparing drinks. Salome suspected that Fiona's kitchen needed a good cleaning—not something she'd want to share with her local feng shui practitioner.

Salome stood at the window and watched the Jaguar roll by, so close she could hear the tires sizzle on the wet street. The passenger in the back looked straight ahead. She sensed an attitude: Nothing around him existed until he looked at it. This was the first of many disturbing things she would come to know about this man.

While waiting for Fiona, Salome wandered around the room, glancing perfunctorily at the stills from Fiona's various documentaries, which covered most of the wall space. Finally, she noticed something new, and in pride of place above the mantel. It was a large framed print circa 1800, featuring all five of the houses located here on Malabar Close. Salome was immediately struck by how little had changed in two centuries. Of course, the trees and gardens were lush now and the original common paved over. But the print served to remind her of the care taken with each house as if it were a revered relative, old surely, but still very much alive.

Salome enjoyed investigating the origins of a house, which was in fact an aspect of feng shui. There was a lot to the old adage, "If the walls could speak what a story they'd tell." Those who first lived in a house always left a mark. Here in Georgetown, where the majority of residences were the equivalent of priceless antiques, most people knew their homes' history as well as they knew their own, and more than likely both were intimately intertwined.

Prompted by the print, she recalled the beginnings of the neighborhood known simply as the Close.

Whitfield Malabar, a wealthy tobacco merchant, built the five three-story houses in a U-shape around a central lawn or common. He moved into the largest house in what he considered to be the commanding position at about the same time that the white-domed Capitol building welcomed its first tenants in November of 1800. He then rented the other four houses.

Life might have continued prosperously and harmoniously but for one thing that no one gave much thought to at first. Whitfield Malabar discovered God. In a display of contempt, he first boarded then bricked up the windows at the back of the manor house overlooking the Potomac River, the waterway largely responsible for Georgetown's merchant class (and Malabar's own wealth). The ornamental garden his wife had so lovingly created was torn out and the land donated to Georgetown University, founded by Jesuits in 1789. Then he built a high stone wall to shield the house from wickedness. Instead of taking care of business, he began spending his days out in the middle of the common, no matter what the weather, preaching fire and brimstone. The renters began leaving until finally Malabar was preaching to empty houses— with the exception of his own.

One icy January day he took ill. The doctor was summoned, shocked to find his patient wearing wet socks. Further inquiry revealed that *all* the socks were wet. A few days later Whitfield Malabar died of pneumonia. Though the doctor suspected the wife had a hand in her husband's demise, ultimately, it had been Whitfield's decision to wear the wet socks while standing in the cold and proselytizing for hours. In his diary, the doctor wrote, "Wet socks do not a murder prove."

Mrs. Malabar saved her family from impending ruin by selling the four houses in the Close. She then reinstalled the windows at the back of the house, and tore down the wall, which she felt had imprisoned rather than shielded her family. Finally, she planted the first of what were to be many rose gardens at the front of the manor house.

Salome turned as Fiona bustled into the sitting room carrying a tray laden with a silver tea service and plates of tiny cakes and sandwiches, pate, cheese, and crackers.

"Good heavens, Fee, you didn't have to go to so much trouble. I really can't stay long."

"Well, it is teatime." Few customs and idiomatic speech remained from Fiona's childhood in Melbourne, Australia, but afternoon teatime was one. "Besides, I haven't had lunch yet."

"Where's Jamie?"

Fiona busied herself pouring hot water in a teacup and preparing a plate for Salome. "We're having something of a separation." She indicated a selection of teas in a silver bowl. Salome took the Earl Gray, and considered the news.

Fiona and Jamie, twenty years her junior, had been living together for two years. Fiona had met him at a lecture she'd given on documentary filmmaking while he was getting his master's degree in cultural anthropology at George Washington University. Despite their age difference, they showed all the symptoms of true love.

"Not to worry, we'll sort it out. Funny, though, his leaving when he did—what is today?"

"Monday."

"Must have been Friday, then. The day after Isabelle's rose garden was torn out. Maybe it's a feng shui thing," she said, deliberate with the pronunciation: *fung shway*. "Proud of me? Been practicing. Even got myself a book. God! I shudder every time I think of all the ways I used to mangle it—fing, fang, fong, shoe, shoey, shee. Takes me back to conjugating Latin verbs."

"Feng shui can improve your love life, you know. I'll be glad to help you out—no charge. But it'll have to wait until I get back. In the meantime, you could start by cleaning the house from top to bottom."

"Get back? But you just got here!"

Salome heaved a sigh. "Because of the extra time in California, I had to reschedule a ten-day speaking tour. Starts tomorrow night in Chicago. Rather, my publicist did. Plus I'll be catching up on private consultations in the Midwest as well."

"A publicist, eh?"

"At the moment, the demand for speakers is just incredible. I've had requests from all over the world. Anyway, I finally decided to hire a publicist to sort things out. I still have my practice to think about. As it is, she's got me booked for two presentations a day, one in the afternoon, one in the evening."

"Hope you're taking your vitamins. Couldn't have picked a worse time to hit the Midwest. Weather's absolutely awful. I know because I'm thinking of heading out there to shoot some footage."

Salome smiled. "Maybe we could meet. What's your project?"

Fiona shrugged. "Drugs in the heartland. That sort of thing." She picked up a wedge of salmon sandwich. "I should probably wait 'til the weather settles, though."

"Unless things have really changed since I've been gone, there's plenty of material right here in the District."

Fiona laughed. "Yeah. No worries on that count. But it's more poignant when some basically innocent farm kid in Iowa gets hooked on coke or heroin."

Fiona fixed a cup of tea for herself while Salome consumed a tiny sandwich.

"What about Judah?" Fiona asked, stirring her tea. "Will he be staying on?"

A retired Metropolitan homicide detective, Judah Freeman had been house-sitting for Salome since October, which happened to coincide with his separation from his wife of thirty years. Though some would call the timing coincidental, to Salome it was an example of synchronicity—that is, certain independent but related situations (in this instance, of a domestic nature) occurring simultaneously and resolved to the mutual benefit. In other words, she needed someone to take care of her house for six months; Judah needed a place to stay. Of course, she had a list of housesitters to call on; for six years she'd been dividing her time between coasts. This last time, however, she'd been pleased to provide comfortable accommodation for an old friend going through a particularly bad time.

"When I spoke with him yesterday, he said he could use the extra time to find a place."

"Well, even though I hardly ever see him, it's been nice having an ex-cop around."

Fiona then segued into neighborhood gossip: Mrs. Ruby Nelson, the seventy-year-old spinster who lived in the house directly across from Salome, recently left on a "singles only" cruise. Fiona, who had lived in this house for years, speculated that Ruby must have started taking hormones as she'd never seen the woman show a stick of romantic interest in men, or, for that matter, women, either. The Richmans, a power couple during the previous administration, and who had bought the house across from Fiona believing they would always be a part of the White House landscape, were finally getting the message that they weren't popular anymore.

"Lately they've been fighting like cats and dogs. Weather's been mild so everyone leaves the windows open. They're so loud it's like they're in the living room. Honestly, I wouldn't be surprised to hear gunshots one of these days."

Finally, she came to the current occupant of the house at the end of the cul-de-sac.

"First off, our new neighbor's name is Duncan Mah. He's half Chinese, half American. I don't know if you knew, but Isabelle's husband, Arthur Malabar, was in the diplomatic corps; never a mucky muck, just a mid-level civil servant. His last assignment, before he retired, was Hong Kong. He was even involved with Nixon's efforts to open up China. Anyway, their daughter, Ann, married one of those hyper-rich Chinese businessmen." She paused to sip her tea.

"Well, they had a son, Duncan, who just happens to be Isabelle's last living relative and sole heir.

"Anyway, since no one came forward to dispute the terms of Isabelle's will, it went through probate slicker than snot. Duncan moved in the first of March, though he's been in and out since November."

"Is he from Hong Kong?"

"According to Isabelle's lawyer, Daniel Hathaway, he has several homes. He—Hathaway, that is—came by after the will was settled and brought me that print." Fiona nodded toward the mantel. "Isabelle wanted me to have it. He told me what he knew about Mah, which I find sketchy: He's unmarried, has an M.B.A. from Stanford, and is a dealer in Chinese art and antiquities. Has shops in San Francisco, New York, and Montreal. And now, he's opened one here in Georgetown, on Wisconsin Avenue just below Calvert Street."

"What's sketchy about that? Have you met him?"

"Can't accuse me of not trying! Once he seemed to be in for good, I went over to introduce myself. An older Chinese woman answered the door. She looked at the pot of daffodils I brought like they were weeds. Said he wasn't available. I could hear someone screaming Chinese nearby—I suppose on the phone. And his car was on the street—obviously, this was before he got the great idea to destroy the garden. I've seen him coming and going but he never acknowledges me. It's like I don't exist."

Having just had the same impression, Salome nodded knowingly.

"And one other thing," Fiona added. "The man's absolutely gorgeous. Want to see?"

Salome's eyebrows shot up in surprise, half expecting Fiona to pull out a pair of opera glasses. "I just saw him leave. At least I think it was he. He sat in the back of the Jag while a young guy chauffeured."

Fiona laughed and shot up from the couch. "Hold on."

The long front room was divided by a set of double doors fitted with panes of etched glass. What had originally been a dining room Fiona had converted into a studio. When she opened the doors, Salome could see the piles of books and magazines, and the newspapers strewn across the floor. An iMac computer, on which she now put together her documentaries, dominated one corner of a wraparound desk. A huge corkboard covered the back window. On it were tacked three-by-five cards. Across the foyer to her left, Salome knew, was additional studio space.

Salome considered the implications of Fiona's career vis-à-vis her shaky love life. From the attic to the basement, the house functioned as a studio in which domestic arrangements were secondary. Salome couldn't help but wonder if Jamie had simply left to find some space.

Fiona returned to the couch holding a mini digital video camcorder, a view plate protruding from one side. She pressed a button and Salome watched a scene unfold. At first, all she saw was the back of a man wearing a camel-hair overcoat enter a shop.

"Where's this?"

"Wisconsin Avenue," she muttered. "Hold on a second . . . there!"

Recognizable by his coat, the man who'd entered now exited, then paused to light a cigarette.

"That's Duncan Mah," Fiona declared proudly, as if she'd created him herself. Then suddenly Fiona stared at Salome. "I'll bet you've been mistaken for any number of dark-haired, light-skinned ethnic groups—Native American, East Indian, Polynesian, Italian, Hispanic—it's the coloring and the bone structure. He's the same, don't you think?"

Indeed, he was uncommonly handsome and his origins not easily pinpointed. He glanced up and down the street, reminding Salome of a tourist stopping to get his bearings. He seemed quite interested in the passersby. Then he moved on, absorbing the surroundings, the camera held above the traffic. The scene cut to Prospect Street, just a couple blocks east of Malabar Close. Duncan Mah

had just walked up the steps from a popular local rath-
skellar. He approached the camera, then suddenly looked
directly into the lens. Immediately, the camera swung up
to the sign, which read THE TOMBS.

"See what I mean?" Fiona said, taking the camera. She
fast-forwarded and the people, Duncan Mah included, began to comically speed up as in silent films.

Salome felt a tremor of unease as she realized what
was happening. "Good heavens, Fee, you've been following him!"

Absorbed by the images on the 3.5-inch screen, Fiona
said excitedly, "Look at this."

Now the camera followed the waist-high hedges along
the east side of the manor house until stopping at the
veranda. Blue tarps covered stacks of something indistin-
guishable. Then, to Salome's astonishment, Fiona kept
the camera trained on the tarps while she actually moved
through a narrow break in the hedges. Holding the camera in one hand, she lifted an edge of a tarp, revealing
what looked to be wrought-iron fencing about eight feet
in length, the top part curved with lethal-looking spikes
at the end.

"Fiona! What if you'd been caught snooping?"

"Hey, snooping's part of my job," she replied. "Would
you look at those spikes? Bloody hell, where does he
think he is, the ghetto?"

She set the camera on the coffee table. "I suppose we
should be thankful he's not planning on constructing a
wall topped by razor wire. In the feng shui book I bought
it says sharp points create poison arrows."

"That's right."

"Look, maybe you could talk to him. I mean, he's
Chinese. Wouldn't he know about feng shui?"

"Just because he's Chinese—or part Chinese—doesn't
mean he's a believer or honors feng shui traditions.

That's like assuming all Italians are Roman Catholic."

Salome regarded the camera thoughtfully. "Keep your distance, Fiona." She checked her watch and quickly set her teacup on the table. "Look, I've got to go, but thanks for the hospitality."

"Just one more thing," Fiona said. She leaned across Salome's lap to the coffee table and tossed aside a copy of the *Washington Post*, revealing an open art book. She set the book between them. On the left was a slick page of text, on the right a colorplate of *Bacchus* by Caravaggio, the original hanging in the Uffizi in Florence.

"The text refers to him as an ephebe—a youth just entering manhood," Fiona instructed. "Just look at the painting for a minute. No question, Caravaggio was a genius."

The subject was painted with an almost absurdly large crown of grapes and grape leaves on heavy black artificial-looking hair, a robe draped over his left shoulder, leaving the right side of his well-nourished torso bare. In the foreground was a bowl containing fresh and rotting fruit, fresh and withered leaves. Above the bowl, Bacchus held out a glass kylix—a cup of pleasure—filled with red wine. But the full, sensuous mouth and heavy-lidded insolent eyes—the look—suggested more than refreshment was being offered.

"Well?" Fiona asked anxiously. "What do you think?"

"His draped body, certainly the musculature of his right shoulder and arm, applauds great beauty while his expression screams of internal corruption." She smiled wryly.

Fiona laughed. "Give Salome high marks for art interpretation. Here," she handed Salome a petit four with white icing. "Have a cake. I was really wondering if you noticed how much he resembles our new neighbor."

"I'd have to get a closer look. At our neighbor, I mean."

"Every woman should, at some point in her life—and preferably when she can handle it—be visited by a man like this."

Salome tapped the picture. "Fee, he's an adolescent!"

"Don't be picky. Imagine him as an adult."

Fiona touched the page, her finger on the hand extending the kylix. "Weird. Here I am middle-aged and I'm finally being visited. Hard to believe I've had this book ten years. Just the other day I was looking for something else and the book just seemed to jump into my hand. I opened it right to this page. Synchronicity, right?"

The mood in the room had subtly altered since Bacchus joined them. Fiona now seemed more serious. Salome looked at the painting again. He had only to sit there leaning on his right elbow, extending that glass—his indolence and a sort of sexual mockery playing with the viewer.

"I might just make a little documentary featuring our Duncan," Fiona mumbled, transfixed by the painting.

"What do you mean, 'our Duncan'?" Salome said, a certain edge to her voice.

Fiona seemed to snap out of it. "Just a figure of speech," she said quickly.

She returned the book to the coffee table. She picked up the newspaper and placed it on top as it had been instead, Salome noted, of simply closing the book.

"Think about it, Fee. You could be arrested for stalking," Salome said, rising from the couch.

Fiona laughed.

"Let's get together when I get back," Salome suggested when they reached the door.

Fiona handed over the yellow umbrella. "*If* you get

back. Honest, there are snowstorms all the way to Alabama."

"Look, I just had a thought. If you're really interested in meeting our neighbor, it might be easier and *safer* to simply go shopping, patronize his store." Maybe if Fiona actually met the man she'd drop the idea of following him around with a camera.

Fiona brightened. "Shopping. Now there's a concept. But I know absolutely zilch about Chinese art."

"Ask him for help."

The two women hugged. When they pulled away, Fiona suddenly held Salome with her eyes. "I'll bet you've got one, don't you? Tucked away where no one would even think of looking?"

"One what?"

"Bacchus of the Uffizi."

Salome rolled her eyes. "Good-bye, Fiona."

A moment later, Salome started to enter her house. She had less than two hours to prepare for a presentation and she needed to clear her mind of the neighborhood's latest arrival. No question Duncan Mah was an eyeful. But that wasn't enough to counteract a deeper, disturbing sensation. Could be jet lag, the Twomey house in Texas, the shock of the rose garden's demise, Fiona's snooping and her obsession with that damn painting—probably a combination of everything. Still . . .

She glanced briefly at the house dominating the cul-de-sac and wondered if a seedling of evil had begun germinating in Malabar Close.

Chapter 2

"FUNDAMENTALLY, feng shui is about ch'i, or energy. There's good ch'i, positive energy, and sha, or bad ch'i, the stagnant, negative, often destructive variety. A harmonious environment depends on the even flow of ch'i and the absence of sha," Salome instructed.

Just a moment before, Cookie Freeman had introduced her and when the applause died down she made her opening statement.

Then, recalling her recent encounter with Caravaggio's *Bacchus*, she had a sudden inspiration. "Energy is to feng shui what light is to a great painter. Without energy there is no feng shui. Without light a painter cannot manipulate form."

She stood at a podium in the main dining room of Cookie's, a restaurant on E Street between North Capitol and New Jersey Avenue, wearing her uniform, the black Chinese-style gown. Every speaking engagement was different and though she had six years experience as a consultant, her speaking career was in its early stages. She usually found herself honing and modifying, adding new ideas whenever they presented themselves, all to further an audience's understanding of feng shui.

A furnished dollhouse was set up on a table to her right, the front wall and the roof removed. To her left was an easel supporting a large square of poster board covered at the moment by a square of black silk.

"Though feng shui has been practiced in China for several thousand years, it's only in the last twenty-plus years that we in the West have come to learn about and benefit from its principles. Of the several schools available, I practice what is known as Black Hat sect, or Black sect feng shui, the primary tool of which is called a Bagua."

With her left hand, Salome reached over and threw back the sheet of black silk, revealing a segmented octagon. In the center was a black-and-white *tai chi,* or yin yang symbol. "If you'll open your red packet, you'll find a copy of the Bagua. Anyone who doesn't have a red packet, raise your hand and someone will bring one to you."

Giving them a moment, she looked around the packed room. She wondered what motivated some of these people to attend the fund-raiser sponsored by the prestigious Black Women in Business Association to benefit a battered women's shelter discreetly tucked away in rural Maryland. Most of the attendees had money; many were black activists, the District's movers and shakers; a few were politicians (or their aides) who never let an invitation or an opportunity to get their name in the news go to waste. And some were lawyers and members of the police department who spent a great deal of time at the nearby courthouse and probably ate lunch here at Cookie's five days a week. Though Salome hadn't flattered herself by thinking that some of these people had actually attended just to hear her speak, she did notice a couple of interior decorators, one of whom, Simon Snow, was perhaps the most influential in the District. Unfortunately, he was also a major detractor, declaring that feng shui practitioners had nothing viable to offer and were merely riding the coattails of interior designers like him.

She'd agreed to be the keynote speaker months ago as a favor to her good friend, Cookie Freeman, estranged wife of her house sitter, Judah. Even if her parent's illness had required that she stay longer in California, she would have made a special trip rather than cancel. Salome and Cookie were old friends and the worthy cause was one close to Salome's heart. Last year, she personally paid for a new roof for the shelter.

"Each section is called a gua and within each is a trigram from the *I Ching*, the Chinese Book of Changes, followed by a corresponding color, element, and body part. For instance," she continued, pointing to "Career" at the very bottom of the Bagua, "you can see that black, water, and ears are all represented in the career gua. Moving clockwise, the next gua is knowledge followed by family and health, then wealth, then fame, then relationships, then children and creativity, and finally, helpful people and travel. The center represents balance and harmony.

"Whenever I do a consultation, I mentally superimpose the Bagua over the property as a whole, then the main house, then each room. The position of the entrance determines the mouth of ch'i and will always be either at knowledge, career, or helpful people/travel. For example, the entrance to Cookie's restaurant is in the knowledge gua. One walks down the richly paneled hallway, passing her collection of African masks—located, incidentally, in the family/health gua—finally coming to the hostess station where the cash register is located, in the most auspicious place for a cash register, the wealth gua.

"So you see, once you've located the mouth of ch'i, it's very simple to determine the location of the remaining guas."

She stopped for a moment. "Any questions so far?"

Cookie, who knew these people, acknowledged a stunning black woman in a red silk sheath seated at one of the front tables. "What if you rarely use the front door? I always enter my house through the garage." Cookie repeated the question for all to hear.

"Doesn't matter," Salome answered. "The position of the front door always determines the mouth of ch'i."

Cookie then called on a man in the back. "I don't mean to sound stupid but what's the purpose of feng shui—what does it do?"

Again Cookie repeated the question then looked at Salome and said, "Mind if I answer that one?"

"Go right ahead."

"A couple years ago, I had the restaurant remodeled. Afterward, business fell off so bad it looked like I might have to close. Well, I've known Salome for years so I asked her to come over and see if she could find out what was going wrong. Well, she did. Turned out, it was a case of 'if it ain't broke, don't fix it.' Basically, the new stoves were placed so the cooks mainly had their backs to the kitchen door. Now this made them jumpy. The food suffered. There wasn't any problem with the stoves themselves; they just need to be moved back where the old stoves had been—in the kitchen's wealth position.

"Second, the cash register had been moved across from where it is now—out of the way, in one of the waiter's stations, my interior decorator having told me that, currently, it was considered vulgar to have the cash register in sight of the diners, especially when they entered."

She nodded toward the cash register. An overhead

spotlight shown down on it, highlighting a multifaceted, thirty-millimeter crystal hanging from a red cord. "Unless I'm running a soup kitchen, I sure as hell don't mind if my customers come in with the idea they're gonna pay for their meal."

That incited a good laugh.

Cookie went on. "Well, it was bad enough having the cash register hidden away, but Salome pointed out that it was also near the hall leading to the restrooms and the stairway leading to the private dining rooms upstairs."

Cookie then turned the discussion back to Salome.

"Bathrooms have special problems. They represent money draining away, which is why we recommend that toilet lids be kept down, something you gentlemen should keep in mind."

That tweaked scattered snickers.

"Whenever you leave the seat and lid up you're putting your finances at risk."

"And your wives, especially at night," the woman in the red sheath called out.

After the additional laughter died down, Salome went on. "Further, all drains in your residences should be plugged and the bathroom door kept closed.

"Now to the stairs," Salome continued. "While Cookie had replaced the old, worn carpeting, the area remained dark, preventing the ch'i from moving. Cookie installed track lights at intervals and a mirror at the top to give the illusion of more space."

Cookie glanced over at Salome and their eyes met briefly; Cookie silently reminded Salome not to mention what they'd discovered in the private dining room. Salome nodded slightly then moved to another subject.

"Part of the remodel included installing a new sound system. Sound itself is a feng shui enhancement used to attract and raise the ch'i in a space. However, the jazz playing the day I was here for the consultation was heavy on horns. Thing is, a horn shoots energy outward. People seated under the speakers were being blasted even though the music wasn't that loud. However, they didn't linger. Now some will argue that turnover is important in a restaurant and if the horns keep the tables turning, all the better. On the other hand, this could hurt repeat business—those who felt uncomfortable wouldn't come back. Such sound is better for a dance club where people are moving around a lot."

"What about elevator music?" someone called out.

"Totally innocuous. It's designed to calm the herd; to make us feel safe as we shoot up and down an air shaft."

Salome now moved over to the dollhouse and switched on a spotlight to illuminate the interior. "This dollhouse has become quite a valuable tool for me to use during local presentations and for certain consultations. I suppose I should mention I even consult over the phone. This saves the client the cost of travel expenses. They fax me a layout of their house or apartment, complete with the positions of their furniture, the most important of which are the stove and the bed. I then set up the dollhouse accordingly.

"The walls are movable and I can create practically any style house I need. At home I have a selection of roofs, windows, doors, etc. and, of course, all sorts of furnishings. I brought it tonight to show you how revealing our residences can be.

"I've set this up like the house of a woman I consulted in another state. She'd been married for a little over a year to a very wealthy man whom she loved dearly. Though they never argued, she felt something was wrong with their marriage. She thought he might be having an affair. So let's take a look and see what the house reveals.

"The entrance is in the career gua. First off, we enter

a wide, airy foyer. Stairs leading to the second floor are off to the left, which is good as you don't want them directly in front of the door. But the first thing we see is a set of luggage placed in front of a partially opened closet. That was my first clue. I found the second clue when I opened the closet door and saw a half-dozen additional sets of luggage.

"Next I asked her to show me the bedroom. It took up the entire back portion of the second floor and had wraparound windows affording a fabulous view."

Salome raised and tilted the entire second story so everyone could see. The furnishings were affixed to the floor with velcro so everything stayed in place.

"Now just look at the layout for a minute and see if you can spot the problems."

Salome nodded to a young white guy neatly dressed in a suit and tie. She took him to be an attorney or maybe a congressional aide.

"Seems to me the bed should be over on the right in the relationship gua instead of on the other side of the room in the wealth gua."

"Good," Salome said encouragingly. "What else?"

"The desk. Why have it by the bed? If this guy's rich why doesn't he have a separate office?"

A middle-aged black woman with close-cropped hair and wearing large horn-rimmed glasses squinted at the house and asked, "What is that in the relationship gua?"

"There's a spiral staircase that leads to the utility room downstairs. And I put little bits of this and that to represent clutter—the dirty clothes and trash that were left there for the maid.

"Be wary of spiral staircases. Because they typically don't have risers, ch'i escapes. Further, spiral stairs act like a corkscrew boring a hole through whatever gua they're in—in this case, the couple's marriage. I suggested she put a light above it and wrap the banister, from top to bottom, in ivy, even artificial ivy would do. And, she needed to get rid of the clutter in that area."

Cookie caught Salome's eye and tapped her watch. Salome lowered the second floor.

"Clearly the problem centered around her workaholic husband. Besides having the set of luggage outside the closet, all the additional sets right there in the foyer, even though put away, subliminally tweaked his desire to travel. Also, I urged her to convince her husband to move the desk and computer to another room altogether. When he was home, he was literally taking his work to bed. It was the only place the couple communicated. In this case, his wife and sex were a part of his wealth, she a possession, an object that functioned for his pleasure.

"Just remember, the bedroom is for sleeping and making love. If space is limited, hang a curtain or in some way isolate the bed. And keep the décor simple and decorate with pairs of objects—paintings, ceramics, and such. And use the color pink. If you must have a mirror, don't aim it at the bed. While mirrors are popular feng shui enhancements, they can definitely disturb sleep. Over time this can create serious medical problems. To those clients who include mirrors in their sexual activities I suggest they keep the mirrors covered at all other times."

Cookie joined her at the podium.

"Well, it seems my time is up. I look forward to the consultation with whomever among you wins the door prize."

"Wait a minute!" someone called out from the audience. "What happened to the woman whose husband left his luggage out?"

"Ah. Well, he refused to change. Wouldn't even move his computer. He obviously liked things as they were.

Seems to me he treated his home like a hotel he could always count on. A place to stay with no surprises. But, a marriage involves the happiness of two people. Three months later, she left him."

"So feng shui didn't help?"

"I wouldn't say that. How often do you hear of something negative turning out to be a blessing in disguise? She knew there was a problem——" Cookie squeezed Salome's hand; another cue for her to finish. "Feng shui showed her the areas that needed changing. When he refused to cooperate, she changed."

After thanking Salome for donating her time, Cookie said, "We'll take a ten-minute break before the auction begins. Please help yourselves to pie and coffee."

Cookie helped Salome clear the props from the podium area. "Sorry to rush, but we're running late." Then, lowering her voice, she said, "For a minute there, I thought you were going to mention those bugs we found in the private dining room."

The bugs were not of the insect variety but those used to listen in on conversations. "Now that was creepy," Salome said. "But I am surprised you talked about the disastrous remodel, especially with Simon Snow in the audience." Snow had been the restaurant's interior decorator, the person who created the problems. "I'll bet he's furious especially since it took a feng shui practitioner to untangle the mess."

Cookie shrugged. "It was worth it. The bastard nearly cost me my business and overcharged in the process. He can be thankful I didn't mention him by name—though certain people knew who I was talking about."

A quick glance around the room told Salome that Snow had a tough enough skin and didn't appear the least bit flustered or angry as he chatted with those at his table. Just then a good-looking young black man moved beside

Snow and served him a piece of pie and a cup of coffee, though he didn't appear to be one of the wait staff.

Several people joined Salome, asking questions about feng shui while she and Cookie prepared the dais for the auction. Someone even thought to bring Salome a slice of Cookie's fabulous rum-flavored pecan pie.

Salome was just finishing the treat when nineteen-year-old Chimene Freeman, Cookie and Judah's youngest daughter, dashed up. She was carrying a large carton containing items to be auctioned. "Mom!" she hissed. "The linguist staff's gone!"

"What?"

"The Ghanaian linguist staff. I can't find it anywhere."

"Oh no!" Cookie moaned.

"What's wrong?" Salome asked, moving closer to the two women.

"Chimene's misplaced the linguist staff—"

"No, I didn't! It's gone. Someone must have taken it."

"Where'd you last see it?" Salome asked.

"In the kitchen. It was with me the whole time." Her eyes darted around the room. "All I did was go to the bathroom. And it's not like it's little. I mean, this big stick covered in bubble wrap."

"Maybe it fell over or something while you were in the bathroom and someone put it in a safe place," Salome suggested.

"Just find it! It's the centerpiece of the auction!" Cookie declared.

"I'll help you look." Salome joined Chimene.

"Tell me something about it," Salome requested while she and Chimene discreetly looked around the various tables. Fortunately, most people were mingling and mostly ignored them.

"Well, it's from the Akan tribe of Ghana. The staffs are a political art form—this one had a bird carved at the top with a snake in its beak—the snake's head on one side, the rest of the body dangling at the other side. There's a little card that goes with the staff explaining the significance.

"Anyway, it says, 'When you hold the head of the snake, the rest is nothing but rope.' Which means, when you attack the right part of a problem the rest is easy."

But the linguist staff never turned up. Cookie substituted one of the masks from the locked cabinet in the hall toward the entrance to the restaurant, which happened to be a family heirloom.

A short time later, Salome joined Cookie at the back of the dining room just before the auction started.

"I don't mean to sound like an ignoramus, but was the staff very valuable?"

"In a word, yes."

"Oh dear."

"In and of itself, certainly. But the wife of the Ghanaian ambassador donated it. She's a friend. *Was* a friend. At least she's not here."

Though it probably wouldn't cause an international incident, the theft of the linguist staff would cause Cookie extreme embarrassment. And considering where the item was eventually found, much more.

Chapter 3

BECAUSE of the rain, the Close looked much as she'd left it when Salome returned a week later, though now it was nearly one A.M. With a rain hat firmly in place, she clutched her hanging bag and house keys and dashed through the downpour to her front door. In one swift, quiet movement, she slipped inside.

Though not quite a disaster, the tour had been an ordeal, cut short three days when floods in Missouri forced cancellations of the last six presentations. Too bad the publicist's fee didn't include accurate weather predictions. Salome should have listened to Fiona. She'd trudged through enough snow in the upper Midwest to fill a life's quota. Delayed flights, broken-down automobiles, scarce taxis, and overbooked hotels notwithstanding, she'd made it to each presentation, some of which were quite intimate indeed with only a few hearty souls in attendance when many more were expected. She'd accompanied her ex-husband on some grueling book tours, but she'd been younger then and rarely did he make multiple appearances in one day.

The toll on her body was one thing but the theft of her briefcase containing a laptop computer and her presentation materials was quite another. Someone had plucked it right off the dais just after yesterday's luncheon engagement at a posh Milwaukee hotel. She'd been chatting informally after the lecture and when she turned to collect her things, the briefcase was gone. Security personnel had been helpful but unsuccessful. Fortunately her cell phone had been in the pocket of her gown and her purse left in her hotel room about a mile away. She'd planned to stay at this very hotel but at check-in was informed there were no rooms available. By the time she left, rush hour traffic had taken over the streets. Snow, with flakes the size of cotton balls, had started to fall. Not a taxi to be had and she still had an evening presentation at a Chinese furniture gallery somewhere in the suburbs.

Salome stood in the dark leaning against the door, trying to recall where she'd started the day. Milwaukee? Chicago? Kansas City? The Twilight Zone? Ah yes, she thought, all of the above. At dawn she'd flown from Milwaukee to Chicago where she made the connection to Kansas City. And when picking up the rental car outside the Kansas City airport the publicist called with the news of the cancellations. The rest of the day had been spent cruising the Twilight Zone, hopeful that she would eventually arrive exactly where she was now. She considered kissing the floor but figured she might not be able to get up again.

Off to the right were the rooms in which Judah was staying, the double doors open. Not wanting to disturb him, she slipped off her shoes, then padded into the living room to the left on her way to the kitchen. There she would have a much-needed shot of something strong and drop off her hanging bag in the basement in preparation for doing laundry in the morning.

The living room drapes were tightly closed and the house completely dark. She hoped she wouldn't do any damage to herself or the furnishings before reaching the light switch in the dining room. Turning on a lamp in the living room would shoot light into Judah's rooms. Finally, she found the proper switch and a moment later, the elegant little chandelier hanging above the cherry wood table came on. She began to move on then abruptly stopped.

Carefully setting down the hanging bag on the hardwood floor at the edge of the Persian carpet, Salome entered the pool of light, raindrops glistening on her hat and coat. Her hands gripped the curved back of a chair. With a shocked expression, she regarded the assortment of macabre photographs—hardly the sort of fare one would expect to be served up on polished cherry.

The hairless nude body looked more like a child's baby doll than that of sixty-year-old Simon Snow, his size diminished by the vast expanse of a king-size bed. He lay on his side in a nest of mussed pink bedclothes. The photos had been shot from several angles. Salome picked up one for a closer examination, thinking her eyes were playing tricks. Snow's hooded eyes stared out from above the smooth skin at the center of his narrow back. Blood trailed from his mouth and down the left side of his jaw staining a small pillow. Shuddering, she dropped it, her eyes shifting to one taken from the front which looked to be evidence that his body had been found during rigor, maybe, she reckoned, six to eight hours after death. His pudgy little hands gripped the shaft of a wooden stake that extended about three feet from the center of his body. If his neck hadn't been broken, he would have faced a fierce-looking bird with a snake in its beak carved at the top. Another picture revealed the sharpened business end protruding another two to three feet from Snow's back.

"Sweet Jesus," she whispered, certain that this was the linguist staff that had gone missing the night of the fundraiser at Cookie's restaurant. Her own concerns of the past week paled in comparison.

Other than a set of ordinary sweats on the gray carpet, the room looked neat, not what one would expect at a brutal crime scene. She was also a little surprised that it was so sparsely furnished, never having associated Simon Snow with minimalism. She'd heard he filled his home with duplicates of the furnishings in the showrooms he owned in Dupont Circle and across the Potomac in Alexandria and Falls Church, Virginia. It was said that he carried an order book around during his frequent and lavish parties and that if you saw something you liked, he'd have a duplicate at your house the next day. Still, she could only assume that this was his bedroom. Having been consumed by her own affairs recently, her focus on local weather, she knew nothing about the crime. But given his association with government officials who could afford his services, including, of course, the wives of members of Congress, the murder might well have made the national news.

On either side of the massive bed were nightstands each with a lamp and a small bronze of identical reclining male nudes displaying astonishing virility. A cart supporting a TV/VCR stood at the foot of the bed and she could see a tape protruding from the VCR's tape compartment. Sheets hung at the floor-to-ceiling windows. Not what one would expect, but there were drapes, pink brocade shot with silver thread, in protective clear plastic bags laid out on the carpet. Several paintings were propped against one wall either waiting to be hung or taken away, the two in front covered by protective wrapping, which lead her to believe they were new.

She moved down to the far end of the table where a three-ring binder lay open. She picked up a loose sheet of paper, recognizing the neat straight-up-and-down printing as that of her house sitter, Judah Freeman. She read:

Certain members of Washington's elite, those without a firm seating in reality—of which we suffer far too many—have presented some really stupid, downright outlandish theories. One of this country's lawmakers actually suggested that Simon Snow stumbled while undressing and fell upon the wooden staff, impaling himself after which he broke his neck. Speculation about the staff itself provided more unwanted insight into how some of these people think, not to mention their ignorance of African culture: The staff has magical, regenerative powers that restore a man's virility if he sleeps with it.

Of course, most are certain Jett Malieu, Snow's twenty-two-year-old houseman, bears most of the responsibility for the crime, though they are reluctant to come right out and say he murdered his employer. Thing is, they consider Malieu a gracious and humble servant who was simply too good-looking for the job. Some speculate that Malieu and Snow had probably been engaged in wild sex when the younger, stronger Malieu accidentally broke Snow's neck. Then Malieu stabbed Snow with the linguist staff to cover up the accident and make it appear that an intruder, the same person who stole the staff the night of the fund-raiser, followed Snow home and committed the crime. Still others feel that Snow came on to Malieu one time too many, the two men fought, and Snow ended up dead.

But consider the source: These speculations come from people who refuse to believe that any of their set could

*possibly be a murderer. Simon Snow has been the fa-
vored interior designer of the District's society folk for
over thirty years. If anyone knew where the bodies were
buried, or in which closets the skeletons were hidden,
Simon Snow did. Which leads me to believe that there
could be any number of people with a motive to silence
Snow.*

Salome put the paper back. From the look of things,
Judah had scored the case. She certainly hoped so. Like
many retired cops, he'd had a difficult time adjusting to
civilian life. It was especially rough for Judah, who'd
become something of a legend on the Metropolitan Police
Force, solving many of the District's most bizarre homicides. For two years now, he'd been working as a private
investigator and in that time hadn't been able to get past
the sordid divorces that had become the staple of his
practice.

She started to move back around the table when she
heard a muffled noise. It was so sudden and unexpected,
she had no idea where it came from. She froze. Standing
there in a pool of light walled by darkness, she felt like
the perfect target. Straight ahead, one of the curtains fluttered, indicating that a window overlooking the back garden had been left open. She'd been so absorbed in the
crime scene photos and Judah's notes, she hadn't noticed.
Now, too, she was cognizant of the rain outside.

As her anxiety shot up the scale, she was torn between
making a dash to switch off the light and staying put to
listen. But maybe she'd imagined the noise. Maybe
something outside had fallen over. Then the decision was
made for her.

With a soft click the light went out. The room went
pitch-black.

"Judah?" she whispered tentatively. Who else could it
be? He must have heard her enter the house, what? Five

minutes ago? But dressed in the hat and raincoat and with her back to the living room, he wouldn't recognize her. She'd told him no guns in the house but she knew he kept a baseball bat handy. Had he just been standing there watching her go through the photographs?

"Judah!" She repeated. "It's me, Salome—"

"Shhh!" A voice hissed.

Salome took a breath to calm herself. Surely Jude wouldn't strike before being certain it *wasn't* Salome. Again she sensed movement, this nearby, to her right. A second later she thought she heard a faint click, coming from the direction of the kitchen off to the right, and thought it might be the back door.

Salome hurried around the table to the window. Pushing the curtain aside, she leaned out. "Judah," she called. "What's going on?"

The rain fell straight down. The fresh air felt damp and warm. She could just make out the low beam of a flashlight heading toward the back wall. Then it went out.

"Damn it, Judah! What are you doing?"

After a moment, she heard his familiar baritone.

"Salome? Is that you?"

"Of course, it's—" She abruptly stopped. Her mouth went dry and her skin prickled with gooseflesh. He was speaking from a place *behind* her.

He turned on the light. Salome straightened and they regarded each other incredulously.

So, who the hell had been in the house?

He stood to one side of the archway that separated the living room and dining room wearing only a pair of emerald-green satin boxer shorts, sweat beading his smooth chest like silver sequins on black velvet. In one hand he held a pair of wire-rimmed glasses, in the other a baseball bat, which, at the moment, looked to Salome big enough to use in the pole vault.

"What the hell's going on? What're you doing here?" He started to put on his glasses.

She dashed into the kitchen, her bemused house sitter on her heels, and switched on the light.

Mini blinds covered the pane of glass in the kitchen door. Salome noticed the cord swinging slightly. The hair rose on the back of her neck and she felt sweat trickle from her armpits.

She grabbed the flashlight held by brackets alongside the door and at the same time turned the doorknob, but it wouldn't give. The door was locked! Now that was strange. The intruder had actually paused long enough to lock the door before closing it.

A moment later, she dashed outside.

Heavy rain continued to fall, battering the flowerbeds and pocking the surface of the small pond. Even with the flashlight on, she could barely see. Still, she checked every corner of the lush garden, even shining the light up through the branches of the cherry tree. But whoever had been in the house was gone. And they had to have been agile to scale the eight-foot stone wall. There was a gate at the very back but it required a key and she found it securely locked.

"What the hell's going on?" Judah barked as Salome stepped back into the kitchen.

Salome pulled off her hat and sopping socks. "We just had an intruder."

Cursing, he reached for the wall phone.

"No," she said, shaking her head vigorously. "On top of everything, I can't deal with any more cops."

"What do you mean—'any more cops'?"

"Look, Jude, let me check around. If anything's missing, I'll report it tomorrow. You awake?"

"This ain't sleepwalkin'."

"Good. I need to wind down a bit. Maybe we can

figure out who might have taken an interest in the house."

While Judah fixed a pot of tea, sliced lemons, and added a jar of honey and a bottle of rum to a tray, Salome looked over the living room. The only item worth stealing was an antique Japanese tea bowl. Apparently, the intruder hadn't been a collector of tea ceremony artifacts for the bowl remained on the mantel above the fireplace. However, maybe he or she liked pearls.

After hanging her wet coat on the coat tree in the foyer, she hurried upstairs, adrenaline working its magic on her otherwise fatigued body. She kept nearly a dozen pearl necklaces of varying lengths and colors along with assorted earrings and rings in a secret compartment in her tiny, cedar-lined closet. A quick look told her they hadn't been disturbed.

She stripped off her travel clothes, which by now felt as if she'd been born in them, and changed into comfortable gray sweats and a pair of fleece-lined slippers. Gathering the dirty clothes, she went back downstairs.

By the time she'd emptied the hanging bag and sorted the clothes in the basement, Judah had tea ready and waiting on the dining room table. He'd neatly stacked the photographs and his binder at the end of the table and had put on a cotton robe.

"Anything missing?" he asked anxiously.

Salome shrugged. "Not that I can tell."

"Look," he said, "I must have left the window open. That had to be the point of entry. I checked around but didn't find anything. Cops might pick up some prints— if you decide to call them."

Judah handed Salome a steaming mug. She sniffed the rum-scented brew.

"What's this?"

"Freeman's miraculous elixir. Drink it and all problems vanish."

Salome smiled. "By the way, hi."

"Hi yourself. What are you doing here? I wasn't expecting you until Wednesday or Thursday. And what have you been doing that involved the police?"

She shook her head. "Nothing serious. My briefcase was stolen and—" she sighed. "—the rest of the trip cancelled." Suddenly she laughed. "Just now it occurred to me that I should have called you today. Never even entered my mind."

Judah regarded her knowingly, then said with a Chinese inflection, "Ah. Senior moment, grasshoppah."

Salome laughed, then sipped her brew. "Do you think the intruder might have been interested in those?" She nodded toward the stack of photos.

"Could be."

"Did you check to see if any are missing?"

"Yeah. Far as I can tell, they're all here."

"Where'd you get them?"

"Buddy of mine."

"You have the case then?"

"Uh-huh."

"You don't sound real pleased about it."

"Oh, I am! Believe me, I am. It's just, well, there are a few complications."

He remained reticent.

"I read some of your report."

That got his full attention. "Oh God. Just forget it, okay? One of my attempts at creative writing."

"Jude, I didn't read it to critique your style. I was just curious about the crime."

"You ever deal with Snow?"

"I knew him but not well. The last time I saw him—alive, that is—was last Monday night at the fund-raiser. He won the door prize, you know. A feng shui consultation."

"Cookie told me."

"I was supposed to call him when I got back and arrange a time."

Both stared at their mugs for a moment.

"That linguist staff," Salome said. "Uh, in the photographs. Was that the one that was supposed to be auctioned? Was it the murder weapon?"

"Technically, no—he died of a broken neck. But yes, the staff was the one supposed to be auctioned that night. The killer crudely whittled the end to a point—no respecter of African artifacts," he added sardonically. "Cookie's prints and those of the wife of the ambassador from Ghana are all over the damn thing. Worse, Snow and Cookie had a rather heated argument after the benefit—but I guess you witnessed that. Everyone else seemed to. One of the evening's highlights."

"Oh, dear. That's right. He was furious that she'd mentioned the bad design job that nearly resulted in the loss of her business. He accused her of making it all up to put me in a better light, seeing as how business improved after the feng shui consultation."

"Well, that confirms Cookie's story. Everyone else— those I've talked to and those the homicide detectives have questioned—has a different version about what they were arguing about. Most seem to think she accused him of stealing the linguist staff."

"So who hired you?" If she were a gambler, she'd bet on Cookie. And anyway, maybe something good would come of the murder and they'd get back together. "Or is that confidential?"

He looked away for a moment. But his reluctance had nothing to do with maintaining the confidentiality of his client.

He refilled his mug with tea and rum.

"Jude?"

He raised the mug in a toast. "Here's to my client."

They clicked mugs.

"Chimene Freeman."

Salome blinked. Now she understood his reluctance. At the same time, a few more things became clear. For one, the photographs being on the dining room table. She'd turned on the foyer light when she hung up her coat, illuminating his front room. Just before heading up the stairs she'd noticed the boxes covering the long refectory table. So, there'd been no space for him to study the photographs. The boxes on the table suggested more—that he'd finally been evicted from the cramped offices on Ninth Street not far from the monstrous FBI building. The office he also used as a crash pad. Lastly, with Chimene for a client, cash flow would all be one-way—out.

"How did Chimene talk you into this? Because Cookie might be a suspect?"

He heaved a great sigh that pulled open the top of his robe. "Cookie *is* a suspect. Just not the prime suspect. That distinction belongs to Jett Malieu, Snow's house-man. It seems Chimene and Malieu have a thing going."

"Oh dear. Did you know about this before?"

"Are you kidding? I thought Chimene was dating a classmate at Georgetown." He looked away for a moment. "She met Malieu during a modeling assignment. Seems they both do modeling on the side for extra cash."

Both were silent for a moment. The next subject was one she knew a proud man like Judah was embarrassed to bring up. But it needed bringing up, quickly and bluntly.

"So how are you doing for funds?"

Jude worried a tooth with his tongue. Then he looked at her directly. "Remember when we talked awhile back, when you told me you needed to stay on in California?"

"More or less."

"Well, remember you suggested I get rid of nine things for nine days?"

"Sure. One of the feng shui cures for getting one's life together."

"Well, I never got around to doing it but somebody else did. First thing that went was the rented furniture. Second, the temp. Third thing, the office. The fourth thing, the answering service. Fifth thing—" He rolled his eyes to the ceiling. "Guess my wife fits in there some place—"

"You know you can stay on," Salome interrupted, not mentioning what she'd already figured out about his change in status. "All I ask is one thing."

"Which is?"

"To work with you on the investigation."

Jude frowned but before he could verbalize a protest she told him about her latest interest in feng shuiing houses in which murders had been committed. "Right now I've got some free time. No one even knows I'm back. And I do need to fulfill my obligation to Simon Snow."

"What obligation?"

"To feng shui his house."

Abruptly Salome stood up. "You're right about this stuff," she said, pushing the mug aside. "I feel like all my problems have disappeared."

"Funny," he remarked. "I feel like mine have just been compounded."

JUST BEFORE SUCCUMBING TO EXHAUSTION, Salome had one last deed to perform. From her night-stand, Salome took a slip of paper the size one finds in fortune cookies and hastily scribbled a request to Kwan

Yin, the Chinese goddess of compassion and mercy. Then she tightly wound the paper around the tiny removable right hand of the Kwan Yin statuette beside the bed and inserted the hand in its slot.

Finally, she said her prayers. Every day, be it good or bad, deserved thanks even if only for every breath taken.

As she drifted off, an odd thought entered her tired brain. What if the intruder hadn't been in the house to take something away but *to leave something behind?*

Then in an instant, the thought dissolved into the black hole of dreamless sleep.

Chapter 4

🜲

THE scent of hickory-smoked bacon dislodged Salome from the snug nest of pillows, sheets, and comforter. It would have been easy and guiltless enough to spend the morning in bed; after all she had no appointments, no place to be, no one depending on her. Not just the aroma of cooking roused her, but the exhilaration of being *home*. After leaving Willow and Jack's, she'd had only a day before heading out again. Now, she had the opportunity to reacquaint herself with this wonderful old house.

In the small bath off her bedroom, Salome showered with Dr. Bronner's enlivening peppermint soap, her thoughts turning to her ex-husband, Gabriel Hoya. It was natural enough for her to think of him—Gabe figured in the argument she intended to present Jude should he be disinclined to include her in the Snow murder investigation.

During the twenty years of their marriage, Salome had worked as Gabe's researcher, providing the factual material he needed on which to base his best-selling fictional mysteries. Judah and Gabe went even further back, to the mid-1960s when they were freshmen roommates at Georgetown University. When Gabe began dabbling in political activism and drugs, he dropped out. Jude kept to his course and graduated with a degree in English. Jude planned to be a writer. Gabe had no plan. Life intervened. Judah fell in love with Cookie and wanted to get married and start a family. He needed a decent job—which pretty well eliminated anything related to writing at the novice level. He joined the Metropolitan Police Force and never looked back.

Gabe needed a job, too. The United States Army stepped in and drafted him. He went to Vietnam. While on R & R in Honolulu his path crossed Salome's at the bar where she waited tables. Over the next five years they maintained a friendship by mail and, when he left the army, he returned to Georgetown University and lived with his grandmother at Number 3, Malabar Close.

Salome's first connection to the house had come when writing the address on the envelopes housing the weekly replies to his letters. When she eventually visited him, she stayed in what was then a guest room, now her bedroom, never imagining that one day the house would be hers through a divorce settlement. She got on well with Ida Pearl Shaw, his grandmother, and of course, Gabe, but she adored the three-story redbrick house with its trim black shutters at the windows and lovely little garden adorning the back. (Sometimes she wondered if she'd actually fallen in love with the house and Gabriel only by association.)

They lived in Malabar Close for the first six months of their marriage while Ida Pearl went on a world cruise. By the time she returned they'd moved to a rental in McLean, Virginia, both working on Gabe's first mystery. It was during this time that she met Judah, who'd agreed to be their consultant on police procedure. For the next twenty years, Salome and Judah discussed every aspect of law enforcement, emphasis on homicide investigations, several times a month either on the phone or over lunch.

If need be, Salome intended to remind Judah that with her on board, he wouldn't be dealing with an amateur. Her bona fides were in the millions of copies of books sold. She couldn't imagine feng shui scaring him off, especially given the successful resuscitation of Cookie's business after the feng shui cures had been implemented.

After toweling dry, she opened the double-hung window to allow the steam to escape and generally stimulate the circulation of ch'i since the room hadn't been used for months. She pulled her heavy, waist-length black hair, still unsalted by gray, into a ponytail, then returned to her bedroom to dress in jeans, a blue work shirt, and thick socks.

Upon leaving the bedroom she entered what she called a "landing library." As the name suggested, in the space between the second floor bedrooms, she had installed pine cabinets to house her collection of books. To avoid the cutting energy associated with bookshelves, the spines of the books were flush with the edge of the pine shelving. Before leaving for California, she'd taken down the healthy plants kept here to neutralize the effect of "dead trees"—of which books were made. One of her practitioner friends actually refused to keep books in his house, saying that doing so was as bad as keeping dried flowers. Salome thought that was going too far and besides she'd been a book lover all of her life. To her way of thinking, what the books *contained* stimulated ch'i.

She made a mental note to pick up her plants from the small greenhouse in Fiona's back garden.

Midway along the landing was a three-paned bay window complete with a built-in window seat made of cedar and topped by a thick cushion and back rest covered in a red plaid (this being the fame position, the color red was called for). The long window seat doubled as storage for blankets and bed linen as there was little closet space, the house having been built when armoires were used. Beside it was a small round table with a reading lamp and a Japanese red lacquer bowl containing an assortment of bookmarks. During lazy summer nights, she enjoyed opening the windows and reading here.

She pushed open the door to the second bedroom, threw back the curtains at the two west and two east windows, then opened each. She could feel the air start to move, the rich, loamy scent of spring rain quickly overpowering the stale, dusty smell of inactivity. Certainly, she had more to do than simply open the windows and added to her mental agenda fresh bed linens, fresh flowers, and a thorough cleaning.

She glanced at the stairs leading to the third floor studio, deciding to save that space for later. Not only did the studio need a spring-cleaning, her computer was up there. She required time without interruption to transcribe her handwritten notes from Texas (fortunately in her purse and not the stolen briefcase) and to create some sort of new file system to organize the murder house case studies.

With a soft rag in hand, she polished the gently curving mahogany banister while making her way down the stairs, carpeted in what was called the Federal motif: dark blue stars on a red background.

A small Persian carpet spilled rich shades of red, gray, and black across the floor of the foyer. A gilt mirror hung above an antique marble-topped chest of carved oak to the left of the door. Here, too, was the coat tree and beneath it an umbrella stand, a small wooden platform for shoes, and a basket of slippers for those who wanted to wear more than socks in the house.

Across from the front door was a hall that lead to the kitchen and just beyond, the back door. As in the Twomey house, this was not good as ch'i would enter the house then sweep down the hall and pass on out the back door. To break the rush, Salome had set up an easel in the middle of the hallway on which she displayed certain paintings, all of which featured water. The foyer being in the career gua, water was the associated element. Before leaving for California, she'd placed her favorite winter scene on the easel: Hokusai's woodblock entitled *The Breaking Wave Off Kanagawa,* Mt. Fuji crowned in snow, about to be engulfed by an enormous foam-crested wave. Some practitioners would see this as bad feng shui, reasoning that the great wave would "drown" other beneficial aspects. But she loved the painting and so, to disperse any disruptive elements, hung a faceted crystal on a red cord above the masterpiece.

Now though, given the change of season, it was time for a different scene and she added yet another "to do" to her growing list.

Through the archway, she entered the living room. Jude had opened the curtains. As she'd been doing since she got up, she regarded the room with new eyes as if she were a stranger and seeing the house for the first time. And certainly, she was curious as to whether or not last night's intruder had been drawn by something in this room.

"Morning, Jude," she called out.

Jude peeked out from the kitchen. "Hey, kiddo. I was wondering if you were going to sleep all day."

"Spoken like a dedicated early riser," she joked. A glance at the clock on the green mantel above the fireplace told her it wasn't even eight-thirty.

"Hey, I've been to the market and back. And I got some news."

"Be right there."

In the knowledge gua of the house itself was a comfortable grouping consisting of a rosewood table, a lamp, and a pair of club chairs upholstered in iridescent sapphire silk, each with an ottoman, the color chosen to stimulate knowledge and spirituality. Against the wall was an entertainment center housing the television, VCR, DVD player, and stereo components plus shelves and compartments for DVDs, cassettes, books, and magazines.

Including the clock, the mantel held framed family photographs and the antique Japanese tea bowl. This was the family/health gua. To enhance these areas of life, a four-foot-wide green silk fan featuring a magnificent hand-painted golden dragon hung above the mantel, which symbolically "fanned" or energized the ch'i in those particular areas. The dragon itself represented powerful, protective life forces.

Positioned in front of the fireplace were a green velvet love seat, a matching armchair, and a small teak coffee table, all passed down from Ida Pearl. To eliminate any lingering ancestor ch'i that might be of a malign nature, Salome had sent the pieces out for a professional cleaning when she moved into the house. Afterward, she performed a blessing ritual using a sage smudge wand.

Finally succumbing to the tantalizing scents coming from the kitchen and curiosity about Judah's news, Salome skipped an examination of the dining room for the moment and went on into the kitchen. Jude stood at the stove in jeans and a T-shirt, a towel draped over his shoulder, looking very much at home. But then, he was a terrific cook. Two of the most popular items on the menu at Cookie's, the cornbread and the pecan pie were Jude's creations.

"Smells heavenly in here. How long have you been up?"

"Since six. Already ate but I'm taking orders. What'll it be?"

"Whatever you had."

He rattled off a list that could have fed four. "At least last night didn't spoil your appetite," she commented and ordered poached eggs, bacon, and biscuits.

"Nothing wrong with getting spooked once in a while. Reminds us we're not dead yet." The crack of each egg on the side of the poacher nicely punctuated the remark.

He pulled a thermos from the freezer and set it on the round table in the airy breakfast nook.

He'd put his plate in the sink but the three-ringed binder, his wire-rimmed glasses, and a half-filled cup of coffee marked his place, a chair with the back to the garden window. She honestly doubted he'd been sitting in that particular place during his stay at the house. But he'd been sensitive enough to leave her favorite seat vacant, the one facing out. She smiled at the sight of the cheery paintings on the wall: small, framed oils and watercolors of predominately pink flowers, which enhanced this, the relationship gua of the house. Jude had even bought a bouquet of fresh-cut daffodils for the table.

"What's your news?" Salome asked while pouring fresh carrot juice laced with ginger from the thermos. Keeping it in the icy thermos maintained its nutritional integrity, a trick she'd passed on to him before heading to California last year.

"Talked to a friend of mine this morning. Wants me to manage his fishing camp on the Potomac about an hour west of here."

"Oh." She felt a twinge of disappointment.

"All I really have to do is make sure the cottages are clean and that no one gets too rowdy." He glanced over at her from the stove. Little geysers of steam shot from the covered poacher. "Give me a place to stay and won't interfere with work."

"This the same place some guy took a shot at you while you were snapping pictures of him and his wife's best friend? The Bait and Mate Motel?" Cookie had mentioned the story during a lament about the seedy cases he took just to make ends meet.

Ignoring her, Jude busied himself preparing her plate. From the oven he took biscuits and a pan of thickly sliced bacon, the grease being absorbed by a brown paper bag. A moment later he set the plate down in front of her.

While she ate, he slid into his seat. He lowered the binder into his lap and, picking up a pen, appeared to be studying a page. Salome figured it was the one she'd read last night.

The breakfast nook quickly filled with their respective thoughts.

When she finished, he swept up the empty plate and washed it. Salome poured herself a cup of coffee and topped off his.

"Jude. We need to talk."

He resumed his seat and regarded her earnestly. For a middle-aged former homicide detective who'd seen it all, he could appear remarkably artless. But then, she reminded herself, though he'd *seen* it all, he hadn't *done* it all. In the years she'd known Judah he'd never done anything to tarnish his own soul.

"Oh! Before I forget, Gabe wants you to call."

Salome frowned. "What's up?"

Looking uncomfortable, Judah shrugged, then said quickly, "Something about certain things you might want. Uh, Elle's redecorating."

Elle was Gabe's wife of only four months. Salome had never met her but felt certain Jude didn't want to discuss the new wife with the old one. "Fine. I'll give him a buzz."

"We're meeting for lunch at The Tombs. You're welcome to come."

"I'll call." Then she segued into the matter of Jude's domestic situation. "I know you're anxious to get your own place, Jude," she began, though it wasn't entirely true. What he wanted was to move back with Cookie. "But it's no hardship on me for you to stay here a bit longer. And after that intruder last night, I'd actually feel a lot better if you wouldn't take off just quite yet."

"That's sweet of you, Salome, but if I hadn't left that window open there wouldn't have been an intruder."

"You can't know that for certain. If the window had been closed they might have picked the lock. For some reason, I don't feel violated, which seems to be a common reaction to a burglary."

"Well, think again. Snow's murder hasn't provided the only excitement around here. Two single women were burgled just a couple nights ago. Close to half a million in jewels taken. And just a couple blocks from here."

"Jeez Louise!"

"Could be you walked in on the same thief." Jude rose and went over to the phone. "Really, Mei," he said using the nickname she'd had since childhood, "you need to talk to the police."

"I don't have jewelry a thief would be interested in! And big jewel thefts aren't accidental."

Jude picked up the portable handset. "I'll call the local precinct. Won't take but a few minutes."

Salome sighed. Of course he was right. This would be a first. Now she would have a record of sorts at the Georgetown precinct. Looking on the bright side, with

Jude available, the process would be less unnerving.

A moment later, he hung up the phone. "Someone will be here shortly. If you'd like, I'll handle things. Of course you'll have to explain what happened since I never had any contact with the intruder."

Judah took a bag of coffee from the refrigerator and began preparing a fresh pot.

"What if they think I'm just some flaky alarmist?"

"Don't be ridiculous. Besides, you've got me to vouch for you."

Salome saw the opportunity and jumped on it. "Well, then. Will you extend that affirmation of my character to my involvement in the Snow investigation?"

Just then the doorbell rang. Jude bolted out of the kitchen.

"Make certain they wipe their feet!" Salome called out. Though she'd probably be within her rights to do so, she decided not to insist that the officers remove their shoes. It would no doubt annoy them and she didn't want to do that.

Judah had been right. They concluded their business in no time, talking and gossiping with Judah while taking prints from the dining room window and the back door. There were two uniformed cops, one a red-haired female with beautiful translucent skin who Jude introduced as Officer Delaney and the other, her barrel-chested male partner, Officer Ford. Jude left the two women alone in the breakfast nook while he ushered Officer Ford around the dining area and the back garden.

Salome offered coffee, which Delaney accepted. Q & A was pleasantly short. At the conclusion, Salome said, "I really don't fit the victim profile."

"Except that you live in Georgetown. Of course, it would help if you owned some important jewelry." Delaney sipped her coffee, then after a moment's reflection said, "Unless Simon Snow redecorated your bathroom."

"He certainly didn't."

Apparently it was all right for her to discuss the subject for she went on. "From what I've gathered, murals in the bathroom are all the rage. All the rage, that is, with those who can afford it. Snow did about a dozen over the past six months."

"I don't even know where and when he was murdered."

"His house here in Georgetown. Last Wednesday."

"And the robberies occurred . . . ?"

"Friday night," Delaney said with a finality that indicated the end of the interview. She rose and actually put her coffee cup in the sink. "Listen, you bring a pot of that coffee, you'll be welcome at the station anytime."

Salome laughed. "You'll have to extend that invitation to Jude. He gets the credit."

Salome walked Officer Delaney to the front, where she could hear Jude and Delaney's partner talking.

"So, this feng shui really works?" Delaney said conversationally.

"I wouldn't be in business if it didn't."

"Got any tips for improving my love life?"

"Change jobs?"

Delaney gave Salome a "don't go there" look.

"Just kidding," Salome replied quickly and offered a general cure-all, a sort of feng shui aspirin. "First, clear away all clutter in the bedroom and that includes removing anything under the bed. Once that's done, clean the room top to bottom. Then give me a call."

"How much does this sort of thing cost?"

"Consider it on the house."

"I'll bet that's a feng shui pun. Right?"

Salome laughed. "Right. But I am serious."

"Great. I'll definitely call."

When the officers left, Salome and Jude returned to the kitchen.

"See, that wasn't so bad," he said. "And it looks like you've got a new friend on the force. What'd you do? Offer your services?"

"You bet. Did you find out anything? Any links between Snow's murder and the robberies?" What Delaney had told her about the bathroom murals she decided to hold as a sort of trump card—which wouldn't matter if he already knew. Still . . .

He scooted his chair around so he was parallel to the window rather than being in the vulnerable position of having his back fully to it.

"So far, it doesn't appear that robbery figured into Snow's death." He looked away for a moment. "It's funny. Working homicide, if we didn't have someone in lockup and the case close to solved in twenty-four hours, the pressure would be on. Now that I'm on the other side, I'm beginning to see how the pressure can work against you, in and of itself another obstacle." He looked back at her. "How often have you heard that if a murder isn't solved in twenty-four hours it's likely that it never will be?"

He shook his head. She could see him building up steam. "What bull! Stinks of politics and public relations and people that know better worrying about how they're gonna look on the evening news. I may be floundering right now but I think I'm going to like working on this side. Working by instinct is one thing but having time to think is a real luxury."

Salome figured this was as good a time as any to make her case, and jumped in before he went off on another tangent.

"Look, Jude, I'm serious about wanting to take my feng shui practice to another level. Since I've got the next few days free, let me see what I can come up with from a feng shui angle. I could help in other areas, too, I mean now that you're totally without office space, staff—" She took a quick breath, then went on. "—and it's not like we've never worked together before. I know you're not all that interested in feng shui—"

"Not true. What happened after you feng shuied the restaurant is proof enough for me. It's just that I'm a Baptist."

The remark sounded so much like a non sequitur and his expression was so serious, she couldn't help but smile.

"Nothing funny about being a Baptist."

"Ain't that the truth—no offense. Religious beliefs don't affect the fundamental principles of feng shui one way or another. But that's a topic for another day. Anyway, we could set up an office in the basement."

"What about bringing evil energy into the house? I mean, I feel bad about having those crime scene photos spread out on the dining room table. Of course, I'd planned to have them out of the way by the time you returned home...."

"Don't worry about it. It's not like I've never dealt with brutal murder before! I've even crafted some pretty foul deeds myself. Fictionally, of course. Primarily, we have to establish a dedicated work area—a command post where the investigative work is focused. There are various things I can do to eliminate negative energy before it builds up. The basement's virtually empty and certainly big enough."

"Why not just set up shop in the rooms I've been staying in?"

"You shouldn't have your work and sleep areas adjacent."

"Salome. This would be temporary anyway. I could set up the computer on the refectory table. The phone jack's close so there's be no problem hooking up the modem."

"There's a phone jack here in the kitchen. Use an extra long cord and hook up the modem in the basement." Salome watched him anxiously. "And keep in mind that money's not a problem with me."

Judah turned away, his focus on the backyard. Pride, she reasoned, would make this decision.

"Officer Delaney told me something that might be pertinent," she said.

"But you're not going to share that with me unless I agree to accommodate this new project of yours."

"Hey. It's a simple matter of quid pro quo. You can't lose."

Finally he said, "Let's take a walk."

Five minutes later, Salome closed and locked the front door. The rain had reduced to fizzy drizzle and the temperature had risen. Though still too early to tell, a warm and lovely spring day might be ahead. And then she saw it—the hideous fence that had been erected in her absence, the components of which had been revealed on the view plate attached to Fiona's digital camcorder. Her heart sank at the sight of the ugly black spikes, bent at the top, surrounding the manor house at the bottom of the cul-de-sac. Indeed she had work to do not only inside but outside the house as well.

"So where are we going?" she asked, trying to reestablish a cheerful demeanor.

"Where do you want to go?" he said coyly. She knew something was up as he'd changed clothes.

"Let's head over to Simon Snow's."

Judah smiled and did something unexpected. From his pocket he withdrew a key.

"Your wish is my command."

"You know, I just don't hear that often enough," she declared, eyes shining and mood instantly restored.

Chapter 5

TO Salome, autumn best accessorized Georgetown: the changing leaves particularly suited to the antique houses, the crisp air stimulating an intellectual appreciation of their stately forms and revered place in American history.

In spring, though, with life in its vibrant stage of renewal, many of the old homes seemed to sag beneath a burden of time, reminding Salome of dowagers hunkered down on a children's playground, of colorful, pretty bonnets framing an aged face. Even the air, redolent with pheromones, turned thoughts toward structural mortality—how much longer would the brick and mortar hold up? How much longer before the brick and cobblestone underfoot turned to dust?

"How on earth did you get a key?"

"Snow's sister-in-law, Ellen Russo. She's taking care of things while Snow's estate's being settled."

"Hmm. Does she benefit from his death?"

"Probably, but I don't see her as the perpetrator. She's a widow and by all accounts she and Snow were close.

She doesn't believe for a minute that Jett Malieu killed him. She said he's so determined to get his degree, she can't imagine him doing anything to jeopardize that all-important goal. If she'd done the deed, I doubt if she'd be so willing to defend Malieu—even going so far as to giving me access to the house now that the cops are finished with it. She seems honestly baffled; couldn't come up with a single name to divert suspicion from Malieu and her."

Judah had exchanged the jeans and T-shirt for flannel slacks, a crisp, yellow Oxford cloth shirt, and a cordovan belt that matched his tasseled loafers. With the collegiate attire, wire-rimmed glasses, and comfortably aged leather briefcase, he looked like a Georgetown professor. How he dressed around here was an important consideration, especially if he wanted people to open their doors to him and talk. Still, there must be quite a few people—good guys and bad—who recognized him. When he was on the force, the brass liked to trot him out before the cameras to discuss whatever murder he was investigating whether he liked it or not. Though erudite, he never talked down to people and he possessed a presence that inspired confidence and trust—all of which made his problems in civilian life that much more poignant. Had he been just a mediocre cop, chances are he'd be having an easier time adjusting.

Now she told him what Officer Delaney had said about Snow's association with the burgled women.

"We'll just have to talk to the ladies," Jude remarked.

"You think they'll open up to a private investigator?"

"If it means they have a better chance of recovering their property. I'll just have to see what I can do."

"What's Ellen Russo like?"

"A well-nourished, gray-haired lady in her late sixties," he said with a smile. "Sharp. She runs one of

Snow's ancillary businesses—ironically, one that sells and installs home security systems."

"His death certainly doesn't speak well for the product."

"He just made money off the systems. Didn't bother with one himself."

"Why not?"

"According to Mrs. Russo, he didn't like to be controlled by technology."

Jude had a slow, deliberate pace that forced Salome to rein herself in, reminding her how infrequently she walked with anyone.

"So what about Jett Malieu? Have you questioned him? Any violence in his background?" Recalling what he'd written, she asked, "Do you think he might have been having sex with Snow and they were using that staff as some sort of prop?"

"Slow down! First of all, he's adamant about not being gay. Secondly, I spoke to him briefly after he was released. That would have been Thursday. Most of my information has come from Chimene."

"That's strange. Especially since he's your client."

"Chimene's the client, Salome."

"I suppose I mean that you're trying to prove he's innocent."

"The kid's terrified. My guess is he knows something and needs to sort things out. His girlfriend's involved—not to mention her father, who's an ex-cop—all of which complicate the guy's life."

"So, what is he like?"

Judah stopped for a moment and pulled an eight-by-ten glossy from his briefcase. Salome whistled at the professional beefcake pose of Malieu wearing only a pair of bathing trunks. After a moment, she realized that he wasn't altogether unknown to her.

"Give him points for not wearing a Speedo." She handed it back. "He was at the fund-raiser, you know. In fact, after my presentation, I remember seeing him serve Snow dessert."

"Really? Both Cookie and Chimene told me he'd been there but no one mentioned him having any contact with Snow. Not that he wouldn't, I suppose. I mean the man was his employer. Thing is, Chimene was responsible for the linguist staff as well as all the other auction items."

"I know. I helped look for it."

"Plenty of people knew about the staff; after all it was the centerpiece of the auction. Chimene said she kept everything in the kitchen. Went to the bathroom and when she returned the staff was gone. Anyone could have picked it up."

"What if Malieu was in on the theft?"

In the near distance they could hear the bell at Georgetown's Healy Tower chime the quarter hour. Jude returned the photograph to his briefcase and they moved on.

"It's a possibility. But to answer that question you asked about violence in his past—he's from West Baltimore, oldest of five kids. No father at home. Took a couple slugs when he was fourteen. His mother couldn't afford more than basic medical care. And he definitely needed to get out of the hood for a while. Anyway, his mother's cousin offered to look after him.

"You ever hear of Diana Daye?"

"As in The Daye School?" Located in Fairfax County, Virginia, the school was one of the most exclusive in the country. The students were girls from wealthy and prestigious African American families.

"She's the one," he said. "Jett stayed in the school's infirmary until he was healed. Of course, by then he didn't want to go home. Diana liked him and didn't want to send him back. Daye's students were well disciplined and she trusted them. It was a risk, but she moved Jett into her apartment, deciding to trust him, too. If he so much as winked at one of the students he'd be back in Baltimore. He did custodial and kitchen work while attending high school in Fairfax.

"His SATs were over the top," Judah went on. "Could have gotten into any school he wanted. He chose Diana's alma mater, Howard University. Where he is currently majoring in accounting."

"So," Salome said as Jude steered them down P Street. "You're saying he's a good guy."

"Not exactly closing in on sainthood, but yeah. He's worked for Snow for two years. Reputedly an outstanding cook—chef—what have you. Caters for all Snow's parties, hiring wait staff himself."

"You two share common ground there—cooking, that is. Might be a way for you to get him to open up."

Judah laughed. Then he regarded her more seriously. "Hadn't thought of that. Anyway, he basically ran the household. A maid came in twice a week to do the general cleaning; her husband took care of gardening chores once a week. Jett had his own rooms, a small bedroom and bath downstairs."

"Where's he staying now?"

"A small apartment near campus. Chimene wanted him to move in with her. I tell you, he scored points with me when he declined that offer."

They sauntered on, passing a few wrinkle-free mansions that looked fabulous any time of year, Jude absorbed in his own thoughts for the moment. Salome now remembered a series of articles on feng shui that appeared in the *Washington Post* last spring. Comments by several interior decorators had been included, Simon Snow among them. Far from complementary, he'd sug-

gested that feng shui practitioners were simply trying to
weasel their way into the interior design trade.

Salome's mentor, Madame Wu, had been one of the
practitioners featured in the series. One morning she'd
called and angrily read aloud a passage attributed to
Simon Snow:

". . . they're ruining it for the rest of us. That ratty old
couch? Well, instead of buying a new one or even having
it reupholstered, a feng shui practitioner will say all you
have to do is move the thing! I mean really."

Salome broke into the silence, "Snow seemed to regard
feng shui as a threat. After all, if someone's seeking
change in their home, it's easier and certainly less expensive to move existing furnishings than to go out and
buy new. And given his various stores, he must have
made very good money by being able to sell the items
he recommended."

"Ironic, isn't it, that he'd end up winning the door
prize."

"I can't help but wonder if Snow really did have something to do with the theft of the linguist staff. If his intention was to embarrass Cookie, it succeeded. That's
going to stay with her for a long time. But if he was
involved, the plan backfired—horrendously."

"While the staff certainly adds a dramatic dimension
to the crime, we can't lose sight of the fact that ultimately
a pair of hands killed the man. It takes strength to break
someone's neck."

"Or finesse. You ever see any Bruce Lee or Jet Li
movies?"

They stood at the bottom of a drive leading up to
Snow's house. Salome glanced around. Since Snow's
murder, she doubted if his neighbors had been sleeping
soundly. She noted the quiet and lack of activity. Though
curtains were drawn, she had the feeling they were being

watched. Then, next door, the gardener popped up from behind a hedge. Jude raised his hand in greeting. " 'Mornin', Carl," Jude said.

"Detective Freeman," Carl said somberly.

"Carl's the first person in the neighborhood I spoke to. Pretty much knows everything goes on around here, don't you, Carl?"

Carl nodded. The proprietary look on his face told Salome he'd probably been working next door to Snow for years. "This is my partner," Jude announced. "Salome Waterhouse."

"Nice to meet you, Carl," Salome said, pleased and somewhat surprised that she'd been elevated to partner so soon. At the same time, it was the simplest way to explain her presence.

"Likewise." Carl nodded.

"Salome and I are going up to the house to have a look around."

"You do that, Detective Freeman. And good luck to you both. Sooner that killer's caught, the happier folks around here'll be, I can tell you that."

As they started up the drive, Salome asked to be filled in on the details of the crime; it was difficult to envision bloody murder in such innocently idyllic surroundings.

Chapter 6

ORNAMENTAL cherry trees lined and over-hung the curving drive, newly opened pink buds clinging to the branches. Clusters of daffodils, their sunny yellow flowers trumpeting the season, grew between the trunks. Salome tried not to let the beauty of the place distract her as she listened to Jude recite a few more details.

Jett Malieu discovered Snow's body around eight P.M. the previous Wednesday. The medical examiner determined the time of death to be not too long after Snow had eaten lunch—roughly sometime between one-thirty and three P.M. The neighbors reported seeing nothing unusual that afternoon, but then most of them were out enjoying a round of post-winter golf, shopping, attending luncheons, and even, in some cases, working. Servants dittoed their employers but pointed out that little could be seen of Snow's detached house for all the trees. Carl, though, mentioned seeing Malieu's vintage orange Toyota Corolla leaving the house around one-thirty P.M., which, in any case, was a normal occurrence. On Mondays, Wednesdays, and Fridays he left at that time to attend his afternoon classes at Howard University. After classes he studied at the library until his evening class and returned between eight and nine P.M. That particular night, Malieu had left dinner for Snow, which Snow could heat in the microwave. Alerted by the uneaten meal, Malieu went looking for his employer and when he found him, called 911.

Carl had also mentioned seeing the florist van arrive while he—Carl—was getting ready to leave about quarter of two. This caused him no concern, as fresh flowers were delivered daily though not always at the same time. However, the florist denied having gone to the house as the morning of the murder Snow had cancelled his standing order, giving no reason for doing so.

"Carl's adamant that it was a Metro Florist van he saw that day," Judah remarked. "I checked with them and they said Snow called up and cancelled that morning first thing. *Someone* delivered flowers, though, because Malieu said there were several fresh bouquets when he arrived home that evening."

"Maybe someone pretending to be Snow called in to cancel." Salome inhaled the sweetly scented air, thinking how fortunate Simon Snow had been to have such natural beauty embracing the otherwise dead asphalt drive. The trees and flowers would attract ch'i toward his English Romantic Revival mansion. It was a two-story boot-shaped house with eyebrow dormers jutting from a hipped roof of irregular shingles, which gave the appearance of thatch. Two prominent brick chimneys stood at the north and south sides of the structure. The "toe" of the boot was in the knowledge gua, leaving career and helpful people vacant. However, a lovely old mulberry tree stood directly across in helpful people, thus nicely squaring off the area.

Auspiciously, fragrant wisteria dripped masses of

lavender-colored blooms from a trellis arcing around the recessed, gabled front entrance. A partially hidden entrance was not considered good feng shui: all too quickly, the energy would become trapped and stagnate, undermining the happiness of the inhabitants. In an instant, Salome flashed on a client, a well-known actress who was fanatical about her privacy. She'd chosen the southern California bungalow in which she lived precisely because the entrance was disguised in an ivy-covered wall. And then she wondered why she was so unhappy. The ch'i couldn't find a way in the house. The woman's life changed dramatically when she tore down the wall, placed a pot of fragrant jasmine to the left of the front door and, to ease her privacy concerns, positioned a pair of Chinese Fu dogs a few feet in front of the entrance.

The use of color, aromatic plants, and water features were among the various adjustments suggested to attract ch'i to the entrance of a house. Here at Snow's, the fragrance of the wisteria served well but more was needed to alleviate the unpleasant feel of the dank, shadowy space directly around the door.

Jude fished the key from his pocket and unlocked the heavy oak front door on which a plain, prim brass knocker was centered.

"Would you give me a minute?" Salome asked.

"What for?"

"I'd rather enter with my eyes closed. To get a feel for the energy before I see anything."

Without further comment, he stepped inside, leaving the door ajar.

Salome softly chanted *om ma ni pad me om* nine times while her hands were held in the proper mudra, left upon right, thumbs barely touching. She then slipped inside and quickly closed the door so the entering ch'i would not interfere with her first impression.

Eyes closed and standing motionless, she met the house's energy. Naturally enough, the temperature registered first. Cold and dank like the entrance. The emotional climate though, felt different and not what she expected since a murder had been committed here. Then, abruptly, she reminded herself not to allow any preconceived ideas to influence her thinking. She needed to treat this house like any other and keep an open mind.

When she adjusted to the absence of anger and hostility, she had a feeling of deception. Then, moving from the general to the specific, she sensed slyness and . . . betrayal.

She opened her eyes. Judah was staring at her intensely. "Well?"

She sighed and blinked.

"Hey, don't hold anything back, Salome. This is new to me. If I look like I think you're nuts, just ignore it."

She told him what she'd experienced. "As I interpret the energy, it seems to me whoever killed Snow wasn't an enemy. At least not someone he or anyone else would expect to be an enemy."

"Uh-huh. Well, that helps a lot. You've probably described most of the people he knew," Jude remarked, his skepticism unmistakable.

"That's why I didn't want to tell you."

"Guess I'll just have to get used to your ways."

Straight ahead was a wide staircase with a plush red carpet. On each banister were large pinecone newels. A gorgeous window of stained glass flowers in reds, pinks, and yellows overlooked the landing.

"You've already been in the house?" Salome asked.

"Yesterday, as a matter of fact. I helped Ellen hang curtains and pictures in Snow's bedroom. The mattress, of course, has been changed. She's going to rent the house furnished. With the change in administrations, there are plenty of people looking for a prestigious address, no matter what happened inside. And, I suppose, there's no shortage of those who'd consider murder an enhancement."

"Right. Let's go to his bedroom first."

They mounted the stairs. At the landing they turned and climbed a second flight. Salome pulled out her camera. Then she remembered she'd used up all her film on the trip. The exposed rolls were still in her bag.

At the top, Jude moved to the left and Salome refocused her attention. She followed his tall form, peeking into the open doorways. When they reached the end, Jude stopped. There were open doors on either side. He entered the room on the left.

Salome automatically conjured a Bagua, aligning it with the front door downstairs, which was in the career gua. That put this bedroom in the relationship gua of the house. The door to the room was in helpful people.

Crime scene photos were one thing; being in the actual space in which a murder had been committed was quite different. Here, if one knew how to listen, the voice of the victim could be heard. In theory, anyway. At the moment all Salome heard was birdsong. For a moment she considered that she hadn't heard much, if anything, from the victims in the Twomey place, either. Doubt started to creep into her thoughts.

"It's bigger than I thought." She sniffed the air. "And it smells of paint."

Salome pulled the notebook and pen from her pocket. For the next few minutes Judah displayed surprising patience as she silently sketched the details of the room. It also gave her time to recharge the positive. Doubt had its uses—primarily as a tool for questioning—but could cloud first impressions.

"From the look of things, he was redecorating and,"

she said, her voice edged with excitement, "according to feng shui principles."

"How can you tell?"

"I'll take you through it step by step. Okay, the bed first." She moved into the room, diagonally across from the door, and ran her hand along the curved satiny, cherry wood footboard.

"This is a Henkel Harris Edwardian-style king-size bed. Looks brand new. Any idea how much this cost?"

"Couple thousand bucks?" Jude shrugged.

"Thirteen thousand."

"Jesus!"

"He probably didn't pay retail. Even so, it's a major expense. Notice the matching cherry nightstands. Both are round, a preferred shape for the bedroom. The erotic sculptures add an obvious sexual dimension. But you know, unless I had a partner—or was trying to attract one—I wouldn't have artwork like this in my bedroom. But that's just me, I guess."

She glanced around. The two paintings Jude had helped hang, interestingly enough, in the relationship gua, and that Snow hadn't lived to enjoy, caught her attention.

"Look at these, Jude," she said. "Cranes. The significance of cranes is that they mate for life. My guess is Snow was looking for a serious, long-term relationship. And notice the use of the color pink in the room. The curtains, the walls have been painted pale pink, and in the crime scene photos the bed linens were pink. In feng shui, pink is the color associated with relationships."

Just inside the room to the left of the door were two bachelor chests pushed side by side. Salome noted the absence of a mirror. With each clue pointing to evidence of feng shui in the bedroom, her conviction grew that Snow had feng shuied the room or had brought in a practitioner.

"In the crime scene photos there was a TV/video player set up at the foot of the bed."

"That's back in the closet."

"What was on the tape?"

"Couple guys doing their thing."

Salome moved to the walk-in closet, Jude coming up behind her. Inside were built-in cabinets that, when pulled out, revealed silk underwear, cashmere sweaters, and so on. On the floor were racks of shoes. An assortment of beautifully tailored suits, trousers, and shirts hung in the discretely scented area. Then, in an alcove, they found the TV/VCR on a wheeled stand and empty shelves above it.

"Where's his collection of tapes?"

"There weren't any. Just the one in the machine."

"Isn't that a bit odd?"

"Jett told the police he never knew Snow to be interested in porn. In fact, at one time he—Malieu that is—was approached by someone who wanted to put him in porn films. He told Snow about it. Snow said pornography was particularly demeaning to gays, that it gave people the impression gays were all sexual predators."

"What about prints on the tape?"

"Snow's, the rest unidentified."

"So no other tapes at all?"

"Not in the closet."

"If he's got the VCR handy, why not any tapes? How about in the other rooms?"

"Downstairs in the den is another VCR and a few videos of old movies. There's also a DVD player and a selection of DVDs. Snow also had a membership at a rental place on Wisconsin. I talked to the clerk. He said Snow rented new releases of movies, lately only DVDs and never any porn. At least while he, the clerk that is, was working."

They'd seen about all the bedroom had to offer.

"So, what do you think?" Jude asked as they moved into the hall.

"Just a minute." She stepped into the doorway opposite Snow's bedroom and regarded a room haphazardly filled with assorted bedroom furniture and large mirrors. Various prints and original art crowded the walls. The windows overlooked the front garden. Almost directly across was the mulberry tree.

"He *did* redecorate, Jude! I bet a good portion of the furniture in here was originally across the hall."

She moved back to the pink bedroom. Finally she summarized:

"The choice of pink, the position of the bed, the art objects all suggest feng shui. One more thing—there aren't any mirrors. According to feng shui, mirrors should be kept out of the bedroom as they disturb sleep. I don't think these factors are a matter of coincidence, Jude. He may have been a detractor of feng shui but something or someone changed his mind."

They went downstairs.

"Oh dear!" Salome exclaimed as they entered Snow's home office. Though auspiciously located in the wealth gua of the house there was a problem.

"What?"

"The desk." She went on to tell Jude that the desk was placed in the worst position in the room—that being so he sat with his back to the door. "This particular position suggests activity going on behind a person's back, and also, being stabbed in the back—which pretty much applies, doesn't it?" She shivered slightly, the image of the linguist staff protruding from the Snow's body appearing in her mind.

She moved to the desk, understanding why he would like that position, for it was directly in front of a window that overlooked the well-kept back garden complete with a fountain in the center.

"Is there a, whaddayacallit, cure?" Jude asked.

She smiled. "Oh yes. You can hang a mirror so you can see anyone entering behind you. There are also small convex mirrors you can attach to a computer monitor. Still, it's best to move the desk altogether, the strongest position being at a diagonal from the door."

She noticed a lonely little computer mouse resting on a blue mouse pad. "Where's his computer?"

"Ellen Russo took the monitor and speakers to use in one of the other offices—I can't remember which one. Maybe his main office in the showroom on Connecticut. Anyway, the monitor's one of those new slim ones. Expensive, and she wanted to put it to use. The police have the rest of the computer. Ellen insists that he could do little more than send email: That he'd gotten the computer more to appear up-to-date than to put it to use."

Shelves of books on interior design, architecture, and art covered most of the wall space. She checked the spines while Jude wandered around the room. There was a grouping of professional-looking tan leather furniture around a coffee table with a few magazines on the polished surface. Neither found anything of particular interest. Salome was a little surprised not to find a single volume on feng shui.

She made a mental note to call her mentor, Madame Wu, and ask if she'd heard of any practitioner Snow might have consulted.

"Why don't we have a look at Jett Malieu's rooms?"

Judah guided her to a little room off the kitchen. It had pale-blue walls, a small closet, a neat single bed with a navy-blue blanket, glaringly white sheets, and a tiny pillow. On the wall next to the bed was a photo, presumably of his mother and siblings, everyone crowded together on a stoop in front of a run-down–looking row house. A small window with a flimsy blue nylon curtain was just behind the head of the bed. Across from the bed was a desk and straight-back wooden chair and a book-shelf where he kept a reading light. A flowered curtain opened onto a tiny, windowless bathroom with a shower stall, sink, and toilet. Both rooms were spotless.

"Spartan, isn't it," Jude commented.

"Considering the rest of the house, Spartan to the point of demeaning." Salome's thoughts turned to that Henkel Harris bed upstairs. "I think I'd be a bit more generous, especially with someone who prepares all my meals."

Jude laughed. "Took the lead detective all of about five minutes to go through Malieu's stuff. Can't accuse the young man of being acquisitive."

Had Salome been a gourmet cook she would have drooled all over Snow's state-of-the-art kitchen. The room itself was located in the family/health gua of the house itself. The stove was a Le Corneau with six gas burners and a deep oven and was positioned so the cook could see whoever entered from either of the two en-trances. There were stainless steel double sinks, a walk-in restaurant-sized refrigerator, and an island/work station in the center of the room. Out of the way in an adjoining space was a solid wall of cupboards with glass panels. Here he kept all serving equipment: gorgeous silver, crys-tal, and china.

"A thief would have had a field day," Salome re-marked. "By the way, Jude, did Snow have any signifi-cant jewelry?"

"Not according to Ellen. But that's a question that may have to be asked again in light of the recent burglaries."

"Jett might know."

"The sooner I get some answers out of that boy, the better," he mumbled.

So, she wondered as she opened drawers and peeked into stocked cupboards, what had been the motive? Why would anyone want to kill Simon Snow? Did he have something someone could only gain by murder? Or was it personal—revenge, maybe? Had a disgruntled client, like, say, Cookie, killed him because of a botched job? Of course she couldn't imagine Cookie resorting to brutal murder. And if Cookie hadn't known about feng shui, she would have simply lost her business, never thinking that the interior decoration had anything to do with it.

They moved on into the adjacent, lavishly furnished living area located in the knowledge gua of the house, the toe of the boot. She figured he primarily entertained here as the space had that cold stillness of an infrequently used room. A stand-alone, circular gas fireplace was in the center of the room, cushioned seating surrounding it. Several sets of French doors opened onto a terrace with terra-cotta pots of newly planted spring flowers.

Jude checked his watch. "I need to get going pretty soon."

"Just a quick look at the den?"

Salome found the den to be the most appealing room so far. Located in the relationship qua on the ground floor, several sets of floor-to-ceiling French doors provided plenty of light. Here he'd chosen a few expensive pieces of rosewood in a Chinese motif and big comfortable divans and overstuffed chairs in pale yellow and white. Accessories included a pair of carved rosewood dragons on the mantel and several vases. Just out of curiosity, Salome lifted a pale-green vase with a gold lip and looked at the bottom. She wasn't an expert on ceramics but if this was an antique, maybe even museum quality, Ellen Russo might want to sell rather than risk having it broken by renters. Her own tea bowl had the one-of-a-kind mark of the artisan. But instead of a marking, she found a small black sticker with gold lettering: *Mah's Chinese Arts and Antiquities.*

Interesting, she thought.

A few minutes later they left the house. While walking down the drive, Jude's pace having picked up now, he asked, "So what did the house tell you?"

"I think the cops should be looking for someone with whom Snow was enamored—almost desperately so."

"You're saying a gay guy he was involved with?"

"Not necessarily. I don't think this person reciprocated Snow's feelings. That's why Snow was trying so hard to attract him. Could be someone who's straight but might be considering a homosexual relationship. On the other hand, it could be someone who played Snow along until he got what he wanted."

"And killed him for it?"

"Or maybe knows who did."

"Okay, well, I guess I'll catch you back at the house," Jude said when they reached the end of the drive.

"Wait a minute. You didn't let me finish. There's a good chance he does business with this person. Might even be a client."

Jude blinked. He glanced down the street then back at her. "Where'd you get that?"

"The impression I get from the placement of the desk. Like I told you, when you sit at a desk with your back to the door, you are symbolically setting yourself up for being stabbed in the back—figuratively—by someone involved with your business."

Salome nodded then asked, "Was it determined that he was actually *in* bed when he was murdered, when his neck was broken?"

"It looks that way."

"What if he was at his desk? What if his killer sneaked

up behind him, broke his neck then carried him upstairs, and staged the whole scene on the bed."

Jude regarded her thoughtfully. "You know, now that you mention it, I wondered about his clothes. The sweats found by the bed. And if what you say is right, that he was hot for someone, he'd have dressed more carefully for a liaison. Even if the purpose is to get naked, you tend to try to look your best before. Cookie used to wear these beautiful silk—" He stopped and looked away.

To get him back on course, Salome quickly asked, "Do you have any police photos of the office?"

"No. But I would have heard if it warranted attention as a possible crime scene."

"When are you going to see Jett Malieu?"

"Soon as possible. I'll see what I can arrange."

"I'd like to go with you, if you don't mind."

"Sure. No problem."

They parted, Jude heading east toward Prospect Street and lunch with Gabriel while Salome decided to wander over to Wisconsin Avenue. She had a couple of places to visit on the popular street.

Jude had gone but a few steps when he turned and called her name.

"Hey, Mei!"

Salome stopped.

"You need to talk to your new neighbor. Guy who moved in to the big house—"

"Duncan Mah?"

"Yeah. Anyway, I forgot to mention it but someone came by this weekend, said the locks on the carriage house were going to be changed. If you want to get your car out, you might have to get a new key from him."

"Thanks, Jude. See you later."

Salome smiled to herself. How synchronistic. After dropping off her film to be developed and buying new rolls, she planned to stop in at Mah's Chinese Arts and Antiquities.

Chapter 7

JUST minutes after leaving the quiet enclave where the most intrusive noise came from a jubilant mockingbird, Salome entered the noisy rush on Wisconsin Avenue. A lunchtime crowd partook of the eclectic restaurants and shops, moving at a pace Salome found invigorating. She always enjoyed window shopping here as much for the unusual merchandise as the exotic mix of humanity.

She dropped her film off at the photo shop, then, recalling Fiona's directions, she headed toward Calvert Street and eventually found herself peering in the storefront window of Mah's Chinese Art and Antiquities. As she entered, a bell jangled on the door. An older Chinese woman wearing a Chinese-style ensemble of short-sleeved blouse and flowing trousers in dark blue entered at the back through a red beaded curtain and smiled. Salome noted that the curtain was in the fame gua. The color red would stimulate the shop's reputation in the community, essential for any business.

The woman wore her hair cut short in a neat salt-and-pepper cap. On her right wrist was a pale-green jade bracelet with a gold hinge and safety chain.

"I'd just like to look around, if I may," Salome said.

The woman nodded and began emptying boxes, surreptitiously keeping an eye on Salome as she roamed around the store.

"How long have you been open?" Salome asked.

The shop room was about eight hundred square feet, track lighting providing illumination. The air was cool and pleasantly scented by sandalwood.

"We open at ten, close at five-thirty."

"No, I mean, how long has the store been here? I've been out of town, you see."

"Ah. March. We open in March."

On either side of the entrance were neatly arranged displays of rosewood chairs and tables and stunning room dividers with elaborate inlay of mother-of-pearl. On the walls were hand-painted scrolls of orange carp and misty Chinese landscapes, blue-and-white porcelain weights and tassels keeping the scrolls from curling. Further inside were shelves of brass, ceramic, and jadeite Chinese deities, including male gods of happiness and fortune with huge, smooth stomachs, and slender Kwan Yins. There were expensive tea sets, vases, and hanging rugs, and locked display cases featuring cloisonné ware, jade figurines and jewelry, and assorted Chinese coins. Of Bagua mirrors, wind chimes, faceted crystals, there were none; either the shop didn't sell feng shui supplies or they'd not yet unpacked such items. Salome had been hoping feng shui supplies would be available; if she needed something she could simply walk over to the shop and have it within minutes. As it was, she made most of her purchases in Chinatown or on the Internet. Of course, this store dealt primarily in high-dollar items. Still she needed some gifts and decided to give Mah's her custom. She approached the Chinese woman.

"I'm looking for a Kwan Yin and a Kwan Kung, not too expensive."

"Okay," the woman said brusquely.

As they moved to the display of Chinese deities, Salome figured she'd have gotten a warmer reception had she not concluded her request with "not too expensive."

Finally, Salome settled on a Kwan Yin in translucent porcelain holding a prayer in one hand. At her feet was a dragon's upturned head, its open mouth waiting to receive the prayer. This she intended to give to Fiona.

"You know Kwan Kung?" the woman asked. She set several elaborately dressed male figurines, each with flowing Manchu moustaches and beards and holding a lethal-looking dragon halberd, on the glass counter. All were a bit more expensive than what she'd first thought she'd pay. It wasn't the money but sometimes people felt uncomfortable receiving an expensive gift, especially if they didn't have the means to reciprocate. And this one was for Jude.

"Oh yes. Patron saint of police."

"And politicians," she reminded, segueing into a spiel. "We sell lots of these in Washington! These," she added, "are very powerful. Especially this one." She gently tapped the one with the fiercest expression. He was also the most expensive.

Indeed, Salome knew, the fiercer the expression, the more potent the figure.

"All right then, I'll take him."

As they walked over to the cash register, which Salome noticed had no enhancements though it was partly in the wealth gua, partly in fame, Salome said, "I was hoping you'd have feng shui supplies."

Then, almost as if the words had acted like a powerful

magnet, a young Chinese woman darted out from the beaded curtain. Though dressed in a cheap paisley blouse and cotton trousers, she was uncommonly beautiful. Her abundant blue-black hair was held back from her delicate face by two cheap barrettes and cascaded down her back to her waist.

Immediately, the older woman rattled off something in Chinese that sent the girl flying back through the beads. The whole episode began and ended in a matter of seconds.

The woman tallied Salome's bill. Salome handed over a credit card. "You see, I'm a feng shui practitioner. In fact, I should introduce myself. I'm Salome Waterhouse."

The woman handed over the slip for Salome to sign, comparing the signature with that on the back of the credit card, giving no clue that she was interested or had even heard the introduction.

"I live on Malabar Close. Number three."

That, at least, got the woman's attention. She looked up sharply.

"In fact, I need to get in touch with Duncan Mah. You know him, of course."

"Yes!"

"Maybe we should start over," Salome said, her annoyance evident. "I'm Salome Waterhouse. I live at number three Malabar Close and am the neighbor of Duncan Mah. And you are?"

"Betty Wong. His auntie."

Both "auntie" and "uncle" were honorifics used by the Chinese to denote practically anyone. So she might or might not be related.

"Thing is, I just returned from my winter home. I rent space in the carriage house and I need to get my car. I was told the locks have been changed. I thought he might be here at the shop and could give me a key."

Betty's eyes widened. "Oh, I see. No, he's not here." She offered nothing further.

Salome took a deep breath. "Fine. Would you call him for me, please? Surely you know his number."

The beads snapped together as Betty slipped through the curtain. Salome heard her speaking in rapid Chinese and didn't need to understand the language to know the woman was frightened.

While Betty was on the phone, the young Chinese girl suddenly reappeared and pulled out white tissue paper in which to wrap the figurines.

"Hi," Salome said. "What's your name?"

The girl looked up and Salome suddenly felt a bone-deep chill. The girl's demeanor now seemed threatening. It was something in her eyes, in the way she regarded Salome—as if Salome was something she might be considering for lunch.

"She doesn't speak English!" Betty snapped. She shooed the girl away and took up wrapping the figurines.

Salome shook off the strange sensation. "Well? Did you reach Mr. Mah?"

"He'll see you in an hour," she intoned breathlessly, as if Salome had just been granted a papal interview.

"Where?"

"At the carriage house."

"Thank you."

When Betty handed over the bag, Salome asked another question even though getting answers from this woman was akin to quarrying marble.

"By the way, did Simon Snow come in the shop very often?"

Betty blinked, hesitating just a bit too long. "Never heard of him."

"He was a small man about sixty. Quite famous around here, certainly since his murder."

A silence followed.

"He has things in his house from this store."

"Maybe someone else waits on him. Not me."

JUDE HADN'T RETURNED FROM LUNCH SO she left the Kwan Kung in the bag to give him later. But she really didn't expect him back anytime soon. Gabriel was no doubt sucking every morsel of information Jude had gleaned about Simon Snow's murder, then adding his own theories. At the same time, she had a feeling Jude might be enlisting Gabe's professional help. After reading Jude's short summation of the crime last night, and seeing him read over it this morning, she couldn't help but think he was finally catching up with his early dream, formed in college, to be a writer.

With the wrapped Kwan Yin in hand, she made the short trip to Fiona's and knocked on the door. While waiting, she looked around. There was no activity in the Close, not even an errant tourist looking for a parking space.

Finally, when no one answered, she returned home, wondering if Fiona had gone to Chicago as she'd mentioned last week. At least that meant she wasn't following Duncan Mah around and possibly getting herself into trouble.

Cleaning the house was at the top of her to-do list so, after tucking the goddess away in the chest in the foyer, she decided to start in the kitchen, having some time before meeting Mah.

While she had no complaints about Judah's kitchen maintenance, cleaning was a sort of sacred ritual, something always performed as soon as possible after returning from California, whether the house needed it or not.

Cleaning was a personal, intimate act that reconnected her with the house.

If more people simply changed their attitude, cleaning wouldn't be seen as an unpleasant or boring chore. She always advised cleaning a house or apartment when one first moved in as a way to learn more about a place. Especially in an impersonal city where one could easily feel alienated, an intimate knowledge of each room and each corner of each room created a fundamental sense of belonging.

And so, she set about her task with joy and once the major appliances, sink, counters, and floor were done, she blessed the room. By then, it was time to meet her neighbor.

THE CARRIAGE HOUSE WAS ON THE WEST side of the manor house and consisted of four spaces roughly demarcated by white paint on a concrete foundation. Currently, the spaces were rented by residents of the Close at a cost of several hundred dollars a month. In the past, Isabelle occasionally rented to outsiders to whom she upped the charges—in parking-deprived Georgetown, still a deal.

Salome stood in front of one of the two wide garage doors waiting for Mah. Though still angered by his destruction of the rose garden, she was curious enough to feel some titillation. She wondered why he hadn't just taken over one of the spaces in the carriage house for his own use, though it would have been at the expense of one of the neighbors, even her.

She saw him come around the back of the manor house, slipping on a pair of mirrored sunglasses as he approached.

"You're Mrs. Waterhouse?" he asked in what almost

sounded like a declaration. To Salome it wasn't just a simple mistake. He should have known her marital status— she only lived a matter of yards from him and paid him well for the use of the carriage house, sending in a check every month. Even though they'd never met, she found his ignorance insulting.

"No."

That took him aback.

"I'm *Ms.* Salome Waterhouse."

He snorted and smiled. It dawned on her that he probably thought she'd mentioned the distinction to let him know she was available. That piqued her further and made her bold.

"Why did you destroy the rose garden?"

He unlocked the garage door and began fiddling with one of the keys, trying to remove it from the ring.

"That should be evident. I need parking for guests and myself."

"You could have used the carriage house."

"Would you have sacrificed your space?"

"Absolutely." Of course it wouldn't have been that much of a problem for her since she didn't need the convenience every day and stored her car half the year.

"That can be arranged right now." He suddenly straightened and stood with his hands held in front of him, his head high. "You may vacate the premises, *Ms.* Waterhouse."

She stared at him, unnerved by seeing her own stunned expression reflected in his sunglasses. After a moment, she regained her ability to speak. "As soon as I have my refund. I sent you a check for the month."

He pulled a cell phone out of his pocket and punched a button on speed dial. "Give Lee five hundred dollars and have him bring it to the carriage house. Call the first person on the waiting list for a parking space. Double the price."

He snapped the phone shut and smiled at Salome. "You see, *Ms.* Waterhouse, you have done me a favor. Helped bring more money into my house."

Working to keep her emotions in check, Salome pulled the cover off her British racing green Austin Healey 3000. Beside it was Fiona's black SAAB. She added to her speculations about Fiona's whereabouts. Quite possibly Fiona was working and ignoring interruptions. Or she might be off on a walk. Salome decided to telephone. Even if she were monitoring calls, at least Fiona would know Salome had returned.

"You plan to evict anyone else?"

He laughed. "It would make good business sense, now wouldn't it. My grandmother extended a courtesy to her neighbors by allowing them to rent parking space at a discount. Wanting to be a good neighbor I chose to continue the policy. Perhaps though, I'll just increase the rent. The neighbors can thank you for bringing the matter to my attention."

A young Chinese man in a dark suit jogged up to the pair. He handed an envelope to Mah. Instead of taking it, Mah nodded at Salome. The young man gave her the envelope and bowed slightly.

"Count it," Mah said.

Salome looked at the young man. Though he studiously avoided meeting her eyes she felt a wave of fear roll off him.

"I'm sure it's all here," she said and slipped the envelope into her pocket. The young man immediately turned and jogged back to the house.

Salome slid behind the wheel and pumped the gas a couple times to prime the engine. After a few tries, the engine engaged. She'd asked Jude to take the car for a

spin every once in a while but he refused, not wanting
to tempt fate. If she'd had an ordinary car, he probably
wouldn't have thought twice. But no way could the
Healey be considered an ordinary ride.

She backed out, for a moment considering running
over Mah's immaculate Italian shoes. He smiled at her
as she passed. He lowered and locked the garage door
then disappeared around the back of the house.

Times like this reminded her that she did have a tem-
per, and a considerable one at that. She pulled up in front
of her house, double-parking next to Jude's car, so hot
with ire she suspected steam must have been shooting
from her ears. Letting the Healey idle, she stepped out
and raised both hands. Flicking the second and third fingers of each hand against her thumbs, she "threw away"
the negative energy while muttering *om ma ni pad me
om.* In a few minutes, she felt cleaner, as if she'd taken
an internal shower.

Then she dashed in the house and picked up her purse.

Back behind the wheel, she fished her cell phone out
of her handbag and punched out the numbers of Dario
Burgos's pager, returning his call of several weeks ago,
having picked up his message off her machine while she
was in California.

While waiting for a reply, she counted the cash. Five
hundred even, in small bills. That gave her pause. Did
Mah keep cash on hand for emergencies? Plenty of people did. But wouldn't it have made more sense to write
her a check, thereby keeping a record? Which reminded
her that she should have given him a receipt.

Just then, the phone trilled.

Dario's voice slid from the phone to her ear like a wet
tongue.

After concluding the call, she pulled out of the Close,

her good humor partly restored, on her way to Foreign Service across the Potomac in McLean, Virginia.

Yes, indeed, she thought, every cloud does have a sweet spot.

Chapter 8

DARIO Burgos pulled off the tight-fitting latex gloves as he sauntered across the floor of the garage toward Bay 6, where Salome had just pulled in.

"Chica," he said and opened the door for her. As she stepped out, he kissed her on both cheeks. "I've missed you." Then his gray eyes followed the rolling lines from front fender to rear. "And the car."

Several expensive automobiles were in various stages of attention, the mechanics' tools gleaming on trays like precision surgical instruments. And indeed, the garage was like an operating room, with Dario Burgos, in his gray overalls—gray being the hue associated with helpful people/travel—with the embroidered name patch, head surgeon. And like medical personnel, all the mechanics wore surgical gloves.

The floor and bays were kept as clean as possible and the air fresh. Today Al Di Meola's classical guitar form of jazz fusion provided a subtle rhythm to work by. The music reflected Dario's taste. But then, he owned Foreign Service, and could play whatever he pleased. Fortunately, his taste in music didn't annoy his mechanics or customers and, it was rumored, actually improved the performance of the exotic automobiles—literally had them humming.

What most people didn't know was that the garage had been feng shuied by Salome. That accounted for the cheery yellow walls, immaculate shop floor, hearty plants, the thirty-millimeter faceted crystals hanging at each clean window, the wind chime positioned to catch the breeze when the bay doors were open, and the sound system. The mechanics liked their work environment though some couldn't explain exactly why. They would simply say that they all got along, Dario was a fair boss, the wages were good, and their patients some of the world's finest.

Before the feng shui consultation, Foreign Service had been scraping by even though the garage had the reputation as one of the best in the metro area. After talking to him for a while, Salome determined that, while he loved working on cars, British makes in particular, he hated the business side of things.

The offices and bathrooms shared by all had been on the right side of the garage in a space taking up the relationship, creativity, and helpful people guas. The door separating the two areas had been open at all times and mechanics came and went, tracking dirt and oil and making it impossible to maintain a clean, harmonious environment for the office staff. This accounted, in part, for the constant turnover in employees. Dario's amorous liaisons with his office workers didn't help matters either.

On the back lot a jumble of cars and trucks had been parked and in the top left corner was a trailer used for storage, as a break area, and for Dario's trysts. At Salome's suggestion, Dario had it remodeled and furnished as an office as it was already located in the wealth gua.

Flower boxes were added and he hired a competent woman to run the show. Not a trace of oil or smell of gas could be detected in the office area. A diffuser maintained a subtle rose scent, the choice Dario's. She had told him it was important to use a fragrance he particularly liked in the offices to equate the money side of the business with a pleasant scent.

Additionally, he enlarged and remodeled the bathroom in the former office to include showers. The extra space was used as the break room and included literature on most makes of foreign cars and a computer to access automotive information exclusively (there were no games or any other distractions on the machine).

These changes occurred seven years ago when Salome was still an apprentice practitioner and just a year short of starting her professional career. It was then, too, that she'd bought the Austin Healey and brought it to Dario for servicing. Immediately noticing the problems with his business, and herself needing experience, she'd asked if she could feng shui the garage. He didn't mind in the least, was happy enough to welcome her car into his family. However, when the suggestions she'd made began to work he made a deal. If she wouldn't feng shui any other garages within fifty miles, he'd maintain the Healey at no charge.

Since then, to Dario, the scent of roses was the scent of money.

He raised the hood and surveyed the vitals. "I was concerned when I didn't hear from you two weeks ago."

"Delayed by illness."

"Not yours, I hope," he said.

"My parents. But they're fine now."

"If I'd known, I would have sent flowers."

"How about you? How's your son?" Not surprisingly, Dario was divorced and had a sixteen-year-old son who

3

lived with his mother, a blackjack dealer, in Atlantic City.

"Georgie's great. And my mother's visiting," he said and grinned broadly, his eyes suddenly sparkling. She thought she knew why.

Dario's mother, Maria Elena Burgos, was a legendary Argentine tangoist who met his father, John Fenn, during a summer tour of the United States nearly forty years ago. His father had seen her while on business in San Francisco and for three months zigzagged across the country attending at least one show a week. Unfortunately, John Fenn was very married to old Virginia money. The tour concluded in a grand fashion with an exhibition at the White House, just miles from Fenn's estate in Northern Virginia. Dario could always claim to have been in the East Room, as that was where his mother danced a milonga for the president of the United States while she was two months pregnant.

When John refused to leave his wife, Maria promised to make his wife leave him. Eventually, they worked out a deal involving money.

Dario was born at George Washington University hospital. After the birth, his mother stayed in Washington for a few months strictly to antagonize his father, turning up at restaurants where he happened to be dining with his wife, finagling invitations to parties he was attending, all fairly simple to arrange through connections she'd made at the White House. She also claimed to have had the president's ear, though rumor had it far more than his ear was involved.

But she quickly lost interest in both toying with John and motherhood. Perhaps if Washington had been as fashionable and exciting as Buenos Aires, life might have worked out differently. Even the president of the United States, though unquestionably powerful, didn't have the zing of his more volatile South American counterparts

whom she definitely preferred. She and Fenn arranged
for Dario to live with a couple, the woman a domestic,
the man a mechanic, in Falls Church, Virginia. After the
age of ten, he began spending summers with his mother
who he adored and found infinitely exciting. Later, when
he entered his twenties, she began visiting him, and, of
course, resuming cat-and-mouse games with Dario's father.

Salome was about to ask what mischief Maria Elena
was up to when Dario suddenly said, "Hey! Have you
heard about Simon Snow?" The question reminded her
that it was here that she'd first met Snow, maybe five
years ago, while both were waiting to pick up their respective automobiles. She remembered that he drove a
silver Aston Martin DB3, a classic best known as James
Bond's ride in the early films when Sean Connery gave
form and flesh to Ian Fleming's inked spy.

"Funny you should ask. I was just in his house. My
house sitter is investigating the murder."

"Well, at least he didn't die in a car wreck. Losing the
Aston Martin would have been a tragedy. Maybe you can
find out for me what they plan to do with it."

"Snow's sister-in-law is handling the estate. Do you
know her?"

"No, but I should have been invited to the memorial
service."

"Why? Were you close?"

"No. Actually, I found him offensive. But I was important to him. Without me that car would have been
ruined. Nothing worse than seeing a precision instrument
in the hands of an incompetent. You wouldn't believe the
state of the gears each time he brought the car in," he
said, shaking his head in disbelief. "And the interior! Jesus. Always a mess. I don't know how he found the ped-
als for all the crap." Suddenly, he made a dismissive

gesture. "Sorry. I know we both have better things to do. So, what's your pleasure?"

"Tune-up and oil change. Rotate the tires. The usual. And there's no hurry. I just talked myself out of my parking place and I'm not sure what I'm going to do."

Dario frowned, his face so full of concern you'd have thought she'd just declared *herself* homeless. "You cannot keep this car on the street!"

"Right. Well, I'd better be off."

"Hold on a sec. I know this is short notice but would you happen to be free tonight?"

Suddenly, Caravaggio's *Bacchus* appeared in her mind's eye, only this time the arm offering the wine-filled kylix was covered by the sleeve of a mechanic's overall. Fiona had been right again.

"What do you have in mind?"

"Dinner and a milonga."

"It just so happens my dance card hasn't filled yet."

"Pick you up at seven-thirty?"

"Fine."

IN THE OFFICE, SHE SIGNED THE NECESSARY work order. Declining the offer of a loaner, she waited for the courtesy van to give her a lift home. Finding the number in her little black book, Salome called Fiona. After one ring, the machine came on. Salome left her message. Whenever she left town, Fiona programmed her answering machine to pick up after one ring—a pretty good indication Fiona was off making a film.

During the ride back to Georgetown, Salome began to think about housing for her car but stopped after a moment. That could wait. Instead she returned to the magical mood spun by Dario and thoughts of an evening with him at the club on Fourteenth Street.

She thanked the driver and, with music playing in her head, went into the house.

To Duncan Mah, though, who just happened to be looking out the second-floor window, she appeared to be dancing.

"That you, girl?" Jude called out as Salome closed the front door.

She started to remind him that she was decades past girlhood then stopped herself. "Girl" was a common enough term of endearment. Besides, fifteen, twenty minutes with her mechanic and she'd already dropped at least a decade.

"How was lunch?"

"Great!" Jude, too, seemed to have had an encounter of the rejuvenating kind, not something she'd normally attribute to lunch with her ex-husband. He was sorting through boxes on the refectory table in the sitting room to the right of the foyer. Salome joined him.

In her declining years, Ida Pearl had stayed in these rooms exclusively. The long refectory table was perpendicular to the foyer. Behind it were floor-to-ceiling bookshelves separated by the front window. Further into the room was a fireplace with a granite mantel over which hung an oil painting of children at the seashore that Salome had brought from California. Comfortable chairs and a table and floor lamp were positioned on a thick Berber carpet in front of the fireplace.

Beyond that was a huge four-poster bed Salome hadn't had the heart to dispose of, though she'd cleansed it of ancestor ch'i with a sage smudge wand and replaced the custom-made mattress. Jude referred to it in and of itself as his "New York apartment."

The adjacent bathroom was tiny, an addition that had been squeezed into the remaining space between the sleeping area and the breakfast nook when Ida Pearl could no longer go up and down the stairs.

"Gabe thinks I'm crazy."

"For what?"

"Working with you. Which convinced me it's the right thing to do. He's jealous, of course. Wants to get in on the action. Anyway, he's got some furniture we can use. That is if your offer of the basement still stands."

"Of course."

"So will you head over to his place with me tomorrow at noon?"

Salome made a face.

"Hey. It's what partners do. And, like I told you this morning, he has some things you might want."

"I was just about to say yes. What about transport?"

"Already got a truck lined up. Just a little pickup. So don't worry, I'm not thinking of filling the basement with furniture."

"Tell you what. Let me give the basement a good scrubbing then we can haul your computer and these boxes downstairs. There's a card table you can set the computer on."

"Leave the cleaning to me, Salome."

Actually, that would be a good idea. Give him a chance to "honor" the space.

"Okay. And don't forget the windows. Just the act of washing them will improve your vision—physically and mentally."

"Whatever you say, kiddo. Oh, before I forget, Jett wants to talk."

"Excellent! When and where?"

"Eight o'clock tomorrow morning at his place. You on for that?"

"Absolutely."

Salome went up to her study on the top floor, staying

only long enough to collect several Bagua mirrors, a hammer, and some nails.

Once outside again, she took a moment to survey the neighborhood. Cul-de-sacs have special problems. Ch'i rushes down the street and, unable to disperse, collects and stagnates. The house at the very end is most at risk, in this case the manor house. For years, Isabelle's rose garden acted like a perfect cure, keeping the ch'i invigorated. Now, though, the spiked fencing would exacerbate the inherent problems. By installing that particular style with outward curving spikes sent poison arrows in all directions. Had the fence been straight, the points aimed skyward, some of the effect would have been neutralized.

At the corner of her house, and positioned so it faced the manor house, Salome hung the Bagua mirror. As a cure, it would return the negative energy back to the source. Normally, she'd hesitate before taking such a drastic step but she had to protect her property, Judah, and herself. She'd been drawn into a battle, one waged subtly but no less powerfully, on another level.

She crossed the street. Since Ruby Nelson wasn't home, was on a cruise as Fiona had said, Salome couldn't do anything about her house. As a rule, she never implemented any feng shui cure without permission.

She presented herself at the Richman's door and knocked. Almost immediately, Hank answered. His face was flushed and the sweet scent of bourbon wafted off him like a heavy perfume.

"Hey. How ya doing, Salome?"

"Fine, Hank, fine. Look, I was wondering if you and Susan would like me to hang a small mirror on the side of your house to deflect the negative energy created by the new fence."

"Huh?" He frowned then turned. "Hey, Suze! C'mere and talk to Salome."

Salome sighed. A moment later, Susan Richman stepped in front of Hank and stepped out, partially closing the door. Her face was pale and drawn.

"What can I do for you, Salome?" Susan asked in a low, weary voice with a distinct southern drawl.

Salome smiled and repeated what she'd said to Hank.

"That's sweet of you but there's no need. We sold the house. Hank's heading back to Arkansas tomorrow."

"Oh dear. What about you?"

She shrugged. "We're getting a divorce. Hank's burned out. I suppose I am, too, but I just don't like to admit it."

"I'm sorry to hear that. Do you mind my asking who you sold to?"

"Not at all." Suddenly, she smiled. "Our new neighbor. Rather, *your* new neighbor, Duncan Mah. Have you met him yet?"

Salome felt the blood drain from her head. She turned and took a deep breath.

"Yes," she finally said.

"Hey, you might think of doing the same thing. He paid almost double what the house's worth. Best thing that's happened to us in months."

"Well. I don't know what to say except good luck."

Susan moved in closer and said confidentially, "I just found out what he paid for Ruby's house."

"Wait a minute! I heard Ruby was on a cruise."

"Oh yeah. Part of the down payment. She's buying a condo in Sarasota, Florida."

Salome now noticed Susan's eyes glittering. Greed, it seemed, had taken over Malabar Close. She felt sick.

She recalled Duncan Mah's smug superiority, trying to give her the impression he was doing his neighbors a favor by renting them space in his carriage house, that *she* was responsible for his sudden decision to raise the rents. What a jerk.

"Hey, are you listening?"

Salome stared off toward Fiona's.

Susan chuckled. "I see. Well if you're wondering how much to tack on to the price, I'd say—"

Salome interrupted. "Have you seen Fiona lately?"

"Not in a couple days."

"Do you know if she's sold her house?"

"I haven't heard anything. Duncan would have told me."

"Well, I need to get going. Like I said, good luck to you. And Hank."

"Take my advice, Salome. Sell! Get yours while the pot's still full."

She knocked on Fiona's door and again received no answer and wouldn't hang the mirror without permission.

Returning to her house, Salome stood in front of the mirror she'd just hung, and holding her hands in the proper mudra, concentrated her thoughts on intention, in this case, protection. Later, under cover of night, she'd properly perform the ritual and a cleansing of the neighborhood when she was certain no one would be watching.

But it was hard to concentrate on anything but the fact that Duncan Mah was taking over Malabar Close.

Chapter 9

☯

THE slinky Capezio dress swirled around her thighs like black liquid as she gracefully twisted back and forth, one step allowing Dario's leg to slide between hers, the next step allowing her leg between his. His touch on her bare back was both light and instructive. Her hand on his shoulder registered the heat beneath his crisp white shirt, the garment exuding the sexiest scent imaginable. Sunlight and a spring breeze had dried the shirt, then all those powerful, spring-released pheromones had been ironed right into the fabric.

The tango was about submission, appreciation, wariness, domination, and of course, seduction. But that was only at the beginning of the evening. By the end, by the last dance, none of that would matter. The dancers would be as one, just two halves of the same form.

Six years ago, Salome had learned the tango, starting with lessons here at the same club, on the night she'd moved to Georgetown, also her first night as a divorcée. Now that she was living in the lap of temptation, that is, within spitting distance of the lively Georgetown nightlife, she could have become a partier. Depending on one's viewpoint—fortunately or unfortunately—she wasn't much of a drinker and couldn't see pursuing such an activity among a bunch of strangers, most of them decades younger. So, she'd taken Dario's advice and learned to tango.

At first she was embarrassed because of the weight she'd gained during the divorce process. Her instructor immediately assured her that it was a misconception that one needed a sleek body to tango.

"Tango," he'd declared, "is an attitude. You can be two hundred pounds and if you know what you are doing you will be sleek as a Jaguar."

His name was Alejandro and he was a Brazilian in his late seventies. Everyone called him "Maestro." Salome called him the Jack La Lanne of dance. He was also extremely patient with her. How many times did she catch her heel and rip out a hem and, worse, knee Alejandro in the groin, committing every unsightly blunder of an earnest novice?

"I'm rusty," Salome said as the dance ended and they walked back to their table.

"Your body remembers."

They'd finished dinner and their plates had been cleared away. Dario helped her into her chair, something anachronistic these days but he insisted on gallant display. If she didn't like it, she had no business involving herself with him and the world of tango. But who in their right mind would say no to a world in which age and experience equated to skill and due respect. In her second home, the California beach community, she often experienced a peculiar malady of middle age—that of feeling invisible. At times it was as if she simply dissolved into the ubiquitous fog. But then, she had no lover there, no one with whom to connect body and soul.

The waiter approached. Dario ordered brandy, Salome a club soda with lime. When the waiter left, Dario sat forward.

"You're a born dancer. When you're eighty you'll still have young men begging to dance with you." He smiled. "Salome." He enunciated each syllable. "You can't help but dance. Your namesake is the world's most famous dancer."

"The *Christian* world's maybe." Then a sudden, unexpected, and seemingly unrelated image popped into her head: the victims' bedroom in the Twomey house with the bricked-in fireplace and the mirrored tiles. Scribbled on the wall, in her mind, was *family gua.*

"Salome?"

She blinked. The vision vanished.

"You left me. Where were you?"

She shook her head. "A room in a strange house. Why it popped into my mind, I don't know. Happens sometimes." She shrugged it off.

The waiter brought their drinks. Dario raised his glass and they toasted.

"So," he began, now sitting back in his chair. "Tell me about your boyfriends in California. Do they dance as well as me?"

Salome had to laugh. Dario's ego was an interesting beast. When he danced he totally lost it. She could see in his eyes that he had dissolved into her. For him, tango was truly an out-of-body experience. But off the dance floor, he needed the same stroking as any other man.

"Let me put it this way, no one dances like you."

"What about that guy you saw last year. An old high school boyfriend?"

"Good Lord. Michael O'Kelly. I'm surprised you remember that."

"Why not? Love rekindled after thirty years."

"You're a romantic. Maybe if he were, we'd be an item. But we're not. I saw him a few times. He's much more interested in money than I am. He rarely talks about anything else."

"Maybe he doesn't have any. You forget that for most people life is a continual economic struggle."

"What about *your* love life?" Then she pretended to look at a watch. "But don't take all night."

He made a face and waved his hand from side to side, a classic Spanish gesture meaning so-so. "Mother's escapades have been keeping me entertained. But with her here I've also been seeing more of my ex. They're great friends, you know. But CeCe, she's a constant reminder of how easy it is to get in trouble with women."

Just then, a sultry Latin melody began. Everyone moved from the tables to the dance floor and once again, the world outside slipped away.

IT WAS AFTER MIDNIGHT WHEN DARIO double-parked the ten-year-old Range Rover in front of her house. Another surprise to those who didn't know Dario: He chose to drive conservative vehicles around town. Yes, he could be a show-off on the dance floor but never out on the street, choosing not to drive an automobile that attracted attention. Exotic cars were not that unusual in the metro area given the diverse international population and especially in Georgetown with its diplomatic community. However, having had experience as a car thief while in his teens, Dario wisely reserved his own collection of exotic vehicles for pleasure drives in the country.

"I could look for a parking place," he said. It wasn't his style to come right out and ask to come in for a while or the night.

"I have a ritual to perform." That wasn't the real reason and besides, it would only take about twenty minutes.

"Feng shui's your excuse?" he said, looking skeptical. "I thought the whole purpose was to attract."

Salome sighed. It was odd how something as simple as a dance had created a relationship based on honesty. Certainly they knew how to sidle around the truth—that was half the fun of tango—but they'd always been honest with each other about sex.

Bill Frisell's *Blues Dream* CD played, hinting at Miles Davis, Judah's musician of choice.

"My house sitter's still here."

"Why? And why should it matter?"

"He doesn't have anywhere else to go at the moment. And it matters because he's one of my ex-husband's oldest friends."

"You've been divorced six years, Salome."

"I prefer that Gabe doesn't know anything about my private life."

They were quiet for a moment, the only sound the purring of the perfectly tuned engine and some fine acoustic and electric guitar and alto sax. Then she thought about the office being set up in the basement. Could be Jude would be coming and going for longer than just a week or so. That thought spurred another.

"But I do have a question for you."

"The car'll be ready whenever you want," he quickly interjected.

"No, not that. Do you remember anything unusual about Simon Snow? Maybe something he always kept in his car?"

"You mean like a gun?"

"Just anything. We're trying to figure out a motive for his murder. Something he had that someone wanted badly enough to kill him for. But yes, a gun in the car would suggest he was scared enough to keep protection handy." Then she remembered his lack of home security and a gun didn't quite fit.

"Let's see," Dario said, staring out the window. He glanced up in the rear view mirror. "Nice Jag."

Salome twisted around. She glared at the automobile sitting in front of Mah's house. "Horrible owner. So, can you remember anything? You know people's cars better than they do."

"Under the hood."

"Well, if you think of something—" she said and leaned over to kiss him.

"His tapes?"

"You mean music?"

"No. Videos. I remember thinking once that they might be porn so I always locked them in the office safe. Not that any of my guys are thieves. Just don't want to tempt anyone. I always put them back when the car was ready to be picked up."

Salome felt the familiar "aha" and the accompanying tug at her gut. "Did they have titles? Anything to indicate what was on them?"

He put his hands on the steering wheel and pushed back against the seat, staring out the windshield. "There was a sticker, something written on it. Nothing obvious like *Debbie Does Dallas*—or I should say, *Danny,* in his case. Wait. The last time he brought his car in . . . Yeah. There was something and a date—folly?"

"Folly?"

He turned to her. "Does that help?"

"I don't know yet. But it's a start."

She leaned over and kissed him.

He pulled back and looked at her for a long minute. "If it helps, I know a guy who needs a roommate. Has a nice condo in Alexandria."

"Would he welcome a former metro homicide detective now working as a private investigator? A big black man who cooks like a cordon bleu chef?"

"Scratch that idea. Not that Jay's a racist but he is a former coke dealer. On a diet. I can still ask around though. What's his name?"

"Judah Freeman. Maybe you've heard—"

"*The* Judah Freeman? Christ! What the hell's he doing without a place to live?"

"Long story involving adjustment to civilian life and a daughter who's a vacuum cleaner when it comes to money."

She opened the door. "And take your time with the Healey. I still have to find a home for it."

"How about I keep it at my place? And when you're ready, you come and get it. And bring your toothbrush."

He didn't leave until she was safely inside the house. She flicked the outside light a couple of times then heard him drive off.

The refectory table in Jude's sitting room now gleamed with a high polish, the lemony scent still lingering. He'd cleaned and vacuumed and was probably down in the basement setting up things.

She didn't feel tired. The tango had raised her body ch'i, plus the added sexual energy could be channeled into the ritual.

After going downstairs to let Jude know she was home, she stopped in the kitchen long enough to grab an orange from the refrigerator and a paring knife from a drawer by the sink. She put both in a crystal bowl taken from a hutch in the dining room, then left them in the foyer while she went upstairs to change.

About five minutes later she swept down the stairs wearing her black feng shui gown. Taking up the bowl, she went outside, leaving the door unlocked and without turning on the light.

The crystal bowl on the stoop beside her, Salome stood quietly for a moment, adjusting to the energy. Taking a few deep breaths to relax, she listened to the aggregate night sounds, gradually shutting off each one—a reveler who'd had a few too many at The Tombs, a distant siren, a sleepless bird, a car starting—until absolute quiet settled over her. With her hands in the proper mudra, she began the mental and spiritual preparation for the neighborhood's cleansing ritual.

"Om ma ni pad me om," she chanted. "I ask for harmony and peace in Malabar Close."

She repeated the chant and request while visualizing the Close in daylight, the sun burning off any and all malefic energies, picturing the rays probing dark and dank places and filling them with bright light. When she'd concluded the ninth and final chant and request, her internal screen projected an image of the Close vibrating in golden light, each house breathing in the same harmonic rhythm.

Holding that vision, she slowly sat down and began peeling nine round pieces of the orange skin. She put them in her pockets and walked to the top of the cul-de-sac. In a clockwise fashion, she moved around, from her house, to Fiona's, to the manor house, to the Richmans', to Ruby Nelson's while taking each circle of orange peel and twisting it to release the essential oil then rubbing it on the sidewalk to mark a place of blessing. She then tossed the used piece up and out in a gesture that chased away evil while visualizing good ch'i emanating from each place. At the conclusion, she could almost see nine pillars of pure energy positioned around the Close.

Ritual reinforces intention. Performing a ritual while focusing on a desired outcome empowers and releases energy into the universe. This was just one of many transcendental cures, or as some practitioners preferred to call them, enhancements, combining a mantra, a mudra, and visualization.

Finally, Salome raised her hands to the deep-black sky. And, for a moment, she seemed to disappear, to become a part of the night itself.

Chapter 10

SALOME knew something was wrong the instant she entered the kitchen at seven the following morning. Jude stood at the sink, dressed in khakis and a fresh blue shirt, gripping the edge, his body rigid. She wondered if he'd already eaten, as he normally didn't cook in his good clothes. Coffee dripped from the machine and other than its pungent, chicory aroma, there was no scent of food in the air.

"Jude? You all right?" she asked, skipping the preamble of a greeting.

He took a deep breath, then blew it out in a stream.

"Sure, yeah. I'm fine." He glanced over at her with eyes that appeared covered in black ice.

"We're still on for Jett Malieu, aren't we?" If he was upset about anything she figured it would be another cancellation by Malieu.

"Yeah."

Or maybe it was something he'd discovered last night, rather, early this morning. When she'd gone down to the basement to say good night, his focus hadn't left the computer screen. He'd acknowledged her simply by raising his hand in a gesture that also might have cautioned her from coming any closer.

"Have you had anything to eat yet?"

"Not hungry. Do you mind fixing for yourself?"

"Good Lord, of course not!"

"Coffee's just about ready." He checked his watch. "We'll be leaving at seven-thirty."

"Okay."

Then he disappeared down the stairs.

JUDE'S SILENCE PERSISTED DURING THE twenty-five minute drive through town, time extended by morning rush hour traffic. Though he didn't comment, she mentioned certain things she wanted to ask Jett.

He found a space on Euclid Street close to Jett Malieu's apartment. It would be just a short walk to the Howard University campus.

Malieu opened the door to his third and top floor walkup. Salome remembered him serving Simon Snow at the fund-raiser and he was just as deferential to Judah and her as he had been to his employer. He was, she figured, a nice person whose good looks hadn't negatively affected his nature.

They passed through a drab living room, the tired furniture years beyond secondhand. Books, magazines, and newspapers were scattered on tabletops with a few clusters here and there on the floor; the overall effect was the opposite of his room at Simon Snow's. A simple bouquet of cut flowers would do wonders for the room. However, as far as she knew, people didn't bring flowers to murder suspects. Maybe, she thought, such people would be more forthcoming with enlivened ch'i around.

With the east and south exposures he got the light

needed for several plants to flourish in the wealth and fame guas in which the tiny dining area and kitchen were located. Salome smiled to herself upon seeing Chimene sitting in the wealth gua; people focused on money always seemed to gravitate to the wealth gua of any room.

A thick book of poetry lay open in front of her and Salome vaguely recalled Judah mentioning that her major at Georgetown was English. Salome wondered if she'd inherited her father's dream of becoming a writer. If so, whether she liked it or not she was certainly accumulating material. Though her eyes were on one of the pages, her body language changed when Judah and Salome entered the kitchen, indicating that poetry no longer held her interest. She straightjacketed herself—wound her arms tightly around her chest, her legs beneath the table twisted around each other as only thin, agile women can do.

"Hi, Daddy," Chimene said without bothering to get up, then glanced sullenly at Salome and back at her father. "What's she doing here?"

The young woman's hostility shocked Salome and she glanced at Jude, almost fearing his reaction. Jagged cracks seemed to be forming on the surface of the black ice, the only indication of emotion. But he remained detached. If his daughter was baiting him, he wasn't biting.

"Direct the question to Salome herself," he said, his voice low and menacing.

"There's coffee and I can make tea," Jett interjected, deflecting some of the negative energy.

"Coffee, thanks," Jude said.

"Chamomile tea for me," Chimene ordered. "With grated ginger." She could be expected to demand something extra for herself. That her father had spoiled her rotten had much to do with Chimene's behavior. At the same time, there was more to her that her father couldn't be blamed for.

"Chimene will have coffee just like the rest of us. This isn't a tea party."

"So what *are* you doing here?" Chimene demanded, her small chin raised arrogantly and pointed at Salome, shooting poison arrows.

Though Salome had known Chimene since the Freemans' youngest child had been an infant, the two had never clicked. Chimene was usually civil but Salome had been aware early on that Chimene didn't like anyone who drew her father's attention away from her. Having worked with Jude for twenty years, Salome qualified.

Salome steepled her hands in front of her mouth, fingers aimed at her adversary, a gesture to deflect the malicious barbs. "Jude and I are working together again."

"Oh right. Not enough that you have him at night but you have to cling to him like some barnacle all day, too?"

Before Jude could say anything, Salome replied evenly. "You enlisted your father's help in the first place and, need I remind you, without a hint of remuneration. This is about business, Chimene, and the fact that I can provide Jude with a place to work. So let's keep focused."

Some of Chimene's hostility faded. Still, Salome didn't want to sit too close. The young woman's fundamental negativity was so strong she sucked energy like a black hole.

"Let's move into the living room," Salome suggested, already scooting her chair back.

When they were finally settled—Chimene and Jett on the sofa, Salome and Judah in a pair of straight-back chairs brought from the kitchen table and everyone with a mug of coffee—Judah began the interview. With Jett's permission, Judah switched on a small tape recorder.

"Son, I know you've done this numerous times already but I really need to know everything you remember about the day your employer was murdered."

"No problem, sir," Jett responded, his clear eyes focused on Judah. "The day was pretty much routine. I got up at seven and fixed Simon's breakfast, then cleaned up the kitchen."

"Do you recall what you prepared?" Salome asked. She had already told Jude to expect her to ask for domestic details that might seem picky or irrelevant. But even the menu was important to establish any recent change in patterns.

"The medical examiner already determined stomach contents," Chimene blurted, showing her contempt.

"That was lunch," Salome shot back. Though she certainly didn't want to, Salome reasoned that she might have to leave if Chimene continued to disrupt. Unless, of course, Jude himself dismissed his daughter.

"I remember. Grapefruit, toast, and coffee. It was the first day of a three-day diet. That is to say, on three, off four. He'd been on it about a month."

"So this wasn't his usual fare?"

"Oh no. The earliest class I've ever had is a ten o'clock. You see, the morning schedule centers around breakfast. It's his favorite meal. Was his favorite meal, I should say," he added glumly. "Sometimes I'd prepare eggs Benedict, sometimes Belgian waffles, blintzes, or crepes. Other mornings he'd want a big southern feed complete with grits, homemade biscuits, and gravy. Of course everything made from scratch."

"Did you eat with him?"

"No, never. He liked to eat at the kitchen counter and watch the morning shows."

"Why the drastic change in menu? Heart trouble, maybe?" Jude asked.

"In a sense but not what you're thinking. He was kind of secretive about it but it's hard to hide love, if you know what I mean." He automatically glanced at Chimene without thinking, giving a demonstration of what he'd just said. "He was trying to lose weight."

"Who was he in love with?" Jude inquired.

"It's weird but I just don't know. I mean, there were plenty of people coming and going as usual. And to be honest, his love life wasn't of any interest to me so I didn't really pay all that much attention. He was very discreet about his homosexuality, you know. Never while I worked for him did he have any raucous parties and if anyone spent the night they were gone before I got up or left after I went off to class.

"Look, I want to make this very clear. I had and continue to have a great deal of respect for Simon."

"What about his involvement with pornography?"

Jett shook his head adamantly. "That tape in the VCR? Had to have been brought by whoever killed him. Simon wouldn't allow that sort of thing in the house."

"So, beside the fact that he was dieting," Salome said, "how did you know he was in love?"

"Certain habits had changed. He was even fussier about his clothes. Had mood swings. One minute he'd be up, the next minute on the verge of tears. Really emotional—the first I'd seen this side of him in the two years I'd been there."

"Drugs?" Jude prodded.

"Far as I know, nada. He did like to have a Manhattan to unwind but cut those out completely when he started the diet."

"You ever look in his medicine cabinet?" Jude asked.

Jett shrugged, looked away, looked down, unable to find a place for his eyes. He made a terrible liar.

"No reason for me to go into his bathroom—or his

bedroom, for that matter. The maid took care of the cleaning chores, changing the beds and such. Her name's Hilda. I've got her number in my book, if you'd like to talk to her."

"That doesn't answer the question, Jett," Jude reminded.

"Okay, so I did. One time when I first started work. He was off on a vacation and I had the house to myself. He had some prescription drugs for—I can't remember what—but no stashes."

"Did you look anywhere else?"

"Probably, but I don't remember anything significant."

"Let's get back to the day of his death. So after his diet breakfast what happened?"

Jett sighed. "Simon went to his office—uh, not the one in the house, the one in the showroom off Dupont Circle. I went to my room to study. I didn't come out until about noon to fix lunch."

"Were there any calls? Deliveries? Any friends drop by?"

"I don't answer the phone when he's not home. The machine picks up the messages. There wasn't a flower delivery that morning though he had a standing order for fresh flowers to be delivered every day."

"What time?"

"Usually comes between nine and ten."

"In your statement, you told the police that there were fresh flowers when you arrived home that evening."

"That's right. But sometimes the deliveries come later, it's just not the norm."

Judah sat back in his chair. Salome picked up her mug and sipped the strong chicory-flavored brew. Even though it had cooled off, it still tasted good.

"The florist says Snow cancelled the standing order the day before."

"Look, Detective Freeman, all I know is the flowers were there. And the gardener from next door, Mr. De La Cruz, confirms the arrival of the delivery van. And he's seen it practically every day for years."

As yet, Salome realized, no one had determined the time of the van's departure. Mr. De La Cruz had been in the process of leaving when the van arrived and no other neighbors had offered any information.

"Look, Dad," Chimene said, "can't you come up with something new?"

Salome took this to be her cue to interject a new angle.

"Tell us about his actions on the days leading up to the murder. Did he behave differently?"

"Actually, he did. It was like he was on speed or something. There was a lot of activity in the house. He had painters in—"

"When did it start?" she asked, believing that she already knew the answer.

"It started when we got home the night of the auction. He got really hot to remodel his bedroom. We moved almost all the furniture out of his bedroom that same night. The next day, he had the carpet cleaned and later on had that huge bed delivered from one of his showrooms. Curtains were delivered, I think, the next day."

Jett sat forward now, getting into the memory. "He was, I don't know, acting like a servant. What I mean to say is, he acted like he was preparing for a visit from royalty or something."

"Not normal behavior?" Salome said.

"Hardly! Everyone else treated him like a royal. He could be rather pompous and arrogant. Whoever he planned to put in that bedroom had him running around like a mouse. And he fussed and fussed about the placement of the bed. Got out that red packet of feng shui information you handed out that night," he said.

"I guess you got him hooked. Bought new sheets, pillows, and a comforter and some pictures and those, uh, bronzes that were by the bed. Or maybe he had those before. The pictures were still wrapped so I don't know what they were of. But, I don't think I've ever seen him happier. Then he started going through the house and changing things here and there. The next day there were pink roses added to his usual order with the florist. He was definitely taking feng shui seriously."

"What about the day of the murder? Were pink roses delivered?"

"No. Just the usual mixed assortment."

Jett said no friends had come by and as far as he knew, no one but Ellen Russo and Hilda had keys to the house. At this point, he retrieved an address book and gave Jude the maid's telephone number, adding that she'd been working for Snow for over twenty years.

Salome then asked about Snow's last meal.

According to Jett, it was eaten sometime between twelve-fifteen and twelve-thirty and consisted of four ounces of fresh-broiled tuna, a piece of whole wheat toast, and a cup of coffee. As Chimene had reminded them, the District medical examiner confirmed the stomach contents and Jett's recollection of the time of the meal helped determine the time of death to within a few hours. Not exact science—any number of ancillary factors including emotional state can affect the rate of digestion.

"After I cleaned the kitchen, which wasn't much of a chore, I studied until it was time to leave for class. Oh yes, and Simon said he'd be home the rest of the day. I even waved at Mr. De La Cruz. It takes me about twenty minutes to drive to school and park."

Jude eyed him strangely. "Then you have to get to class."

"Yeah. Another ten minutes or so. Believe me, I've been doing this for a while. I know how much time it takes," he replied.

Salome thought Jett seemed to be as much a person of routine as his former employer. Keeping to a schedule certainly made it easier for the killer to know where everyone would be and when.

"Go on."

"On that day I had a two o'clock, a three o'clock, and a four o'clock. Then a study and dinner break until my evening class."

"Uh-huh. Well, you didn't make the two o'clock, did you?"

Both Jett and Chimene looked startled.

"With nearly a hundred students taking the course, no one could really confirm or deny you'd actually made it. And it's easy to get the days confused. Still, everybody needs money, right? Slip a twenty to a friend and they'll vouch for you. Hard to prove they're lying.

"No, you went to see a certain African American woman who goes by the name of Jimmy to negotiate the price of the linguist staff."

Chimene gripped Jett's arm. "You don't have to say anything more!" Then she glared at her father.

"You want my help, young man, you'll talk to me." Then he turned to Chimene. "You're the one who invited me into this mess. What the hell did you expect? That if I did find out I'd keep quiet about it?"

Judah went on relentlessly. "Where'd you hide it? Under the bed? In your closet?"

Then he turned on Chimene, his anger finally exploding. "Why'd you put him up to it?"

Chimene went very still but didn't deny anything. Then she rose and walked to one of the windows. After a moment she answered, ruthless in her honesty.

"You haven't been much of a provider, now, have you, Dad. I saw the opportunity and took it. Remember, you always told us kids to seize opportunities 'cause they don't come as often to black kids. That staff was worth plenty and it was insured. The ambassador's wife didn't lose a thing but some face."

"What about your mother?" Judah hissed. "What did she lose?"

Chimene looked away.

Jude directed his attention back to Jett. "So where did you put it?"

"Under my bed. No one goes in my room," he said softly, his head hanging.

"Unless you killed Simon Snow, son, someone definitely went in your room. Someone who knew you'd be gone and maybe even that you'd stolen the linguist staff. Then again, maybe they were just looking for something special of yours, anything they might use in the commission of the crime. Something with your prints on it.

"And, of course, you unwrapped the staff to take Polaroids for Chimene to show the prospective buyer."

"Okay, yes, Chimene and I met Jimmy and showed her the pictures. She wanted delivery the next day."

Chimene glanced over at Jett, eyes brimming with contempt. Salome was glad Jett kept his attention on Jude and didn't see her expression. Even so the couple's relationship had just taken a lethal blow. Easy to see she believed Jett had betrayed her. She'd also learned that manipulating her father wasn't as easy as she might have thought it would be.

"We didn't leave prints," Chimene said, her tone mocking. "Remember, my dad was a cop."

"Let's finish up here, shall we?" Jude suddenly looked haggard, the truth having exacted a price.

"Okay. I made it to my four o'clock then I went to the library at five to study for my seven o'clock. We had a test and I aced it. Left class about fifteen minutes early.

So I arrived back at Simon's some time after eight. See, he eats out almost every night so dinner has never been a problem. Until the diet, that is. Since I've got evening classes during the week, he fixes his own dinner on the diet nights, which I prep before leaving."

"So what happened when you got home?"

"Well, I noticed the kitchen was clean. He leaves the dishes for me so I figured he hadn't eaten yet. I went looking for him to see if I should go ahead and heat up the meal."

"Did you go directly to his bedroom?"

"No, I went to his study. Sometimes he has clients over to go through swatches and things. He always takes care of business in the study. Maybe afterward they'll relax with a drink. Anyway, he wasn't there so I checked all the other rooms downstairs.

"You have to understand something. I rarely go upstairs. I figured he must have gone out to eat so I went to my room.

"Of course, I looked under the bed to check. Couldn't believe the staff was gone. I mean, that really scared me."

"Did you think Chimene might have come over and taken it?"

Jett sat straighter. "No, sir! That didn't even cross my mind. I thought he—Simon—had been in my room and found it. Guilty conscience, I guess. So I went upstairs." He paused to lick his lips. "Then, of course, I found him."

"And never did tell the police about the linguist staff."

After a long pause he said no.

"How did you find out?" Chimene asked her father, a tiny glimmer of respect in her eye.

"Good Christ. I was a cop in this town for thirty years. Maybe you two will keep that in mind. Now, Ms. Waterhouse and I have some other people to see."

Salome and Judah rose. Jett shot from the sofa. Chimene didn't move from her place by the window.

"I want you both to stay in town."

"The police already said that," Chimene said.

Judah regarded his daughter with so much disappointment Salome had to look away. Her eyes fell on the TV and VCR, which tweaked her memory. With all the emotion in the room she'd nearly forgotten to ask.

"What about Simon's videos?" Salome quickly asked.

"You mean movies?"

"Actually, did you ever come across any that might have been of a personal nature? Ever see one with a sticker that had "folly" or a similar word written on it?"

He frowned and shook his head.

"But he did have that VCR in his bedroom. Kept in the closet."

"He must have brought tapes up from the den to watch in bed."

Jett walked them to the door, appearing shorter and smaller than when they'd arrived. "Are you going to tell the police about the staff?"

"At the moment, no."

Suddenly Chimene spun around. "Are you going to tell Mom?"

This is not your business, Salome reminded herself. *How Judah deals with his daughter is personal.* Still, that didn't keep her from wanting to grab him and drag him off before Chimene's charm overpowered his good sense.

"No, baby. You are."

Back in the car, Salome said with open admiration, "You're certainly full of surprises."

Judah turned the key in the ignition and said grimly, "It's a gift."

Chapter 11

"I accessed her credit card records," Jude began, replying to Salome's inquiry as to how he knew Chimene and Jett had taken the linguist staff.

They were headed south on Sixteenth Street, the mid-morning traffic light, Meridian Hill Park on the left.

"I see."

"Don't get all indignant about legalities, Salome."

"Whatever works. I'm not judging, just curious."

Just before they reached U Street, Salome suggested they stop in at Snow's Dupont Circle showroom. She wanted to check the feng shui, to see if anything suggested danger as did the position of the desk in his house. He mumbled in agreement and headed on down New Hampshire Avenue, a straight shot to Dupont Circle.

"I take it you've done this before? Accessed her credit info?"

Jude glanced over at Salome. Then he turned his attention back to the traffic and sighed deeply. "Chimene's money problems have impacted my marriage, certainly my finances, and now Jett. And you, too, inadvertently.

"My daughter has cost me most of my savings. Money's made her very vulnerable. She's had loan sharks after her. Cookie's furious at me for paying off Chimene's debts. If Cookie had her way, Chimene would enroll in a junior college and get a job to pay off the money she owes."

"What does she spend it on? You pay her tuition, right?" Salome was thinking drugs but didn't want to go there. If he wanted to bring it up, fine.

"Apartment, car, clothes, hell, just the usual. And she does make good money from modeling assignments. They're just not frequent enough." He quickly moved on, maybe sensing Salome's thoughts.

"Anyway, after Cookie gave me a list of all those who attended the fund-raiser, I checked with some people who collect African art. Of course, only a certain kind of collector will be willing to buy something as hot as that linguist staff. And my daughter didn't have to look hard. She knew just who to go to. It was all set up a week before the fund-raiser."

"How much was the collector willing to pay?"

Easy to see he was reluctant to answer. "Double what Cookie expected the staff to bring in."

Thirty thousand, Salome thought. Well, that explained Jude's current financial problems—which as he pointed out, affected her as long as he lived in her house.

Jude turned into a side street and within minutes slipped the anonymous blue Toyota into a parking space. They walked a few blocks west to Connecticut Avenue, the street on which Snow's store was located.

At the corner, Salome stopped and grabbed Jude's arm. "Jude, if there's ever a trial, it's going to come out that Chimene and Jett stole that staff. You can't continue protecting her at your own expense." Getting carried away, the words were out before she realized. "That girl's eating you alive."

Jude looked up and down Connecticut Avenue. "I think the store's this way," he said, nodding north. "Come on." He gently held her arm, walking slowly, each step deliberate.

"I've still got juice in this town, certain resources I can tap. Chimene's my daughter and I'll do whatever it takes to protect her."

They arrived at the store only to find it dark. Pressing their faces to the glass, they peered inside.

"My God, Jude. It's empty!"

Jude pulled out his cell phone and tapped a number. He leaned against the glass with the phone to one ear, his hand cupped against the other to shut out traffic noise.

"Ellen Russo, please," he said. After a moment he concluded the brief conversation by leaving a message, no doubt with the receptionist at the home security firm.

Since neither of them had eaten breakfast, Salome suggested they go on to a deli/café she knew of just down the street. He insisted on paying, so she let him.

The weather was warm and muggy and they sat at a table outside. While enjoying fresh croissants and lattes, they watched the parade of locals, at this early hour mainly students and artists.

"So what do you suppose happened? I thought that was Snow's main office?"

Judah shrugged. "The receptionist said that yesterday the stock was transferred to the Virginia stores. Ellen must have decided to consolidate stock and keep overhead low by closing this store ASAP. It's odd she didn't mention it when we met at Snow's. Oh well, the woman's got enough on her mind."

Jude started to rise. "I'm going to get a coffee to go. "You want one?"

"I'm fine."

While he was in the deli, Salome pulled out her cell phone and punched in the familiar number of her mentor, Grace Wu, better known as Madame Wu. Grace would want to hear how the recent tour had turned out as she'd always taken a keen interest in Salome's practice.

For four years Salome had studied with Grace, learning from a master who'd been practicing feng shui for half a century, first in Hong Kong and later right here in the District. In the beginning of Grace's local practice, only a select few enjoyed the benefits of the largely unknown art and science of feng shui. But in the past twenty years, as more people became familiar with feng shui, her business grew. Then a few years ago, Grace opened a school and shop in San Diego, California, dividing her time, like Salome, between the two coasts. Grace's District residence was just a few blocks from Dupont Circle but Salome wouldn't just drop in. That would have been bad form.

"Good morning," Salome said when Grace came on the line.

Salome painted a general picture of last week's feng shui activities, emphasizing the positive aspects. After a couple of minutes, she began to feel that she didn't have Grace's full attention.

"Have I caught you at a bad time?"

"No, no, dear. But I do have to leave shortly for a luncheon engagement," she said. Even after decades in the United States, she still had traces of a British accent.

"Actually, I was just thinking . . . since your trip was cut short, and you are in town, I'd be very pleased if you'd attend a party Thursday evening."

"With you?"

"Well, uh, yes and no," she said, sounding flustered. "I will be there but I have to arrive early for a brief consultation. My nephew's in town and he's keen to expand the business. Anyway, he needs to talk to you about a new project. And I want to introduce you to my client with an eye toward her becoming your client. My driver can collect you at around seven-thirty. Will that be all right?"

"It's kind of sudden. But sure. What sort of party? What should I wear?"

"Oh dear!" Grace sucked in a breath. "Absolutely the best. Do you have any good jewelry?"

That seemed an odd question but Salome replied, "Pearls mainly."

"I could lend you something of mine," Grace mumbled, giving the impression that she was talking to herself. "No, pearls will be fine."

"Just one more thing, Grace," Salome said, remembering her other purpose in calling. "Do you know of any consultants Simon Snow might have contacted before his, uh, death?"

"Horrible, wasn't it. But no. He had nothing but contempt for people like us."

"Well, I'd better let you go—oh, where is this party?"

"Tres Soeurs. You can understand what I mean about dressing your best."

Salome lowered the phone, stunned. Jude arrived with a fresh to-go cup.

"You look like someone just hit you in the face," he remarked.

She returned the phone to her bag, shaking her head slightly as she slowly rose from her chair. "You'll never guess where I'm going Thursday night."

"You're right, I'll never guess."

"Tres Soeurs mansion."

"Whoa! That's about on par with a ticket to the White House."

As a Georgetown graduate in the same class as former President Bill Clinton, Jude had attended a number of White House parties. Salome, too, while married to Gabriel. Though her ex-husband hadn't graduated in the same class, Gabriel started Georgetown in the same year as Clinton. Most importantly, though, Gabriel's success as a mystery writer accounted for his inclusion in a number of functions since Clinton was an avid reader of mysteries.

The District's own mystery bookstore was just up the street and since they were in the neighborhood, Salome wanted to stop in. "We've still got time before we have to head over to McLean, don't we?"

"Sure. And I know exactly what you're thinking. But let's not stay too long. I still have to pick up the truck and we'll want to change clothes."

A few minutes later they entered the bookstore on Connecticut Avenue, the scene of many of Gabe's signings. Salome loved the cozy store with its faux fireplace and comfortable chair and table stacked with books set up near the front door. She bought a half a dozen books written by her favorite female authors and a couple of the store's distinctive black T-shirts with a white logo.

Finally, as they returned to the car, Salome mentioned something that had been bothering her since they left Jett's apartment.

"Jett said something that struck me as peculiar."

"What's that?"

"Well, it was when he was talking about the flower delivery."

"Okay."

"He said, 'Mr. De La Cruz *confirms* the arrival time of the van.' Not *observed* or *said* he saw the van at such and such a time. It was like De La Cruz was backing up a fact Jett already knew."

Jude stopped.

"I mean, if Jett left the house at one-thirty, how could he have known the van arrived at one-forty-five?"

"Damn," Jude muttered.

Salome shrugged. "It might be nothing."

Neither said a word until they arrived at the Toyota. Jude unlocked the trunk and put her heavy bag of books inside.

Whether the observation had merit or not, Judah was certainly thoughtful on the way home.

NEARLY A YEAR HAD PASSED SINCE SHE'D seen Gabe. Now, as often happened when she thought of him, certain images from their domestic life popped up on her mental screen: She saw all the socks and under-pants and T-shirts she'd picked up off the bedroom floor—over the years, enough to fill a department store. She saw the packages of crackers, potato and corn chips left open to go stale in the kitchen, on his desk, on the floor beside his recliner. She saw the cheese never re-wrapped and turning hard in the refrigerator. She saw thousands of rubber bands choking the front door knob where he put them while bringing in the morning paper. She saw the newspaper trails from the kitchen table to the bathroom to his home office. She saw all the card-board rolls empty of toilet paper but left on the roller. She saw the wet towels bunched on the bathroom floor. . . .

Around twenty minutes after crossing Chain Bridge, Jude slid the borrowed green Chevy pickup in front of a stately, salmon-colored brick mansion. Four white columns extended across the wide porch, the center two supporting a small second-story balcony.

Salome gathered her purse and a bag containing the T-shirts for Gabe and his new bride, and stepped out of the car. In the six years since their divorce, she'd occasionally visited him here in McLean. More frequent were his visits to the Georgetown house and understandably so: the house had been in his family for years and many childhood memories were contained therein. She realized, too, that she would never be entirely rid of Gabe as long as she lived in Malabar Close. That didn't bother her; she would always care deeply for him. They had simply lived and worked together for too long. Perhaps if, during their twenty-year marriage, they'd taken separate holidays, the marriage might have survived.

As they started up the walkway, Salome instantly knew something wasn't right in Gabe's life. Whether he'd tell her about it was another matter, but she figured the problem was career-related. Of course, she hadn't even crossed the threshold yet, but what was in the beds leading to the front door told a story. Where once spring tulips, daffodils, and heavenly scented narcissus bloomed now were assorted cacti accessorized with some spongy-looking rust-colored rocks, probably lava. She stopped and regarded the plant life indigenous to the southwest United States. The tall cacti with their imposing spikes probably wouldn't last the typical, hot muggy summer, in which case, the energy in the career gua (of the entire lot) would improve.

Another new addition was the shiny brass plaque beside the front door, a feature often seen in Georgetown to proclaim a home's provenance. This one read: PAS-QUINADE PLACE.

Oh dear, she thought, concern for Gabe rising another notch.

"What the hell's 'pasquinade'?" Jude asked and rang the bell.

"A parody or satire," Salome replied.

Jude raised his eyebrows, surprised.

"I may not have a degree in English from Georgetown but I do read, you know."

"I didn't say anything," he said defensively, raising his hands in a classic gesture of innocence. "It's just kind of an odd name for a house."

"Gabe once wanted to use it as a title for a stand-alone novel. But his editor didn't want him writing anything but mysteries in the series . . . so I take it you haven't been here since he put up the plaque?"

"Not since the wedding in January."

On the other side of the heavy oak double doors they could hear banging and cursing, the sound moving closer. A moment later, Gabe threw open the doors, his face beet red, which, in contrast, made his steel-gray hair appear almost white.

"About time!"

It took a moment for a semi-smile to replace the angry expression on his face. She knew a string of curses were backed up behind his lips. Finally, he took a deep breath. On the exhale he spoke, "Hi. Thought you were the movers."

"We can come back if this isn't a good time," Jude offered.

"Oh, hell no!" Gabe glanced behind him then, looking defeated, stepped back from the door so they could enter. "Come on in. Mei. You're looking well."

Boxes and furniture cluttered what was normally a wide, elegant foyer. So large was it, Gabe and Elle's recent wedding had been performed in front of the staircase directly opposite the front door with fifty guests looking on. Now you could barely see the top of the black upright piano placed just under the stairs where they crossed the great window that rose from the half landing to the top of the second floor.

"Movers? I thought redecorating was on the docket," Jude said.

Gabe's hands dove into the pockets of his twill trousers, then he pulled them out and adjusted his belt as if unaccustomed to wearing one.

"This was all supposed to have been picked up four hours ago. All going to Elle's mother's house."

"She must have a big place," Salome said, thinking about the battered women's shelter, which could use some nice furnishings. But, of course, Gabe's new family came first.

Gabe suddenly blurted, "It's only natural that Elle would want to put her own imprint on the house. Pretty much everything's going. But like I told you, I put some things aside," he said to Jude. Then turning to Salome he added, "and, uh, you know, things we had."

It occurred to her that Elle might have chosen items Gabe actually wanted to keep and in his typical lateral approach, he was asking Salome to hold onto them in case something happened—like his marriage didn't work out.

"Fine," Judah said, slapping his hands together. "Let's get to it."

Gabe and Salome eyed each other for a long moment. Then he lifted one of her long braids.

"Amazing. Still no gray."

Actually she was surprised to see him nattily dressed especially in the middle of the day. For years, unless they were on tour, he wore nothing but sweats or, in the summer, loose-fitting shorts. They had even archived his sweatpants when the butts were completely worn out. She glanced at his feet. He wore tasseled loafers. Where, she wondered, were his trusty Birkenstocks? Elle's redecorating seemed to include her new husband.

"Shall we get this show on the road?" Judah prompted.

"Follow me. I've made a path of sorts."

As they wound their way through the jumble to the stairs, Gabe said, "We're giving—rather, Elle's—giving the house a face-lift. A new, more youthful look."

They mounted the stairs. Through the window Salome could see a mammoth hole in the backyard past the deck.

"Where is she?" Salome asked.

"Out playing tennis, I think," Gabe said.

At the landing they turned left and in a moment were standing in a large stark room, notably, in the relationship gua of the house. Salome tried to appear nonplussed. Opposite the entrance was a slab of glass as long as a door supported by a stand of twisted metal tubing. Behind it was a high-back swivel chair, which he definitely needed for support since desk and chair were positioned in front of a huge floor-to-ceiling window, currently without any window coverings.

"My new workplace."

"So where's the work?" Jude commented half in jest.

"Give me a break, man, I'm just getting settled here."

The walls were a naked, sterile white and the room smelled of paint. Just inside the door was the desk on which he'd written nearly two dozen mysteries, half of them best-sellers. Boxes were stacked on top. Salome peeked in one, astonished to find several of his framed book jackets.

"These should go on the wall, Gabe, on either side of the door in the career gua."

"Elle thinks they should be tossed."

"Maybe this room needs a decorative change but to throw away these things is like turning your back on success, on the work that got you where you are."

He looked away.

Her attention returned to the desk. Even glass coffee tables created a subtle sense of instability and insecurity. For a writer like Gabe who, despite his success, often doubted every word he wrote, this could lead to disaster.

Salome walked over to the window. She looked down on the huge hole. From up here she could see about a foot of water in the bottom. She glanced at Gabe.

"The twenty-five-meter pool," he said proudly.

"Taking up swimming, too. Good for you," she added, glad to be able to find something positive to contribute.

"Actually, it's for Tyler. Uh, Elle's twelve-year-old son."

"Oh!" Salome felt her cheeks redden and turned away. She'd never gotten pregnant and while it never escalated into an issue, they'd both been a little disappointed. "I'm happy for you, Gabe. What's he like?"

"We haven't actually met yet. He's in prep school in Massachusetts. But he'll be spending the summer with us."

Gabe was looking more uncomfortable by the minute. "You guys want a drink?"

"You still make a mean lemonade?" Salome asked.

"Not in a while."

"Water, then."

"No, no. I'll fix the lemonade. Jude?"

"Sounds good to me."

"Just go through the boxes. Pick out what you'd like."

Gabe scooted out of the room. Salome started to follow.

"Mei! Where're you going?" Jude hissed.

"To find the bathroom."

More to the point, she found the bedroom at the other end of the hall.

"Oh my God," she whispered. This was not a room

that would nurture a marital relationship. One entire wall was mirrored, but at least, she reasoned, the mirror was solid and not in tiles, as in Dwayne Twomey's house, which suggested severe fragmentation.

Stepping farther into the room, she noticed that the mirror concealed walk-in closets. One section was ajar. She intended to just have a peek, but when she saw the contents, she went ahead and entered. Elle had a monumental wardrobe, clothes neatly categorized. Beneath each outfit were a couple of shoeboxes, the footwear matching the outfit and providing a selection. There was a section of leather jackets only and two dozen boots to go with them.

At least Gabe had not been forgotten. Though his two racks represented about a tenth of the overall space, the items were all new: shirts, trousers, and even a couple of handsome suits. He'd tossed his only suit when his first book sold and she hadn't seen him wear one since.

Leaving the closet, she stood at the foot of the king-size bed covered with a satin leopard-skin motif comforter. Without moving her head, her eyes rolled up toward another mirror. On the ceiling. What had he said? *A new, more youthful look.* At least the bed was positioned at a diagonal from the door. But she wondered if he had trouble sleeping with all the mirrors around. Even without such an addition, he'd been a poor sleeper. And plants were everywhere, another feng shui no-no in the bedroom. Since plants give off carbon dioxide at night, it wasn't a good idea to fill a bedroom with them.

The adjoining bathroom was bright and airy and she felt a little envious upon seeing the Jacuzzi. And indeed, you could see it everywhere as here again, the walls were mirrored. The toilet had its own tiny alcove—give Elle a point for that.

"Who the hell are you?"

Salome nearly jumped out of her skin. With all the mirrors you'd think she would have seen the woman but she'd been peeking around the corner into the alcove when Gabe's bride made her appearance.

"I'm Salome Waterhouse." Nothing like catching your new husband's ex-wife snooping around the bedroom. At least Elle hadn't caught her in the closet.

Like Chimene earlier, Elle's look shot poison arrows.

"If you're here about Gabe's stuff, you're in the wrong room."

Casually, Salome lifted the pendant necklace, a silver disc with a Kwan Yin discreetly etched upon it, from beneath her T-shirt. She'd put it on when changing clothes specifically to deflect any negative energy she might encounter in this very house and wished she'd worn it to Jett's, though she'd hardly expected Chimene's hostile reception.

"You'll have to excuse me, I was looking for the bathroom." Then she added with a broad smile. "And it seems I've found it."

"There's a bathroom right next to his office. I'd rather you use that one."

"I didn't see it."

"Let me show you."

Like Gabe, Elle was a ceiling duster, over six feet tall and, at the moment, dressed in a tennis ensemble, a sweater casually draped across her shoulders, the arms loosely tied in front. She was in her forties, had ash-blonde hair and, Salome thought, looked older. But, Salome had heard Elle was a journalist, not a career easy on a person's looks.

As they entered the bedroom, Elle pulled off the sweater and tossed it on the bed next to a tennis racket, pausing to check her image in the mirrors, an automatic action that revealed her vanity. Sure, she had impressive height and neatly cut and streaked thick blonde hair, but her features were plain. Salome reminded herself that vanity is hardly exclusive to the beautiful and plays its tricks indiscriminately.

Elle pointed to a door across the hall from Gabe's new office. "Maybe you need glasses."

Salome stepped inside the small, unadorned bathroom. "Thank you." She pulled the door closed.

The seat and lid were up. Salome lowered both and sat down. She wished she'd let Jude come alone.

Elle, Jude, and Gabe fell silent and stared at Salome when she entered the office. A moment before, Salome had heard Elle talking about her tennis game. Three tall glasses of lemonade sweated on a tray on the glass desk. Salome headed for the drinks and took one. Gabe plucked the glass out of her hand.

"You don't want that one," he said, keeping it for himself.

She figured it must be laced with gin or vodka. "Actually, I'm not really thirsty." To divert attention from herself she said, "Jude, why don't you and Elle help yourselves."

"Oh, I'm not really thirsty, either," Jude said, not taking the hint.

Obviously, Gabe hadn't expected his wife to be around when he'd brought the drinks.

"Well, I am!" Elle announced. Her attention shifted from Salome as she took the beverage and drank a third.

"Elle, this is Salome. Salome—"

"We met." Elle wrinkled her nose. "She was in my— our—bathroom." Then she cocked her head. "Hmm. I've seen you before."

"Salome's my ex-wife, Elle."

Surely, Salome thought, there must be a picture of her somewhere in the house.

"It'll come to me." She smiled up at Gabe. "So where the hell are the movers?"

"The sixty-four-dollar question," Gabe remarked and drank more deeply this time.

"Did you call?"

"Several times."

"Mother'll be furious if they arrive after dark."

"Maybe the van broke down."

Elle sighed. Then suddenly her expression brightened and she snapped her fingers. "That's it!"

Jude and Salome started. Gabe actually jumped, spilling some of his drink.

Ignoring Gabe, Elle focused on Salome, a smile blooming. "Foreign Service! Been bugging me since I caught you snooping. You were there yesterday."

It took just a second for Salome to realize what the woman was talking about. An unpleasant chill snaked between her shoulder blades.

"So. Dario services you."

"My car. He's a skilled mechanic."

Elle snorted. "A god damn car thief is what he is!"

Maintaining composure, Salome was a study in restraint. "Good heavens, that was years ago. He was a teenager."

"If he wasn't the only game in town, I'd certainly take my BMW elsewhere."

"He *isn't* the only game in town. There are two other service centers within a mile." She knew, of course, having sworn to Dario she'd never feng shui the nearby competition. And plenty of women were attracted to Dario; they just needed the right car for him to reciprocate.

"Maybe you resent him for not taking a personal interest in German makes. But since they're so ubiquitous, he'd be foolish not to provide service for them."

Just then the doorbell chimed.

"Finally!" Gabe said and started for the door.

"I'll take care of it," Elle said, moving so fast she seemed to leave a vapor trail.

Jude and Gabe started breathing again.

"She's quite the spy," Salome observed.

"Comes naturally," Gabe said. "She used to work at Langley."

Langley, Virginia, being the home of the Central Intelligence Agency.

"That should be fun for you. Lots of new material."

"No great secrets divulged. Yet. But I'm working on it. She writes a biweekly society column for a local rag now. Knows everyone worth knowing. We go to about three parties a week. Bet I spend more time in Georgetown than you do."

"Wow, Gabe. A social life, too. Life can certainly take some strange twists."

"So what were you two talking about?" Gabe asked as Salome went to one of the boxes and looked inside.

"Cars." Salome pulled out a small plaque she'd made Gabe years ago. On it she'd carved the Latin phrase *Pono eum in scribendum,* which translated to "put it in words." She felt stung and wished he'd simply thrown it away rather than letting her know he no longer wanted it.

"Admit it, you're jealous of her."

"Not even close."

He moved up beside her and looked at the plaque. "I thought you'd like to have it," he said. His breath smelled strongly of juniper. Bombay gin, she thought ruefully. Fast acting, too.

She put the plaque back in the box. The sooner she and Jude gathered their plunder and left, the better.

"Just look at her. In her forties and she can still pass for a supermodel."

And she's got you for a lover while I've got Dario.

Gabe's eyes narrowed. "What're you smiling about?"

Chapter 12

☯

FEELING like a small house squeezed between two skyscrapers, Salome sat in the center of the cab clutching the bag from Mystery Books. The T-shirts didn't seem like a good idea after all, possible fodder for a snide remark. Gabe had decided to invite himself along though he wasn't actually needed to move furniture. Jude had had the foresight to borrow a dolly along with the truck, as Salome couldn't be expected to handle heavy items.

Before they left "Pasquinade Place" Gabe acted in keeping with the mansion's new name. After Jude and Gabe secured the boxes and desk in the bed of the truck, Gabe hijacked two wonderful old red leather chairs, a pair of two-drawer file cabinets and a rolled-up Persian rug before they reached the mover's van. Salome had watched in amusement as Elle, prickly as the cactus in the front garden, lambasted him for denying his mother-in-law these necessities. Her reaction aroused Salome's suspicions: What was so important about a few pieces of secondhand furniture? But maybe it was simply about power as they settled into their marriage.

"So what do you think of the new desk?" Gabe asked as Jude drove along a two-lane rural road common to Northern Virginia, this pastoral paradise in particular. Here, Salome often felt as if she were looking at a Currier & Ives print featuring early American–style mansions and lush green lawns and pastures. It was hard to believe that just a few miles away were little buttons and keys that could end life on earth; hard to believe that in these very mansions nuclear war was discussed just as the original owners had once plotted a revolutionary one.

"It's big."

"Oh, come on, Mei." He shifted in the cramped quarters, angling his back to the door so he could look at her.

"All right, Gabe. I think you're in for some trouble. Certainly if you take my advice and get rid of it, your wife won't be pleased. If you keep it, your work will suffer. You might even become embroiled in a scandal. Given that the desk is in the fame gua, the problem would likely stem from your celebrity. That glass is distorted, implying that the truth of the matter may never come out. But you won't get much support from friends—as having the window at your back suggests. And watch out for eye problems; my guess would be cataracts."

The twisted metal supporting the glass slab suggested more but, unless he really pressed her, she wouldn't expound. Since metal is the element of children and creativity, both would be linked to his problems and certainly exacerbated by the twisted shape. Quite possibly his new stepson would be involved. And Gabe's own sexual plumbing.

"Sorry I asked."

"What happened to your old office? Why did you move upstairs?"

"Well, that's Tyler's room now and Elle thought my bedroom—now my office—was too small for us but a good space for me to work. The light in there is really good, you know. . . ." He suddenly threw back his head and laughed. "Why didn't I see it before. You're pissed, aren't you. All that feng shui you did back when I moved in the house has been undone."

On her left, Salome felt Jude stiffen. He twisted his hands on the steering wheel. "Look, I don't want anyone getting the idea I'm taking sides here, but if I recall correctly, it was after Salome feng shuied that house that you signed a multimillion-dollar contract with a new publisher. What, five years ago?"

"You don't think my writing had anything to do with it?"

"That's not what I'm saying."

Gabe poked Salome in the arm. "Hey, you're suddenly awfully quiet."

Salome looked up at him and smiled. "Actually, I do have a question."

"Fire away, old girl."

"How did Elle's first husband die?"

The cab went dead quiet. Then Jude laughed. Gabe announced that he'd married a divorcée and not a widow.

"It was a joke, Gabe," Salome remarked.

When they arrived at Malabar Close, the two men carried the carpet down to the basement while Salome stayed with the truck, which, due to a shortage of space, was double-parked beside an unfamiliar car.

A moment after the two men entered the house another car entered the Close, pulled around and double-parked behind the truck. The driver alighted, now recognizable by his kinky, unruly blonde hair enhanced by dreadlocks.

"Jamie!"

"Hey. Salome. So you're back." He stuck his hands in his pockets and approached. "Or are you moving?"

"Unloading some furniture, that's all."

"You seen Fiona?"

"No. But her car's still here." She nodded toward the carriage house.

"That's strange."

"Why?"

"I've been trying to reach her for days."

"Last time I saw her she mentioned something about going to Chicago. Is there a problem?"

"Yeah. There're some things in the house I need and I haven't been able to find my key. Say, you keep one for her don't you?"

Both women had keys to each other's houses, but Salome had never lent Fiona's to another person.

"Hey. It's not like I'm a stranger."

They walked to Salome's house and she took the key ring with the two keys on it from the marble-topped oak chest. Together they went next door.

First Salome knocked.

"She didn't answer the phone when I called fifteen minutes ago," Jamie said.

When it became obvious that no one was going to answer, Salome inserted the proper key and unlocked Fiona's door. Jamie entered.

"Fee? You home?" he called out. He peeked in the rooms on either side of the foyer, calling her name.

Salome waited in the foyer while he ran upstairs. By the feel of the energy, Salome sensed that Fiona hadn't been home in some time. A glance at the coffee table told her the Caravaggio book remained as she'd last seen it, opened and with the same copy of the *Washington Post* on top. Oddly, though, the print of Malabar Close, Isabelle's gift to Fiona, was gone from its place above the mantel.

Jamie skipped down the stairs, redirecting her attention. He carried a carousel of slides. "I looked in her bedroom and the suitcase she keeps under the bed is gone. Hold on a minute."

He opened the doors to her studio and after a quick look around, returned to the foyer. "Her camera's gone so that pretty well determines that she's off someplace."

"What about her car though?" Salome asked while locking the door. "The locks on the carriage house have been changed and maybe she couldn't get in."

They walked back toward the street.

"Probably took a taxi to the airport. It's what she usually does."

As he opened the door to his car Salome said, "If you hear from her tell her to give me a call, okay? I'd feel better if I knew where she was."

Jamie nodded and with a wave sped out of the Close.

WITH THE CARPET LAID IN THE BASEMENT, the furniture followed. Then Jude and Gabe left to return the truck, Gabe driving Jude's car.

Armed with Murphy Oil Soap and furniture polish, Salome cleaned the new furnishings then purified them with the fragrant smoke of a sage bundle. By the time the men returned, Salome had finished. The new work area was officially christened with the pizza and beer they'd picked up on the way back.

She thought about giving Jude the Kwan Kung but decided to wait until Jude was by himself. Gabe might have something rude to say about the deity and she didn't want its entrance to be spoiled by anything negative.

While eating a slice and sipping a beer, Jude started to set up his computer on the new desk, not wasting any time. Salome and Gabe occupied the twin leather chairs.

"I always liked these chairs," Salome said, rubbing the

arms. "My dad has a pair just like them in his home office."

"Thanks for taking them. And the other stuff, too." Gabe looked around the basement office. "Wow. This is so cool."

Jude carried the monitor over from the card table.

"How about letting me in, too?"

"Let you in?" Jude said, now kneeling on the floor and hooking up the monitor to the back of the tall, gray computer box. "This isn't a clubhouse, man."

"Hey, you know I've got great contacts."

Jude frowned. "What're you thinking of, resurrecting *The Mod Squad*?"

"Why not?" Gabe shot forward in the chair, eager as an adolescent. "I happen to know you look great in an Afro and Salome always looked sexy in bell-bottoms."

"Oh please," Salome moaned. She grabbed her bottle of water and empty plate. "I've got work to do."

Jude shook his head in disbelief. "Gabe. Old buddy. This is my *business*."

As Salome started up the stairs, Gabe continued. "Come on, Jude. You let Salome in."

"Whoa. Salome's got her own thing going. And she's been generous enough to let me temporarily use this space." Salome wondered if that was said for her benefit. But she didn't have time to listen to their banter.

A few minutes later, armed with her own particular weaponry, and wearing a full-sleeved Japanese apron that tied in the back, she started to clean the dining room, a portable boom box playing her favorite music to work by: taiko drums.

Working quickly and efficiently, windows, hutch, table and chairs, and chandelier sparkled and shone. She moved on into the living room, tackling the dirtiest chore first—the fireplace.

At one point, Gabe entered. "May I use your phone?" he shouted over the shrieking vacuum cleaner and thundering drums. "Jude's cell phone ran outta juice."

Salome nodded, half surprised he'd bothered to ask. By asking, though, he showed he respected her space and did not have any lingering sense of ownership. She started to wonder about his marriage, then decided to drop it in favor of reacquainting herself with the fireplace.

After changing from the smudged sooty apron into a clean one, Salome continued in the living room. It was when she started polishing the shelving of the entertainment center that she made a discovery. Here as in the landing library Salome kept the spines of the books flush with the edge to alleviate cutting ch'i. But a number of books had been pushed back to accommodate a brand new volume lying flat on the shelf, a copy of *Interior Design With Feng Shui* by Sarah Rossbach. Her copy was well-worn and with other reference books in her third-floor study.

Puzzled, she carried it down to the basement and directed her question to Jude.

"This your book?"

"Nope. Why?"

She shrugged and started to leaf through the pages but stopped almost immediately. "Jeez Louise!" she exclaimed.

"What is it?" Jude and Gabe asked in unison.

With her mouth agape, Salome held the book up so they could see. The center section had been neatly cut out to accommodate what looked like a piece of plastic about two inches by two inches.

Gabe took the book from her and removed the little square. He held it up. "It's a film cartridge. Fits in those new digital mini camcorders."

Salome's suddenly beamed. "Jude, I think this clears up the mystery of our intruder." She shook her head. "It must have been Fiona! Damn. I should have figured that out. She used her key to my back door!"

"Why not just bring it over?" Jude asked.

Filled with excitement, Salome pulled off her apron. "Obviously, she didn't want anyone to see her. Including you. We need to get on over to the camera store."

AFTER SALOME PAID FOR THE PICTURES SHE'D had developed, Gabe did the talking, sounding like a knowledgeable buyer as he asked the sales clerk to show him various cameras. As luck would have it, the clerk was a fan and had been to every signing of Gabe's at the Connecticut Avenue bookstore for the last five years.

"My mother turned me on to your books," the boyish-looking clerk declared somewhat breathlessly.

Gabe handed over the cartridge. "We need a camera that this fits into."

While the clerk turned and unlocked a wall case behind the counter, Gabe said somewhat wistfully, "Ah, a new generation of readers. I'd mention this to my editor but that will only remind her of my age. And mortality."

"Will this be a clue in your next mystery, Mr. Hoya?" the young man asked with wide eyes as he set a small camera on the counter.

Gabe put a finger to his lips. The clerk nearly swooned.

At first, they didn't quite understand the significance as they watched the image on the view plate of a camera identical to Fiona's.

Fiona had continued to follow Duncan Mah, recording him entering and leaving his house, restaurants, shops, and generally going about his business in Georgetown.

After about five minutes, Gabe and Jude began to sigh and shift around, showing signs of boredom. The clerk said these cartridges had up to an hour and a half playing time.

Judah bought batteries for his phone.

But Salome knew Fiona's obsession had to amount to something and she continued to watch Mah.

"Look," Gabe said, pulling out his wallet. "Why don't I just buy the damn camera."

At that moment, Duncan turned one corner in particular and a moment later began walking up a drive familiar for its cherry blossoms. The little LCD readout recorded the date and time.

"How do you stop this!" Salome blurted.

The clerk helped her, then at her instruction, rewound until she told him to stop. "Look, you guys!" she said, trying to keep her voice down. But it was difficult.

Fiona had just documented Duncan Mah entering Simon Snow's house on the day before the murder.

THE THREE OF THEM FORMED A SOLID UNIT as they hurried back to the house, oblivious to the foot traffic and the grumblings of other pedestrians forced to step into the street to move around them. Gabe carried the bag holding the new camera.

"Maybe it's just a simple matter of this Duncan Mah character being a client of Snow's," Gabe offered.

"Yes, but Fiona considered this significant enough to plant the book late at night and run the risk of being caught by Jude. It was a fluke that I happened to come home when I did. I wasn't expected home for several days.

"Fiona Cockburn," Gabe announced with some authority, having known her for years, "is a woman given to the dramatic. Good grief, she's a filmmaker."

"Well, I think it's more than that," Salome went on stubbornly. "I think *she* was being watched."

Judah suddenly straightened and took a deep breath. "Ah, paranoia! The stuff D.C. is made of; as essential to the District as sunshine is to L.A."

"Hey, I like that," Gabe said, always on the look out for a line to steal.

"It's yours. And thanks for the camera."

"Glad to oblige." He put his arm around Salome and squeezed her shoulder. "See, Mei, I am an asset."

"But we'll never be able to use you for undercover work."

They came to the top of Malabar Close. At the bottom of the cul-de-sac, the bent spikes of the fencing glinted in the sunlight. Salome felt a weight on her heart, fearing the previous night's cleansing had had little effect. But these things didn't work overnight and she reminded herself to be patient.

Gabe picked up on her thoughts. "It is shame about the rose garden. Totally changes the Close. Still, I wouldn't worry too much. Just look at Evermay over on Twenty-eighth Street."

Gabriel was talking about a Georgian mansion built around the same time as the houses in Malabar Close. No one protested as Gabe retold the familiar story. The owner, one Samuel Davidson, not a friendly soul, constructed a high wall and ominous-looking black gates and actually issued a warning in the newspapers urging sightseers to avoid the place, Gabe now quoted, "as they would a den of devils or rattlesnakes."

"Makes me wonder what's lurking behind *these* gates," Salome commented. "I haven't seen any snakes yet."

"Oh, come on, Mei. The devil's already been done in Georgetown," he said, referring to one of the most successful American horror films, *The Exorcist*. "Don't sound so grim. After all, Georgetown's just a little village. Why wouldn't this Duncan Mah know Simon Snow? Snow wasn't exactly a recluse."

Just then Judah's cell phone rang. He answered and handed it off to Gabe. " 'She who must be obeyed,' " he announced, taking a quote made famous by John Mortimer's English barrister, Rumpole, and which Salome recalled from H. Rider Haggard's early-nineteenth-century adventure novel, *She*, a favorite of hers.

A grin slowly grew on Gabriel's face. He mumbled some personal endearment then passed the little phone back to Jude. "Like I said, I am an asset."

"Is this what I think it is?" Jude asked.

"You're expected! They'll both be home until eight. I suggest you change clothes. These are Georgetown ladies." Then he handed the bag to Salome. "Now, I've got to get home to Momma."

"What's going on?"

"Jude'll fill you in."

"Don't you want a ride?" Jude asked.

"I'll catch a cab. Besides, you two need to get going." He slapped Jude on the arm then gave Salome a swift peck on the cheek.

"Just one more thing, Gabe. I suggest you reconsider the new name for your house."

"What the hell's wrong with Pasquinade Place?"

"It just might attract off-the-wall activity into your—"

"Don't be ridiculous! It's just a god damn word!"

"There's more to these things than you realize, Gabriel!"

But Gabe suddenly bounded off. Then he stopped, turned, and cried out, " 'The game's afoot!' "

Chapter 13

☯

WHILE quickly changing into her third set of clothes for the day—this time, a pair of slacks and a silk blouse—Gabe's parting Sherlockian quote echoed in Salome's head. She was reminded of the many fictional investigations she and Gabriel had worked on over the years, in particular the times of intense nonstop activity as the characters tracked down leads. Not to forget the leads that went nowhere—she hoped this wasn't one of them—a product of Gabriel's enthusiasm and almost adolescent desire to participate in a real investigation.

However it turned out, the fact remained that the two women who had been burgled the previous Friday night were friends of Elle. Earlier, while Salome had been cleaning upstairs, Gabe had called Elle and Elle in turn had contacted the women. On Elle's recommendation, the women agreed to talk to Jude and Salome. That is what the call had been about, with Gabe having given Elle the number of Jude's cell phone and instructions to call the minute a meeting had been set up.

Salome appreciated Elle's effort but still couldn't

shake her suspicions that Gabe's new wife was up to something. Then again, Salome had to admit she might be overreacting to the glass desk and what it implied.

KENDALL WRIGHT AND MEG MORAN LIVED but a short distance from Malabar Close in a block of two-hundred-year-old Federalist row houses. After a brisk five-minute walk, Judah and Salome entered the neighborhood.

From one of the narrow, black-shuttered windows a fluffy white cat watched a baby robin learn to fly. Window boxes and pots of spring flowers dappled the street with color. Trees heavy with bright green foliage muffled the sounds of the city. This was one of those places where one could easily drift back in time, replacing the purr of an expensive car with the *clop-clop* of horses' hooves on the cobbled street. Salome thought she remembered Gabriel pointing out several of the row houses as having been part of the Underground Railroad when slaves were smuggled out of the South to destinations north and west.

Her brief reverie ended when Judge engaged the shiny brass knocker on the front door of a house in the center of the row.

Kendall Wright, who looked like something out of a pastry shop (unlike the usual press photos sprinkled weekly in the society section of various papers), answered the door herself.

"Mr. Freeman. Ms Waterhouse. Please come in."

In her mid- to late thirties, she had extremely white skin and platinum hair that fell past the shoulders and down the back of a chocolate-brown satin dressing gown. Maybe because she was craving a sweet, Salome thought of an éclair with whipped cream filling or maybe a cream puff slathered in chocolate as she and Judah followed this extremely wealthy confection into the narrow, fully restored sitting room. Salome admired the fine molding at the ceiling, rich mahogany wainscoting, and green marble mantel.

Kendall lowered herself onto a red velvet love seat (notably in the room's fame position) and indicated a matched pair of armchairs upholstered in pale-blue brocade. She picked up a crystal bell from a coffee table between them and rang it—an action that seemed automatic, something she did by rote once or twice a day—while keeping her full attention on Judah.

Whether dressed for the hunt in red jacket and jodhpurs or a formal gown, she was known for her trademark ponytail and had revived that particular style in the Washington metropolitan area. Salome had been wearing her hair in a ponytail for decades, but it took marketing ingredients like social status and relative youth and the timing—during a slow news period—to set a trend.

Now sitting across from the attractive, divorced wife of a former ambassador to the court of St. James, Salome recalled a headline in the Style section of the *San Jose Mercury News* a couple winters past: *The Ponytail Is Back!* And there was a photograph of Kendall Wright in a ball gown dancing with the president at some White House Christmas party, her thick white mane pulled back and held in place with a black silk ribbon. The author had written, inaccurately, that the hairstyle had not been heard of in nearly half a century. As was often the case with overblown society stories, the reader was left with the impression that Kendall Wright's fashion sense and social life were directly linked to some munificent effort like ending world hunger.

A maid wearing a black uniform and white lacy apron appeared carrying a tray containing a silver tea service, a plate of dry-looking toast, a bowl containing restaurant-size packets of marmalade and butter pats. Kendall flicked a wrist and the maid vanished. Then she poured.

"Help yourself to cream and sugar," she said in a sweet, girlish voice with a Virginia hunt-country drawl.

Salome did. While doing so she noticed that the marmalade and butter were not only designed for restaurant use but had actually come from one, a five-star bistro just a few blocks away. Yet another clue as to how the fabulously rich stay that way.

"Thank you, Mrs. Wright," Judah said. "We appreciate you taking time from your busy schedule to talk to us."

Salome could tell he was adjusting tone and delivery to find just the right blend. But, of course, he was a pro. Nor was this his first this time trying to extract information from the insular and insulated. People like Kendall Wright rarely deigned to discuss their affairs with the common folk, even if the outcome would be to their benefit. Again Salome was reminded that they had Elle to thank.

"I know you've gone over this with the police—"

"Don't forget the damned insurance people!" She interrupted. Her cheeks colored faintly as if a drop of blood had been added to skim milk. "They treat *me* like the criminal." She paused. "As I'm certain you and your assistant absolutely will not do."

Assistant? So, Salome thought, Elle had gotten a dig in.

"If you'd just—" Jude interrupted himself and suddenly changed tack. "Mrs. Wright, would you mind if I remove my jacket?"

The pale blue eyes widened in appreciation. "Why, of course not, Detective Freeman."

Salome sat back, enjoying this parade—or charade—of manners.

He nodded a thanks while carefully removing the tweed sport coat, which he handed to Salome. Though unprepared, she didn't betray a flicker of surprise.

"As I was saying, if you'd just take us through the events leading to your discovery of the theft."

"Maureen—Meg Moran—and I had dinner at the Four Seasons, then spent the evening at the Kennedy Center."

"Lucky you. Itzhak Perlman and Yo-Yo Ma performing."

Judah's homework was impressive but was the sort of thing he'd know.

"Indeed," she said casually, as if attending a concert performed by the world-renowned violinist and cellist comprised a normal evening. "My driver had the night off so we caught a taxi home.

"I wasn't in the house thirty seconds when I realized something was wrong."

"Was the door unlocked? A window open?"

Kendall eyes shifted to Salome momentarily. "Intuition. Something felt different."

Salome smiled and nodded slightly, providing the necessary backup.

"Where was the maid?"

"Out to dinner and a movie with my driver. They're married." She paused, as if to let them know, should they ever be in the market, married couples made the best servants.

"Anyway, I made myself a cup of tea and took it upstairs to the bedroom. I undressed, combed out my hair and then went to the safe to put away the jewelry I'd been wearing. Nothing fancy, just some pearls." She pursed her lips. " 'Course that's all I've got left now, isn't it!"

"You felt something was wrong and yet, you stopped to make a cup of tea?"

Both Salome and Kendall tensed. Everything had been going so smoothly, Salome wondered why Jude would introduce a suspicion. Maybe to let her know she couldn't manipulate him, that he was nobody's fool.

Kendall's hand's fluttered in front of her dressing gown. "Tea calms my nerves, Detective."

"I understand. It's not easy being a single woman living alone."

She managed a brave smile.

"Mrs. Wright, would you mind showing us the safe?"

She laughed. "Now that's a word I don't use anymore! In the future, I will have a lock box."

They mounted the narrow stairs. Row houses were not known for their size but their historical value. Though she didn't know for certain, Salome figured that, like many wealthy Georgetown residents, Kendall Wright had a country estate in Maryland or Virginia, her weekend "getaway."

Kendall lead them through a neat bedroom furnished plainly with a quilt-covered four-poster cherry wood bed, a matching tallboy with polished brass fixtures, and a ladies' writing desk.

Salome and Jude exchanged glances when Kendall didn't stop but lead them through an open door, and into the bathroom.

A trompe l'oeil mural of a Caribbean beach, a ship flying a skull and crossbones anchored out in the turquoise bay surrounded a gleaming claw-foot tub about seven feet in length. Towels were cannily placed so they appeared to be lying on the sandy beach. A handsome pirate sat on a closed chest, his legs splayed, leaning to the left on one elbow. His posture and expression suggested he might be negotiating with whomever was talking a bath. A real chest, identical to the one in the mural, sat open beside the tub. On the top tray were a highball glass, an ashtray, and a stack of romance novels.

Kendall went straight to the pirate and bent down. She appeared to be fondling his crotch. A door sprang open. Inside, they could see a small nine-digit keypad, the cover raised at the moment.

"Well," Judah said.

"The family jewels and all that," Kendall said. "It was such a cute idea I couldn't resist."

Judah squatted down to examine the safe.

"Real or paste?" Salome asked.

"Unfortunately, they were the real thing. Contrary to what most people think, those of us blessed with beautiful jewelry like to have it close by. I mean, why else have it if you can't wear it whenever you want. Of course, when I was married, my husband insisted that it all stay in the safe-deposit box. But then, men see jewels as investments. Maybe if they wore them now and then they'd understand how we women feel."

"Who talked you into this?" Jude asked.

"Simon Snow." She sighed and rolled her eyes to the ceiling. "God rest his soul. Thing is, you see, these hand-painted murals have become quite the thing among our set. Simon would do whatever you want whether it was a copy of a famous painting or something from your imagination. And, he actually believed it provided a secure place for a home safe. He told me he only suggested the safe to a couple of clients. And then, of course, I find out Maureen—Meg—had one, too."

"Who did the actual work? Did he have help?"

"Oh no. Simon worked alone. Other decorators who do this sort of thing have a crew come in to do the work. Simon was very exclusive. Only he knew the location of the safe. So, of course, he was the first person I thought of when I found my jewelry gone. Then I remembered that he was dead."

A few moments later, they left the bathroom again, following Kendall through the prim bedroom. Downstairs, Jude collected his jacket and thanked Kendall for the refreshments.

"To be perfectly honest with you, Detective Freeman," Kendall said when they were at the front door. "I think Meg—Maureen that is—is involved."

"How long have you known her?"

"Years." Her chest heaved. "She was my best friend."

Clearly the burglary had resulted in more than a hefty financial loss.

"What makes you think she's involved?"

"When she saw what Simon had done to my bathroom, she absolutely had to have the same thing done. My feeling is that somehow, she talked him into revealing my number code. Then she hired someone to steal the jewelry at a time when we both would be out for the evening and Chaz—that's her husband, Charles—not in town. He spends most of his time in New York anyway. But they're going through a bad patch that the insurance money on her jewelry would go a long way to mend."

"Did she instigate the evening out?"

Kendall looked off for a moment. "I think so. Yes, it seems to me she did. We do so many things together. I should say, we *did*."

"We appreciate your candor, Mrs. Wright. And it goes without saying, everything you've told us is strictly confidential."

She opened a drawer in an antique table and handed Jude a small card.

"Call me anytime, Detective. Anything I can do to help . . ." She let the sentence trail off in, to Salome's way of thinking, a less than subtle invitation.

Chapter 14

"LOOKS like you made a friend," Salome said, once they were outside.

Judah glared and, instead of walking up the street to Meg Moran's, led the way to a bench in a small park diagonally across from the row houses. He pulled a handkerchief from his back pocket and wiped his face and the back of his neck.

"Christ, it was hot in there."

"Indeed. I thought you'd blown it when you made that comment about her going off to make tea when she felt something was wrong."

"Just didn't want her to get too comfortable. And I don't trust women who wear satin robes in the late afternoon to greet a visiting cop—rather, a private detective. Though it looks otherwise, they're trying to hide something."

"She might have just been getting ready to go out."

"Maybe."

"Why didn't you ask about what she did after she discovered that her jewelry was gone?"

"Because I didn't know the answer myself." He gave her a candid look. "I *always* prepare for an interview. This all happened too quickly. But since it was dropped in our lap I couldn't very well say no or ask for a time more suitable for us. I suppose that's something I need to get used to in the private sector. Being more spontaneous." He sighed. "I do miss the power that shield gave me."

"How'd you know who was performing at the Kennedy Center that night?"

"I checked it out when I heard about the burglaries." Then, his eyes drifting to the row houses, he asked, "So, what does your feng shui tell you about her?"

From their position they could see anyone coming and going.

"Doesn't take a feng shui practitioner to see that she's a romantic, probably attracted to dangerous men—like you, or rather, I suppose in your case, men who *represent* danger—though not as permanent partners. And she has something of a sense of humor."

"Where do you get that?"

"Placement of the safe? The family jewels?"

"Oh. Funny to a woman maybe."

"Her bedroom contradicts what her bathroom says but I'd trust the bath, it being her private sanctum." Salome unzipped her handbag. She handed Jude a small plastic bottle of water taken from the refrigerator before they left the house.

He straightened. "Oh Lord, thanks! Shouldn't have had that beer this afternoon."

Salome went on. "The prim, puritanical bedroom strongly suggests a façade indicating a preference for unimaginative sex—though she might indulge in something kinky but not in her own bed. It would be interesting to know the sort of men she dates."

She paused, then smiled. "However, I don't mind venturing a guess. I'd say they're respectable, career-oriented," she stopped, considering. "But not just any career. No military. Lawyers, men on the clever, deceptive end of the food chain. And definitely single. No matter how attractive, she wouldn't be seen with a married man.

"What's interesting, too, are the dried flowers. Did you notice them?"

Judah shrugged and returned the bottle, half the water remaining.

Salome continued her train of thought as she absently put the bottle back in her purse. "She had them in the entry way, in the living room, and in her bedroom. Dried flowers accessorize a room in an unusual way. But they should be used sparingly as they do not attract positive, energetic ch'i. After all, they're dead."

Jude looked at his watch. "We better get going. Thanks for the time-out."

As they returned to the street, Salome continued. "Kendall's bedroom is in the relationship gua of the house itself. Now, that's a good thing. But, taking the bedroom on its own, we see something else.

"We entered her bedroom through the knowledge gua. Her bed is in the fame position. To the right of her bed is the nightstand with the spray of dried flowers, in the relationship gua. But, also in the relationship gua is the door to the bathroom. So, on the one hand, she sees the excitement in relationships as dried up—something she's not going after with much enthusiasm. Ah, but then, there's the door to a completely different world. Opportunity."

"The bathroom itself, then," Judah said. "Where is it in the overall scheme?"

"Part in relationship, the largest area in children and

creativity. A fanciful side of life. If she has children, they're probably at some boarding school. The bath suggests what replaces children, as well as her creative side."

She took a breath. "So, now I will go out on a limb and suggest that the thief is a lover, someone she doesn't want anyone to know about, someone selfish, probably emotionally immature—"

"A younger man, right?"

Salome smiled. "Maybe. That's not to say all men younger than Kendall Wright are selfish and emotionally stunted." Her smile grew even larger as Dario's image tangoed across her mind.

"You speaking from experience?" Judah said.

Salome may have been good at interpreting the messages people projected in their houses, but Judah was no slouch, especially when it came to reading people. Make that *reading minds,* she thought.

"Anyway, Jude," she said, skipping over the question, "he'll be someone she considers fun and as we've already surmised, that equates to dangerous; someone who probably puts their energy in what they do and has little or nothing left over for the emotional department."

"If he's the thief, then he's a damn good con man."

"And he'd have to know about Meg Moran's safe, too, and her jewelry."

"Which would most likely place him in their social group. I just can't see one or both of these ladies picking up some dude who ends up taking off with their jewelry."

"Like Brad Pitt's character in *Thelma and Louise.*"

"Unless you change Thelma and Louise into to a couple of malcontented Georgetown socialites."

"In which case, you're right. He'd have to blend into salon society."

"Or be an integral part of it."

*   *   *

BUT CASTING MEG MORAN IN THEIR VERSION of the award-winning film would have to wait.

"I'm sorry," the maid said after answering the door. "Mrs. Moran had to leave suddenly. But she said she'd be glad to talk to you tomorrow at noon."

Salome was disappointed but Judah seemed relieved.

"This'll give me a chance to do some background," he said. At the next intersection he stopped. "Anything in particular you'd like for dinner? Or do you have plans?"

"No plans. But, Jude, you really don't have to cook just because I'm home."

"Mei. Lately, cooking functions as my social life. Sad but true."

"Well, you can count on me to enjoy it. Look. Why don't we have a confab over dinner? Go over what we've got, which will help determine where we need to go—who we need to talk to, that sort of thing."

"Sure."

As he started to head back to Wisconsin Avenue and the Safeway there, she remembered something.

"One more thing, Jude."

He held up his hands. "Hey. I'm not going to take your money for food!"

"No, no. It's about the camera Gabe bought."

"Yeah?"

"Well, you know of course, he'll be back to return it to the store."

Jude stared at her for a moment then threw back his head and laughed. "Jesus. I'd forgotten about that."

"I almost did, too. But it just occurred to me that we should take the camera over to Jett's to see if he recognizes Duncan Mah. Then, of course, I remembered that whatever Gabe buys on the spur of the moment he invariably returns."

"Right. I'll give Jett a call now."

The sun was thinking seriously about calling it a day as Salome headed home. Jude strolled toward Wisconsin Avenue, the phone to his ear.

SALOME PUT ON A POT OF COFFEE, THEN went upstairs, all the way to the top of the house, carrying the boom box and a wicker basket filled with cleaning supplies and fresh rags and sponges. She still felt disappointed that the meeting with Maureen "Meg" Moran had been postponed, having wanted the conversation with Kendall to be fresh when she met Meg, to compare their stories. But maybe it was for the best; she had only to recall the investigative tactics of one Antoinette de Beauharnais.

The product of a Creole madam and her underworld paramour, Antoinette had been birthed on the very desk now positioned in the basement. A redheaded dynamo whose silk caftans could shelter any number of the street urchins who, like the Baker Street Irregulars featured in the Sherlock Holmes stories, did her bidding, Antoinette stormed across the pages like the Goddess of Chaos. Gabe loved entangling the New Orleans P.I. in the most convoluted plots, which, of course, Salome had had to edit, a task that had often left her close to screaming and from which had grown Salome's compulsive need for order.

Salome's upstairs sanctum took up the entire third floor. The air was stuffy and close. After setting down her things, she switched on a boxy floor fan and opened the two dormer windows to get the ch'i moving. She took down the two crystals hanging from nine-inch red cords from their positions at the windows and dropped them into her apron pockets. Later, she would clean them and replace the old cords with new.

Then she turned on all the lights.

Years ago, a false ceiling had been installed to cover the beams, which just happened to be good feng shui. Ceiling beams produced destructive ch'i. In a bedroom, for instance, where a bed might be underneath a beam, Salome always suggested that two flutes be hung and angled upward with the mouthpiece in the lowest position. This would redirect the energy up and away from the bed's occupants. To ignore such a problem could result in ill health (in the part of the body the beam crossed), or divorce for a married couple as the beam symbolically split the couple.

A ceiling fan hung in the center of the room. The blades, though, created "cutting ch'i" and could be harmful to anyone working nearby. However, such an apparatus was necessary to keep the air circulating, even with central air, particularly during Washington's dreadfully hot summers. To neutralize the harmful effects, Salome had hung a crystal from the chain and now she removed it to be cleaned with the others.

Instead of a desk, Salome used a long table and a high-back leather chair on rollers. It was positioned in the wealth gua at a diagonal from the entrance in the room's career gua. On it she kept her computer, and on a stand beside it, a printer/fax/copier. Various supplies and materials handed out to individual clients and to attendees at presentations were in boxes neatly stacked on nearby shelves. A short bookcase filled with copies of her most frequently used feng shui reference books was under the window. A phone/answering machine console and a bronze Kwan Yin graced the top.

Positioned around the room were other long tables

where she made adjustments to the dollhouse and drafted floor plans. Propped against the wall just inside the door was the easel she used at local presentations. There were also dozens of cabinets filled with tiny furniture and assorted feng shui supplies: all sizes of mirrors, wind chimes, crystals, and multicolored tassels; inexpensive and expensive flutes, bright-red and soft-pink silk roses, bags of polished stones, and even rooster feathers used in a particular ritual that rid a person of old enemies. There was also a screen, a slide projector, and dozens of neatly labeled boxes containing slides. With a client's permission, she took pictures of the exteriors and interiors of the houses she feng shuied. In six years, she had amassed a sizable collection. For local presentations and seminars where time permitted, she used the slides to show before and after the feng shui enhancements had been implemented, mostly dramatic improvements.

She placed the boom box on her desk and under the influence of the rhythmic drumming of the taikos spent the next couple of hours bonding with her special space by cleaning it.

"OH!" SALOME EXCLAIMED, SURPRISED TO find not one but two men busy in the kitchen. Her mouth salivated as she inhaled the wonderful aromas coming from the stove.

"Me, I'm just the hunter/gatherer. Jett's the artiste: endive salad, crab cakes, fresh creamed corn . . ."

Jett Malieu looked over at Salome and said softly, "Hello, Ms. Waterhouse. I hope you don't mind me coming over like this."

"Good heavens, no. And please, call me Salome." She passed quickly between the two men—Jude prepping at the sink, Jett in command of the stove—on her way to the basement to deposit the cleaning supplies in their proper place. "So what's up?"

"I invited Jett for dinner and what do you know! He offered to cook. So, here we are."

"Uh, has he seen the—" Before she could say "video" Jude cut her off.

"We are cooking, kiddo," he said, giving her a look. "Dinner will be on the table in fifteen, twenty minutes. That sound about right, Jett?"

"Yes, sir."

"I'll stay out of your way then." While descending the stairs Salome had a vague feeling that Jude was practicing to be a father-in-law. No question, he'd be a good one. But what about Jett? she wondered. Was this handsome young man preparing dinner a murderer or a victim of circumstance? And why did he now choose to spend time with Judah when previously he'd been so reluctant?

Well, she said to herself, I suppose we'll find the answers at dinner. She just hoped the answers wouldn't spoil anyone's appetite.

IT APPEARED THAT THOSE ANSWERS WOULDN'T arrive until after dessert. Judah kept the conversation focused everywhere but the investigation: basketball during the salad, college life over the entrée, and what it's like to be a male model (humiliating but well paying) with the peach cobbler.

Finally, coffee. Salome excused herself and returned a moment later with the mini camera. She moved beside Jett and played Fiona's cassette.

"Do you recognize this man?"

"Sure. That's Duncan."

Salome's heart skipped a beat. She and Jude exchanged glances. His seemed to say, "Don't press."

"Was he a frequent visitor?" Salome asked as she skirted the dining room table on her way back to her seat.

"He has an antique store. Chinese stuff. Simon bought a few things for the den."

"When did they meet? I mean, for the first time?"

Jett took a breath and looked away, shaking his head slightly. "I really couldn't say. Christmas maybe? I was pretty focused on finals so during the Christmas parties I didn't pay a whole lot of attention—except, I mean, to do my job."

"If you fast forward, you'll come to a scene where Duncan Mah is approaching Simon's house. The LCD readout gives the date and time."

A heavy silence hung over the table as Jett fast-forwarded. Even the lingering scents of dinner seemed to add to the weight.

"Uh, that was the day before the, uh . . ." He trailed off. He put the camera down.

"What do you remember about that day?"

Another silence while Jett tried to put the pieces together, the question being if it was truthfully or otherwise. "You know, I don't know if he came in. Wait! I was at my desk. I heard the doorbell and started to get up. The door was open—the door to my room. Then Simon was there and said he'd get it. He'd been in his office. You know, he must have been expecting Duncan because I usually answer the door unless the maid's around. Then I just went back to work. I probably would have noticed if the two of them went into the office or something. That's why I think Duncan didn't come in. If they'd gone in the kitchen I would have heard them."

"But you didn't hear their conversation?"

He shook his head. "The front door's too far away."

"Why do you think he came to the house?"

Jett shrugged. "Maybe something about furniture. He

usually came over with a couple guys to carry in new pieces."

"Who do you think killed your employer?"

He sat back as if she'd slapped him then snorted and shook his head.

"Salome," Jude said, "would you bring in the coffee?"

Salome ignored Jude and pressed. "Can you think of any motive?"

"It baffles me. Honest. I just don't know."

"You mentioned yesterday that you thought Simon was in love. Do you think he might have been in love with Duncan Mah?"

"The coffee, please!"

So, she thought, Jude wants to change the subject. But why? Then she realized that she was beginning to sound like Fiona, that is, fixated on Duncan Mah. Well, maybe she was. But there was just something about him. . . .

"So why this change of heart?" Salome heard Jude ask. She picked up the coffeepot and hurried back to the dining room, not wanting to miss any part of Jett's answer. He was so soft-spoken you had to be within a few feet of him to hear what he had to say. Whatever he did after graduating from college, better not require voice projection. Maybe not a problem since he was studying accounting.

"I don't like my lawyer."

"Why?"

"Well, for one thing, he's the one who told me not to talk to you. He said you're still a homicide cop, after all, and your only goal is to put me *in* jail, not keep me out." He paused while Salome refilled their cups. "And I think he's really more interested in impressing Chimene than anything else. I just don't know what to do. I mean, Chimene was so intent on you working on this investigation on my behalf and then she recommends this guy. And now she's pissed at you because she thinks you and Ms., uh, Salome are living together.

"I just feel kind of throttled by both of them. And I don't mean any disrespect to her. I love her. But I feel like a wimp. Hell, I'm acting like a wimp!"

"Do you trust me?"

"Yes, sir, I do."

"Mind telling me why?"

"Because," he said earnestly, "you were a honest cop and a unifying force in the black community. I think you have the best interests of young black men at heart."

That sentiment cut into the atmosphere in a decidedly poignant way. Whatever negative feelings Jude had been harboring about himself just took a direct hit. Salome had to keep herself from leaping across the table and kissing Jett. At the same time, if she ever found out he was manipulating Jude, she'd be first in line to punch him out.

"Gentlemen," she said, rising from her seat. "I hate to eat and run but I've got some work to do." Jude gave her an appreciative nod.

Back upstairs in her workroom, Salome turned on her computer. This would be a good time to transcribe the notes she'd made at the Twomey house and go through the photographs and choose those that were good enough to have made into slides. And after that, if she was still up for it, she'd concentrate on the feng shui of Simon Snow's house. It would be interesting to note if there were any similarities between Twomey's and Snow's despite the obvious differences. Which reminded her she hadn't taken pictures at Snow's, having had no film. At some point, she needed to return to remedy that.

*　　*　　*

AROUND TEN O'CLOCK SHE WENT BACK downstairs. Jude was in the basement at the computer, light from the monitor giving his black skin a futuristic blue tint.

"Got something for you." She set the bag from Mah's shop on the table.

He methodically removed the tissue paper and held the fierce-looking figurine at arm's length.

"It's Kwan Kung. He's a protector of policemen and even private investigators and will attract support from important people."

Jude set the figurine on the desk and made a face.

"Oh, and you needn't worry. He doesn't care if you're a Baptist or a Buddhist."

Jude just stared at the god.

"He stays," Salome declared and put the god on a shelf above the washer and dryer so he faced the front of the house.

"Well," she said, and slipped into one of the red leather chairs. "I guess we didn't get to have our little confab."

He pushed away from the computer and glanced at his watch. "We can talk tomorrow but I'm pretty well convinced Jett didn't kill Snow. He's a good kid."

"Seems to be."

"But he knows who did."

"How do you know?"

"It's a gift."

"Jude!"

"Experience, Salome. The best gift a detective can have. And, I agree with you about his usage of 'confirm' though I didn't confront him with it—I want him to trust me completely. He knew someone was coming by the day of the murder but I believe he didn't know the purpose. I suspect he left a key somewhere."

"Do you think he's in danger?"

"Let's just say he won't be seeing Chimene for a while."

"This is getting a little scary, Jude."

"Look, I've got to go to Baltimore in the morning. Would you mind talking to Meg Moran on your own?"

"No problem."

"Just don't blow it."

"Thanks for the vote of confidence."

"If you've got a minute I'll give you some background on the lady."

What he had amounted to about five minutes.

Salome stood up. Jude yawned.

"Well, don't stay up too late."

"Night, kiddo. And thanks for my new friend over there." He nodded toward Kwan Kung. "Right now I'll take all the help I can get."

Just before climbing into bed, Salome wrote a new prayer for Kwan Yin, something short and to the point. *Keep us all out of harm's way.*

Unfortunately, it was too late.

Chapter 15

❂

SALOME woke around seven filled with youthful exuberance. She didn't know why exactly but maybe it was the morning sun. One could analyze the sensation to the extent that it disappeared. Salome gratefully embraced such mornings, which, at her age, were no longer commonplace.

After showering and dressing in fresh jeans and a lightweight white blouse, she skipped downstairs, expecting Judah to be in the kitchen.

The house was quiet and Judah had already left, presumably for Baltimore. Surprisingly, coffee hadn't been made. But then, maybe she was already taking him for granted.

She fixed herself half a grapefruit and a bowl of cereal, further noting the absence of signs that Jude had eaten breakfast. She began to wonder if something was wrong, then decided she was overreacting to a simple break in his routine.

It was hours still until the noon appointment with Meg Moran. The second floor and the foyer still needed a thorough cleaning but she had no desire to stay inside. Salome decided to spend the morning paying her respects to the city.

While gathering her things, the previous night's mental note came to mind. After seeing Moran she'd head back over to Snow's to take pictures. Surely Jude wouldn't mind her letting herself into the house. And she'd met Carl the gardener. It wasn't like she was an intruder. Now all she had to do was find the keys.

Leaving her shoulder bag in the foyer, she went down to the basement. In the top drawer of the desk she found the keys and, ignoring a little twinge of guilt, set out.

IF YOU KNEW HOW TO LOOK FOR IT, YOU could see ch'i in action everywhere. And springtime in the District provided the perfect stage, even on the subway.

She walked to the Foggy Bottom/GWU Metro station and there joined the crowds on the trains that streaked beneath the city streets. The sprightly ch'i of the freshly showered and dressed combined with their daze of recent waking, reminding her of watching lightning bugs on hazy summer evenings.

She got off at the Smithsonian stop and grabbed a cab to the Tidal Basin. There she began a slow saunter along the eastside path heading south toward the Jefferson Memorial, the Roosevelt Memorial on the opposite side. There was no wind. The surface of the water itself was an achingly beautiful piece of art reflecting the blue sky and millions of pink cherry blossoms. Salome's emotional energy escalated at the sight, this being one of her favorite scenes. But the perfection lasted only about two weeks, the peak period of the blooms only a few days. Apparently, she'd been lucky to be in town for the peak period. The newspapers, of course, would have all the information as tourists flocked to this spot annually. At least it was still too early for the crowds and she wandered on, her mind empty of all but the grandeur of the 3,700 cherry trees all performing the rites of spring in unison. It was Beethoven's Fifth for the eyes.

The cherry trees were originally a gift from the mayor of Tokyo, shipped to Washington in 1912. There had been a shipment in 1910 but those trees were infested with insects and President Taft ordered them destroyed. The most common were the Yoshino trees of which Salome had one in her back garden. The National Capital Parks Central tree crew took care of the trees, and it was illegal to pick a blossom.

Like a tourist herself, Salome had been making the pilgrimage for over twenty years. Salome was an American, of course, born and bred in California. But it was here, at this time of year that she felt a strong spiritual link with her Japanese ancestors. Her mother had never come to Washington, had never seen this sight, and never wanted to. She and her parents and siblings had been interred in Poston, Arizona, from 1942 to 1945, and at the camp her parents had died. Though she, too, was American, born in the United States, Satomi Waterhouse had never quite forgiven the government for what they'd done to Japanese-American citizens.

Momentarily overcome with emotion, Salome hurried to a nearby bench and sat down. She daubed her eyes with a linen handkerchief brought purposefully for the occasion. She always shed tears, wanting so much for her mother to see this place, to feel its inspirational power.

Finally, she took a deep breath, thanked the spirits for allowing her to commune with them, then made her way to her second favorite place in the District to recover the morning's good humor.

The Albert Einstein Memorial was located behind thick hedges on Constitution Avenue near the National Academy of Sciences and Engineering, between Twenty-second and Twenty-first Street, in the knowledge and spirituality gua of the plot—which always gave her a thrill when she thought about it.

With the disingenuous ease of a child or an old friend come to call, Salome climbed up into Albert's lap, seating herself on the thick bronze thigh. An open book permanently occupied his other thigh. His pose was relaxed, the bronze sculpted so his clothes and face appeared wrinkled, the statue centered on three wide and curving steps. Across from him were benches, and the overall impression was intimate and conversational. There was nothing stuffy or remote and one didn't hold the great man in awe as one did Lincoln at his memorial just across Constitution Avenue. Here visitors felt playful.

"Well," she began, "you'll never guess what's been happening. . . ."

The Memorial was not on the beaten track and it was some time before a gang of kids who immediately began crawling all over the statue interrupted her.

She took a cab back to Georgetown. At one of the many upscale cafés, she enjoyed a light meal, and a little before noon, went back to the row houses. On the way, she reviewed the information Jude had supplied about Maureen "Meg" Moran.

Meg was married to the president of a media conglomerate headquartered in New York City. They owned an apartment on Fifth Avenue, but Meg preferred to live in Washington. Since Washington social life normally occurred during the week, she usually spent weekends with her husband in New York. From what Judah had learned, the arrangement seemed to suit the couple, separation being the secret to their happy union.

Meg opened the door.

What a formidable combination, Salome thought after introducing herself, not just considering Meg Moran's looks and money but Meg and Kendall together. Where Kendall was pale, Meg was tanned. She probably vacationed during the winter in the Caribbean, a popular destination for those on the eastern seaboard. She was older than Kendall, in her forties. Her hair was brindled, a striking combination of coppery red with white streaks, cut short. She wore fashionable, slightly flared black hip huggers and a white knit top. The band of flesh belting her middle told Salome that she spent a lot of time at the gym. Her exposed belly button, an outie, sported the tattoo of a coiled snake and made the loudest fashion statement, one that spoke even when she was naked.

"Where's Detective Freeman?" She seemed disappointed to find Salome alone.

"Last minute change in plans."

"All right then. I'll show you the scene of the crime."

Unlike Kendall, Meg eschewed antiques and embraced color and contemporary furnishings—at least downstairs, for Meg did not take her upstairs. Salome could think of no reason to ask to see the upper floors unless she decided to introduce feng shui at some point. For now, she had to read what she could from the bright splashes of red and yellow in the living room and then the photograph-filled corridor through which they passed on the way to the back of the house.

At the end of the corridor, the open door provided the first impression of the room in which Meg had so incautiously kept her jewelry.

Greeting them was the Mad Hatter, the bucktoothed rabbit from Lewis Carroll's *Alice's Adventures in Wonderland.* At a height of about six feet, he'd been painted with a sly expression, bowing slightly, his left arm extended in a sweeping pose of invitation.

"Would you leave your shoes at the door," Meg said over her shoulder as she entered. She herself was barefoot.

They trod upon thick sheepskin rugs in the large, windowless space. A Jacuzzi dominated the room from its central position. On a stainless steel cart beside the tub was a set of headphones and a remote control device. Built into the interior wall was a stereo system, the cord to the headphones snaking underneath the off-white rugs.

Above the tub was a chandelier made of multicolored crystals. Determining the head of the tub by the location of the headphones, Salome could see that while listening to music Meg would face a mural of the tea party the Mad Hatter was hosting. In her blue dress and pinafore was Alice. Here though, she'd been painted with Meg's oval face, full lips, and large black eyes. Disconcertingly, the eyes were all pupil. In fact, all the guests at the long table had the same dilated eyes. Alice poured tea. Guests had a cup and saucer as well as a personal sugar bowl on the table in front of them and each held a spoon. There were lots of spoons on the table.

"Interesting variation of the tea party," Salome commented.

Meg stood to one side, her arms crossed at her chest. She gave her guest a humorless, on-again, off-again smile. The telegraphed message seemed to say: *Yes, I know. What was I thinking?!*

"Simon Snow painted the mural?" Salome asked to get the conversation rolling.

"We *discussed* the mural. He designed the bathroom. I did the painting. He didn't like the idea. I didn't like his suggestions—you know, warm rustic scenes of Tuscany. That sort of thing. But it's my private bathroom. I didn't see any problem at all. He was just being politically correct. Believe me, I never imagined that the police would ever set foot in here."

"And the safe?" Salome prompted.

"Why don't you figure out where it is? I'll give you a couple of minutes. Would you like anything to drink? And please, don't ask for Coke. It's just not funny at the moment." She started to leave.

"I really don't need anything to drink," Salome mumbled while looking carefully around the room, not distracted by the mural or Meg, for that matter.

After a few minutes, she moved over to the stereo system. She pulled out a component nineteen inches wide, standard rack size. She found the keypad beneath a concealed hatch of thin metal.

"How'd you know? Shit. You went right to it!" Meg exclaimed.

"You don't need two tuners," Salome replied evenly. "And, the SOC techs—scene of crime technicians—were a little sloppy." She kneeled down and pointed out a dark smudge on the edge of the rug. Such things rarely escaped the keen eye of a dedicated cleaning person. "Fingerprint powder."

She got to her feet. "With luck I picked the right tuner. And, I figured there's a window behind the mural which you had to cover with plasterboard. So you couldn't hide it there."

"I'm impressed," Meg said weakly.

"Did Snow suggest the tuner or was this another of your ideas?"

"I think it was him but it wasn't the first choice. He thought a couple of the sugar bowls would be cute. But like you said, there's a window behind the mural."

"So how many people knew about it?"

"Me and Simon. Oh yeah, and my husband. But I had

to tell him. You see, some of that jewelry, well, it's, shall we say, very special."

"What about servants?"

"No one's allowed in here but me. I, uh, do the cleaning myself. While the maid's here I keep the door locked. Look, if you don't mind, let's finish this in the living room. I don't like to spend time in here anymore."

Salome collected her shoes and they headed back to the living room, Salome curious about the "special" nature of the safe's contents.

Meg's bottom had just made contact with the brilliant yellow sofa in the middle of the room when she dropped her head in her hands and began to sob.

Salome got up from the overstuffed red chair in which she'd just sat, skirted the slab of white marble that topped the coffee table and handed Meg her used linen handkerchief.

Meg daubed her eyes and nose, not noticing that the linen was already damp. A moment later she managed a weak smile, gripping the handkerchief as she would a lifeline. "I shouldn't be telling you this," she began, then sniffed and fidgeted for so long Salome finally said, "Tell me what?"

Salome felt certain her performance in the bathroom had insured Meg's confidence. Now it was just a matter of pulling out the information.

And, she was glad Jude wasn't here. He had no compassion for anyone involved with drugs—users, dealers, or anyone who condoned or promoted liberal sentencing. The artwork in the bath and Meg's unwise comment about the drink choice would have brought out Jude's hostility.

"Chaz told me not to tell the cops. But I can't help but think someone should know."

She stopped fidgeting. Her expression became determined. "Among the jewelry was a necklace of twenty perfect emeralds, each surrounded by diamonds, any one of which would be considered "important." She stopped and took a deep breath. "Supposedly it was a gift to Alexandra, wife of Czar Nicholas, stolen when the family was arrested, I think around 1917. Doesn't matter now. Anyway, when the Soviet Union collapsed, it was smuggled out of the country. My husband bought it from a Russian émigré in Brighton Beach who needed the money to pay off a loan shark. He was murdered shortly after. Not my husband, the poor bastard who sold it. I brought the necklace here to get it out of New York. Thing is Chaz thinks the murdered guy might have stolen it himself. Worse, from someone in the Russian mafia.

"You can see why I don't want the police to know. It would be too easy for word to get back to the Russians where it went."

"Do you mind telling me how much your husband paid for it?"

"Fifty thousand," she said without hesitation. "At auction it would go for much more and that's without mention of its provenance. When you add that to the equation, it could be worth an absolute fortune."

Salome suddenly realized she hadn't been breathing.

"Compared to the necklace, the other things that were stolen amount to nothing more that costume jewelry."

"Well, if the thief knows what he's got, he certainly won't try to fence it. Not here anyway. And I'm assuming your husband didn't make the purchase himself."

"Good God, no!"

"Does he often buy on the black market?"

"Does it matter?" She regarded Salome defiantly.

"Maybe. Look, Mrs. Moran, the thief could be someone he does business with. Could even be the middleman who physically carried out the transaction."

"From his end, Chaz is making discreet inquiries."

"What about Kendall?"

"Kendall? She doesn't know about the necklace."

"But she knew about your safe, right?"

"Not it's location. Though, God knows, you found it fast enough."

"Were you familiar with her safe?"

Her tan deepened. "In the pirate's crotch."

"She tell you?"

"Look, I *know* her. She's a close friend. She didn't have to tell me." Suddenly, Meg stood. "Do you think we could continue this another time? I need to get to the gym."

"Just a couple more questions, Mrs. Moran," Salome insisted. "Do you know of anyone who might have a reason to murder Simon Snow?"

"Not a soul. It's so bizarre! He's—he was—harmless."

"He knew about the safe. Did he know what was in it, the necklace in particular?"

"He knew what sort of jewelry I have, I mean, the safe had to be the right size. And I like to wear my jewelry. Kendall and I aren't like the rich old ladies who're petrified someone's going to break into their homes or mug them as they get out of their limousines. I'm fortunate to be wealthy and by God I'm going to enjoy it. So many people I know are simply imprisoned by their wealth. Not me. I won't live that way."

"The night of the robbery. What happened?"

"Kendall and I went to dinner. I think at the Four Seasons. Then we went to the concert at the Kennedy Center. Got home about eleven."

"Just quickly tell me what happened when you came home."

Suddenly, Meg Moran fell silent. She rubbed her mouth with her fingers. Finally, she stood up. "It's all in the police report. Look, I really have to be going."

But Salome had just had an idea. "Who knew the code to open the safe?"

Meg blinked. "Only Simon. No, his sister-in-law, too. He installed the safe, you see, but he got it from her. Everyone knows Ellen. She's run Simon's home security business for years. I trust her." She gave Salome a wan smile. "You see, we're just one big happy family."

"Do you think someone from that happy family let themselves into your house and stole your jewelry?" Salome asked just before they reached the door.

"No!"

"Does your husband know the code?"

"Well, yes."

"How did the thief gain entry?"

"I might have left the back door unlocked. Or maybe the maid did. It's never been a problem. I've never gone with the full security treatment—it's too much of a bother and I've always felt safe."

Salome handed over a slip of paper with Jude's cell phone number that she'd jotted down over lunch.

"If you think of anything, call Detective Freeman. Maybe you'll think of someone you showed around your new bathroom. Could be someone you thought was a friend. Know what I mean?"

"Sure," she said, moving quickly toward the door. "God. I can't believe I'm actually trusting private detectives! But if Elle says you're okay, I guess you are. But, please, don't go blabbing about the necklace—especially to Elle."

"Don't worry," Salome said, hoping to sound like Jude. "We're the good guys."

Once outside, Salome closed her eyes and breathed deeply and gratefully of the fresh air. Then, almost automatically, her eyes scoured the street, looking for anyone sitting in a parked car. Someone who might speak with a Russian accent. Her heart rate increased and fear actually accelerated her step.

When she put some distance between herself and Meg Moran's, Salome began to relax. Neither Kendall nor Meg wanted to talk about what happened *after* they discovered their jewelry was missing. Salome found that odd. Had they gone out again? She wished she knew the time they'd notified the police. Had they called each other? Called the police at the same time? Jude, she reasoned, probably had a copy of the police report or, if he didn't, soon would. The actions of the women after the fact might not be important, but still, she'd like answers to each question as it was raised.

Regarding the case from a feng shui angle, she found it interesting that Snow's bedroom and Kendall and Meg's remodeled bathrooms were all in the relationship guas of their respective houses. Salome wondered if all three had something going with the same person.

Some of the morning's earlier enthusiasm returned as she approached Snow's house. She felt strongly that those safes played a part in the mystery of his death.

She took pictures of the front walkway then concentrated on the recessed entry. Once inside, she again noted the absence of hostile energy and felt no fear being alone in the dead man's house.

In about ten minutes she'd finished a roll, mainly snapping pictures of his study and kitchen. Then she entered Jett's room and changed the film and took a few pictures.

Where she'd first been struck by the room's austerity she now saw it in terms of military precision, the quarters of a person who would do his duty. But to what or to whom? Where did his loyalty lie?

Now, too, she had another question about the photograph on the wall beside the bed, in the room's family/

health gua. Why hadn't Jett taken this family photo with him? She'd seen no family pictures in the Euclid Street apartment. Did he simply no longer want a reminder of their poverty, which he himself had escaped? Or was there a different reason? Perhaps, she mused, his family's circumstances had changed.

Upstairs, she padded down the hall toward the last bedroom on the left, her passage muffled by the thick carpet. The silence now became unnerving. She steadied herself by murmuring *om ma ni pad me om*. She didn't want to rush and maybe miss something.

Salome stopped at the door, recalling how the room had looked in the crime scene photos, thinking about Snow himself. His business relied on trust. He would never jeopardize that.

There had been no indications he'd been tortured for information; his neck had been neatly broken. As Jude had said, that took strength but she had thought of finesse, of the martial arts. With such skills, someone could snap a person's neck in an instant and without even breaking a sweat.

For a moment, she stared at that thirteen-thousand-dollar king-size bed, in and of itself a crime scene.

She raised the camera to her eye.

Click.

She turned and looked into the room across the hall. Here he'd moved all the old familiar bedroom furniture to make way for a change. She took a picture of the jumbled mess.

Click.

It was definitely bad feng shui having so much clutter in this, the helpful people gua of the house. She would have advised him to eliminate the clutter before he redecorated the other bedroom. But he'd been in a hurry.

She moved back across the hall and entered the bedroom to take a few pictures of the closet's interior: the closet, which served to store and sometimes hide things.

Click. Click.

Absently, she made a mental list: TV and video equipment, the empty shelves above, the pornographic videotape the police had found. What had Dario said? That he put videos from Snow's car into the office safe.

She returned to the hall and stood between the two rooms looking back and forth between them, something stirring in her brain.

Back and forth; one bedroom filled with castoffs, the other with the new.

Before and after.

"Before and after," she muttered. "Come on, Waterhouse, make the connection."

She raised the camera to take another picture, then noticed she'd used up the roll. She started to pull out a fresh roll when she flashed on Jamie trotting down the stairs at Fiona's. He'd been carrying a slide carousel. Then she thought of the pictures of the Twomey house she'd looked at last night, of those she'd set aside to be made into slides.

The burning sensation that always accompanied an "aha!" moment started on her arms as all the diverse bits crashed together resulting in one blinding moment of clarity. Out of chaos, enlightenment! Had her visit with Albert Einstein somehow stimulated the mental pockets where the images and information were held?

As Salome ran down the stairs and out of the house, it was all she could do to keep from shouting her discovery.

Chapter 16

VIDEOTAPES. Simon Snow had been murdered for his videotapes. Salome was sure of it.

Her shoulder bag banged against her side as she trotted down P Street and toward home, the scenario unfolding in her mind.

He probably enjoyed watching them in bed, seeing his own creativity at work in other people's houses. He made before-and-after tapes for his personal use just as Salome did, the difference being she used slides, and shared them with an audience. While working in someone's home he no doubt was left alone for large periods of time and could easily record the work's progress with no one the wiser. Salome felt certain Simon Snow didn't always receive permission to videotape the homes of his clients, particularly the rich and powerful, and particularly rooms in which personal items like expensive jewelry were kept.

She stopped for a moment and pulled out the bottle of water left over from yesterday, emptying the contents into her suddenly dry mouth. Then she moved on.

Without those tapes Snow wouldn't have been of much

use to a criminal. And lately, he'd started a trend with those bathroom murals. Possibly he'd even been imprudent enough to keep the codes to the safes with each tape, though that seemed to be a long shot. Still, he wouldn't expect anyone else to ever see the tapes. Perhaps he just kept a record for himself in his business files. The codes alone wouldn't do any good unless someone knew the location of the safes, which was why those tapes were so valuable.

And the pornographic tape, she felt certain, was simple misdirection.

She couldn't wait to tell Jude. It was mid-afternoon and hopefully he'd returned from Baltimore. If he hadn't, she'd give him a call.

When she reached the top of the Close, she spotted his blue Toyota. With a little cry of triumph, she dashed to the front door and bounded into the foyer.

And immediately heard sobbing. She set her purse on the oak chest and went into the living room.

Chimene sat in one of the blue club chairs, her head at her knees. From the adjoining chair, Cookie Freeman purred a mother's litany, "It'll be all right, baby. Don't you worry, now. . . ."

"Cookie! What's going on?" Instantly, she thought that Chimene had finally confessed to her mother that she'd stolen the linguist staff the night of the auction. But why here?

Cookie looked over just as Judah exited the kitchen carrying a tray of drinks, his expression grim.

"Hello? Would someone please tell me what's going on?"

Chimene jerked her head up. Her walnut-colored skin appeared leeched of color. Salome was shocked by her eyes. Instead of expressing emotion, they were vacant as if her spirit had floated away on the tears. She seemed to be operating purely on a physical level, that once all the tears were used up she'd collapse like an empty balloon.

Jude set the tray on the table.

"Jude'll tell you," Cookie said.

With his hand at Salome's elbow, Jude redirected Salome back toward the front door.

"Let's take a little walk, okay?"

Once outside, Jude seemed to relax a little, but then the emotion in the house was pretty overwhelming.

"Jett's in serious condition at Georgetown hospital. Broken bones, a concussion."

"Jeez Louise! A car accident?"

"In a sense. Hit and run in front of his apartment. A witness described the vehicle as a white florist's van with Metro Florist written on the side."

"You think it's the same one De La Cruz saw the day of the murder?"

He didn't commit either way. "Probably been dumped by now."

"When did this happen?"

"Last night, after he left here. He'd just parked his car and was crossing the street to his apartment when the van comes barreling out of nowhere. Press didn't get wind of it until around noon."

As they sauntered up the street, he said he'd been driving back from Baltimore when Chimene called him on his cell phone. She'd gotten the news from a neighbor when she went to Jett's after her classes.

Jude shook his head. "Can you believe it, she'd gone over there to break up with him." He sighed and they headed toward Prospect Street. Under other circumstances, they might have gone into The Tombs and talked over a cold beer.

"I picked her up and we went to the hospital. One good

thing—Diana Daye has provided him with excellent health insurance."

They'd stayed just long enough to learn the particulars of Jett's condition then Jude whisked Chimene out of there before any reporters found out she was Jett's girlfriend. Father and daughter arrived at Salome's about thirty minutes ago. He'd then called Cookie. It was when she saw her mother that Chimene finally broke down.

"Did she tell Cookie about the linguist staff?"

"Not yet."

"So what do you think about the hit and run?"

"Could be a warning. Someone probably knew Jett talked to me. Thing is, as long as he's a suspect there's no good reason to kill him. The driver was probably just overambitious."

"Unless whoever's behind all this doesn't want to give him any more money."

Jude stopped and frowned at her. "Where'd you get that idea?"

"Well, what you said last night about him knowing who did it. Your trip to Baltimore." Then she quickly filled him in about "borrowing" the key to Snow's house and letting herself in to take pictures and her impressions of Jett's room, the family photograph on the wall in particular.

Jude refrained from scolding her for taking the key.

"You see, I figure someone paid him to gain access to the house. He probably gave them a key or left it so it was easily found. Anyway, he used the money to move his family out of the old neighborhood. And the money paid for his silence."

"My, my," Jude mumbled.

"Anything you disagree with so far?"

"No."

"Are you ready for more?"

She told him about meeting Meg Moran and the safe in her bathroom, concluding with discovering the motive for Snow's murder after taking pictures upstairs.

"I know it, Jude! I feel it in my gut!" she cried. "Those videos would have essential information about the interiors of the homes of some of the wealthiest people in the area. A virtual gold mine for a burglar!"

He reached over and squeezed her shoulder. "Okay, okay. Let's head on back, now. I need to shower."

"What about Baltimore? What did you find?" she asked anxiously.

Jude gave her a tired smile. "You're right. Mrs. Malieu and family moved last week."

Back in the house, Salome went into the kitchen to make a cup of tea. A minute later Cookie appeared. She leaned against the doorjamb.

"You want a some tea?" Salome offered.

"Oh, no. I gotta get back to the restaurant. Make some arrangements for the evening. Jude and I are driving Chimene to my folks' place in Virginia Beach."

Salome turned away so Cookie wouldn't see her smile. Despite everything that was going on, she couldn't help but think that this would be Jude's chance to get back in Cookie's good graces.

"Weekend coming up, she won't miss but a day of school. We can pick her up Sunday night."

"Sounds like an excellent idea."

"Uh, Jude told me what Chimene said to you the other day. About you two having a thing going on."

"No big deal."

"Yes, it is. That girl needs to learn some respect. I just want you to know I appreciate what you're doing for him."

"I really haven't done anything, Cookie." She poured the hot water into the pot with loose leaves of Earl Grey.

Jude suddenly appeared behind Cookie.

"Speak of the devil," Salome said. She could see the strain on his face from the day's events—Jett's misfortune and Cookie's reappearance. The tension in his shoulders suggested that he was restraining himself from touching his wife. The man was in desperate need of a hug.

"Hey," he said. "You tell Salome about what you found?"

Cookie shook her head slowly and rolled her eyes, her expression changing to amusement. "Well, yesterday after lunch was over, I hopped in my car and drove to Thieves Market off Route One. I was looking for some furniture for the shelter. Honey, you will never guess what I found."

"What?" Incongruous as it may have been to associate the piece with the seedy Thieves Market in Northern Virginia, the emerald necklace Meg had described glittered in her mind's eye.

"If you're willing to take the time to look, you can find a treasure or two there. And I did. Furniture I recognized from when you and Gabe were married! Remember those stacked East Indian tables with some sort inlay?"

"You're joking?"

"I kid you not."

"Oh my God." Salome burst into laughter. After a moment, both Cookie and Jude were laughing, too. They all needed to vent some steam even if it was at Gabe's expense.

"Are you going to tell Gabe?" Salome asked Jude.

"Not me. No way. And you'd best keep your mouth shut, too. Funny, though, isn't it? Fits right in with what you said about his choice of names for the house."

"Whose idea do you suppose it was? Elle's or her mother's?"

"For Gabe's sake," Jude commented, "I hope it wasn't Elle's. If she could do something like that, she could do anything. Can you imagine?"

When Jude, Cookie, and Chimene left, Salome took her tea upstairs. It would be her first time at Tres Soeurs, one of Georgetown's grandest mansions. After such a full day, she looked forward to a change of pace in a place where crime would be as remote as Mars.

Or so she thought.

SALOME TOOK EXTRA CARE DRESSING PER Madame Wu's admonition that she dress her best. She decided on a black satin Chinese gown with a stiff Mandarin collar, tight bodice, short sleeves, and side slits from ankle to thigh. For jewelry she wore opera-length pink pearls, matching earrings and a ring with a large single pearl surrounded by seed pearls. She carried a scalloped clutch of red beads and draped a black Tibetan pashmina stole around her shoulders. She dressed her hair in braided loops secured to each side of her head and made up her face to emphasize her Asian features. Regarding herself in the mirror, she decided she looked elegantly professional.

At seven-thirty sharp, Timmons, Madame Wu's driver, rang the bell. He escorted her to the limousine and opened the passenger door. The person attached to the hand that reached out to help her into the backseat appeared as surprised by her as she was of him.

"Charles Wang," Madame Wu's nephew said in a voice that sounded professionally trained. "You must be Salome." He assessed her in a slow, cool manner as if deciding whether or not to buy.

She took in his appearance much more quickly, but then she wasn't in the market. He wore his hair in a

currently fashionable short cut. Huge brown eyes captured most of the real estate on his face. In contrast, his
nose and mouth seemed to be nothing more than accessories. He wore a black tuxedo with a red cumberbund.
Wearing red at the waist was very good for health. When
her parents became ill, she had made narrow waistbands
for each by braiding three lengths of red ribbon (thirty-
six inches for her mother, fifty-four inches for her father,
numbers that added up to nine, the "magic" number),
which they wore beneath their clothes. This "cure"
helped the body retain the strong ch'i necessary for good
health.

Wang looked to be in his mid-twenties and had the
confident, polished air of the financially successful. For
someone so young to be financially linked to Madame
Wu he must be a whiz kid.

"You're younger than I expected," he said bluntly,
which she attributed to her hairstyle, one that was both
flattering and youthful. Then he added enigmatically,
"But that's not a problem."

"What does my age have to do with anything?"

"Auntie Grace didn't tell you?"

"About what?"

"I'm in charge of publicity for *Madame Wu's House
of Wisdom*," he began, referring to Madame Wu's shop
and feng shui school in San Diego. "We're going to pro-
duce a series of hour-long videos called *The Bagua*. The
first one will be an overview of feng shui and the Bagua.
The remaining nine will cover each gua. I'll be doing the
voiceovers. And I'm co-producer."

"The idea is certainly timely."

"We're really excited. But we've got to get just the
right person and rather than using a professional actor
Auntie Grace wants an experienced practitioner." He
paused. "My aunt thinks you'd be perfect. So far, I'm

inclined to agree. You have the look. Of course, I'll have to see how you move. Have you done any acting?"

"At boring parties," she remarked offhandedly.

"This one might fit the bill."

"You're not suggesting I *perform* tonight," she said. "I'd rather have fun."

"I guess we'll just have to see. But I'd better warn you, I'll be watching. So, try not to feel self-conscious."

"Surely your reason for attending the party isn't to see whether or not I move like a wooden soldier."

He laughed. "Hardly. I'm here to look for financing. And you're just one of the selling points."

The drive from Malabar Close to the estate on the Potomac Palisades took a little under fifteen minutes. Early in the drive, just west of Key Bridge, they passed Three Sisters Islands, a Potomac landmark unrelated to their destination. In the 1970s the three rocks were going to be the foundation of a bridge and parkway that would have crossed Georgetown to ease traffic congestion. Fearful that the construction would sully Georgetown's historical integrity, the proposal had been shot down. The Three Sisters Islands served as a reminder of the stubborn nature of Georgetownettes (as Gabe referred to the residents) and their zeal for preservation.

Before they knew it, the limousine passed through a high gate and entered the grounds.

"My God," Salome exclaimed. As a part-time California resident, her impression was couched in concern for energy consumption and the cost, rather than the dazzling display of the tens of thousands of colored lights. From the air it must appear that some holiday was being celebrated in a small village.

Charles glanced out the window nonplussed. "So," he said, "don't be surprised if you catch me pointing you out to people. So try to act like a professional."

"No stripping or dancing on tables?" she said wryly.

In truth, she found the offer exciting. But a little flattery followed by instruction on behavior didn't sit well.

Timmons helped Salome from the car. She stood quietly and, ignoring Charles, stared at Tres Soeurs, French for "three sisters."

Both the shape and the location were perfectly suited to attract money. The house itself was in the shape of a magnet. It faced the river, thus drawing in the money energy. In the courtyard between the two wings were pots of flowers surrounding a central fountain. On passing, Salome noted the coins glittering on the mosaic-tiled bottom.

"Guess they'll never want for spare change," Charles observed.

A doorman collected the invitation and they entered a wide foyer of white Carrara marble that bridged the two wings. Salome wondered if dissention existed between the residents, as, though a money draw, the magnet shape did not bode well for domestic tranquility. A cloakroom was across from the wide entrance.

"So what is the occasion?" Salome asked.

"April McGann's birthday. And some sort of folly is going to be unveiled. So let's get on with it."

They needed no directions. The party was being held in the high-ceilinged conservatory in the right wing; all the glass and towering palms reminiscent of the 1920s, which, as Charles mentioned, was when the mansion had been gutted and rebuilt by the three daughters of a railroad tycoon after his death.

Salome knew a little about the family history, since it was part of Washington lore. Two of the daughters promptly dedicated their lives to lavish spending and dissipation. The third daughter was something of a mystery, a churchgoer who quietly kept the household together. It was even rumored that she was illegitimate and when her sisters died suddenly, that she had a hand in their deaths. Suspicion stemmed partly from the fact that she married one of the sister's paramours, also a dissolute whose life she turned around. Together they rebuilt the family fortune and had three daughters, April, May, and June, the current residents.

A pianist seated at a grand piano provided the music for what Salome estimated to be about two hundred guests and waiters; the latter, dressed in crisp white shirts, black bow ties, and black slacks, kept the former supplied with strawberries, chocolate truffles, and champagne.

Salome recognized a few of Washington's glitterati: the telegenic first lady and her wired Secret Service minders, a clutch of Georgetown hostesses who she often saw heading for lunch or shopping together on Wisconsin Avenue or M Street, a couple of cabinet members, a famous actress, and the remainder, well-shod behind-the-scenes power brokers.

"Lots of movers and shakers," Salome noted.

Charles viewed the older crowd. With youthful arrogance he quipped, "More shaking than moving."

Charles plucked a champagne flute from the tray of a passing waiter. "See you around," he said, then melted into the crowd.

Not being a fan of champagne, Salome headed for the bar set up in the back, appropriately, she thought, in the helpful people gua of the mansion itself, where she asked the barman for a club soda with a squeeze of lime.

"Salome!" the familiar voice declared.

Salome spun around, relieved to see her mentor, Grace Wu.

Grace was a tiny woman in her late seventies. Despite her age and gender, Grace carried herself like a young warlord. She wore a hand-painted shift of pearl-gray silk with matching stole. A necklace of star sapphires captured the swirled design in the dress. As usual, she wore her thick silver hair styled in a figure eight at the back of her head—eight being the money number.

"Madam Wu," Salome greeted with a certain restraint. Had they been alone, the two women would have hugged. In public, Madam Wu maintained physical distance. Anyone with experience in tai chi could actually feel the older woman's impenetrable wall of energy.

"You look wonderful," Salome whispered.

"As do you, my dear." Her's eyes glittered approvingly. "What lovely pearls." After a beat, she asked, "I take it you've talked to my nephew?"

While casually discussing the proposition, the two practitioners meandered toward the crowd, the music a relaxing accompaniment to what would be a hardworking evening for guests like Charles Wang.

Then the conversation turned to feng shui. "So, how was the consultation?" Salome asked.

"Limited to April's bedroom." Grace sighed, leaving the impression it had been something of an ordeal.

"My God, Salome. What a ghastly place. No wonder her love life's in ruins." She paused to sip her drink, water with a slice of lemon floating on the surface. Salome reflected that even something as innocuous as a glass of water appearing to be a thing of tranquil beauty in Madam Wu's hands.

"What were the problems?"

"Keep in mind that I'm sharing this with you in strict confidentiality!"

"Of course."

"But you need to know. I recommended you as her consultant since I'm retiring from private practice."

Salome tried to reign in a rising excitement. Automatically, she looked around with an eye to feng shuiing this and every other room in the mansion.

"Anyway. Where to start . . . first the heavy black furniture—and not an elegant hardwood like ebony. Even she didn't know what it was, only that one of her ancestors—clearly one of the many with too much money and too little taste—brought it over from Eastern Europe. The elaborately carved posters of the bed are huge, like totem poles, the figures grotesque demons. And perched on the top of each are hunched gargoyles. The only good thing that can be said about them is that they're looking out into the room. Protective sentinels, one could say . . . to give it a positive spin."

She shuddered, causing a little wave action in her glass. "The headboard was no better: a sort of frieze depicting an ancient battle. Can you imagine? Swords and spears right at her head each night? I mean, my God, the poison arrows! She said she never even noticed the headboard and when I asked about nightmares she said she never had them."

A waiter appeared with a bowl of strawberries and another of truffles on a silver tray. Smiling their thanks the two women helped themselves to chocolates. Madame Wu bit into hers and moaned in ecstasy. "Oh my, that's it, isn't it," she declared.

"In what part of the house is her bedroom located?" Salome asked after Grace had completed her pleasure with a sip of water.

"The third and top floor of the left wing—the *entire* left wing. Twenty-foot ceilings. I felt like a dwarf. It had once been a ballroom, so you can imagine. Heavy, worn Persian carpets in desperate need of deep cleaning strewn around the room. Of course, it would take a small army to move them—not to mention the furniture. However, she does have it partitioned by two magnificent Chinese screens."

For a brief moment Salome noted envy in her mentor's eyes. Then it abruptly disappeared.

"Anyway, she has a study at the front, facing the river. Lots of light and the furnishings are far less severe. Good ch'i circulating. A few problems—like a rickety table covered in her collection of paperweights and on the verge of collapse—but nothing major.

"But back to the bedroom. Completing the suite is an equally appalling armoire and bureau. And she has one of those floor mirrors that swing around—narrow and on a stand. Positioned at an angle to the bed—reflecting those demons and gargoyles right back at her." She lowered her voice momentarily. "Spending the night with her would be like visiting hell.

"She recently purchased a bloodred satin comforter—to give the bed, in her words, a sexy touch."

Grace stopped. She glanced off in the distance, shaking her head, clearly baffled by some people's concepts of what is sexy and attractive in the bedroom.

"So what is it she wants? What are her intentions?" Salome asked. Normally she wouldn't have asked. Practitioners did not discuss such deeply personal particulars except in a general way. But since Grace had recommended her, she had a need to know.

"Love. There's some new man in her life she's trying to impress. Can you imagine, all her wealth and she can't figure out something as basic as what it takes to attract a man. Actually, it's the wealth that's gotten in the way of common sense."

"Where is she?"

"Upstairs dressing. She plans to make an entrance when the folly's unveiled. I should say, she's fussing over what jewelry to wear. I couldn't believe it when she pulled this plastic shopping bag out from under the bed. Full of jewels! She'd taken everything out of the bank this morning. One necklace in particular nearly blinded me. It belonged to her mother, called The Three Sisters. On a chain of square-cut diamonds are an emerald, a ruby, and a diamond, each about forty carats. . . ."

At that moment, they were jostled by Kendall Wright and Meg Moran. To Salome's further surprise, Duncan Mah was sandwiched between them. Before anyone even spoke, the two women grabbed a waiter and exchanged empty tulip glasses for full ones. The women's demeanor suggested they'd exchanged many glasses already. Duncan held a half-full glass. Salome had the impression it was more a prop than anything. She sensed he wasn't much of drinker and that his flushed face was more the result of the attentions of his two companions who were attached to his flanks like suckerfish on a shark.

Apparently, whatever chasm the burglaries had created had been bridged and their friendship restored.

"And what might you be doing here?" Meg demanded. Of the two women, she was the bolder, not only in speech but dress. She wore a short, form-fitting, off-the-shoulder black cocktail dress, a plain platinum wedding band her only jewelry. Before Salome could answer, Meg extended a naked arm and grabbed Salome's pearls. "Pretty, pretty," she slurred. "I used to have some. Emphasis on the *used to*. Better quality, of course."

Just as Salome reached for Meg's hand, intending to remove it from her necklace and thus avoid what could be a scene involving seventy-five pearls bouncing on the hardwood floor, Kendall reached across Duncan's chest and swatted Meg's wrist.

"Stop it, Maureen!" She turned to Salome. "I'm sorry, Ms. Waterhouse. We've been out drowning our sorrows. A little too enthusiastically, I'm afraid." With the finesse of a diplomat, she then introduced Duncan.

Salome found herself in a delicate bind here, not certain it was a good idea for the two socialites to know she was actually a neighbor. She also didn't want Grace to know about her role in the investigation of Simon Snow's murder. In the past, Grace had protested Salome's involvement in the investigation into the murder of her tenant in California, saying that, as a feng shui practitioner, Salome shouldn't engage in such activities. This was the reason she hadn't and wouldn't tell Grace about the new project studying houses in which murder had been committed.

"This is Madam Wu."

Grace extended her hand. "Please, call me Grace."

"Oh my. You're the feng shui lady," Kendall said, slipping a glance at Meg to be sure she was behaving. "I've heard about you—I mean, who hasn't. Is that why you're here? Are you feng shuiing Tres Soeurs?"

"April and I are friends. But like everyone else, Salome and I are here simply to celebrate April's birthday."

"Don't tell me April's jewelry's been stolen," Meg slurred.

"Good heavens," Grace said. "Why on earth would you say that?"

"April as a rule doesn't socialize with private investigators," she snorted as if she'd been speaking of a life-form commonly associated with the pelagic depths of the sea.

Grace appeared puzzled.

Then Duncan added to the confusion, which this time included Kendall and Meg. "I trust you've found adequate accommodation for your car, *Ms.* Waterhouse."

"Yes, Mr. Mah, I have."

"Had I known our mutual destination was to be Tres

Soeurs I would have offered you a lift. And please, no need for formality. Call me Duncan."

Though drunk, Meg was still quick on the uptake. "Ah. You rented a parking space in Duncan's carriage house." Then she frowned. "Where the hell do you live?"

Duncan shrugged Meg off his arm and moved beside Grace, apparently wanting to distance himself from his drunken admirer. He began a conversation in Chinese, speaking rapidly but pleasantly. Madam Wu glanced quickly at Salome, sending a message of apology. She'd never been comfortable speaking Chinese in a group of English speakers. It was matter of politeness.

Meg spotted a waiter and headed toward him. Kendall smiled wanly at Salome. "I really am sorry. Meg's a little stressed out. Is Detective Freeman here, too?"

"No, he's not." She was relieved they'd gotten through this little episode with her pearls intact and her address still unknown.

Kendall's eyes widened and she spoke in the slow manner of the suddenly enlightened. "Oh, I know why you're here! It's the folly, isn't it!"

Salome smiled to cover her ignorance.

Then Kendall leaned close and whispered, "Did Simon include a safe?"

Salome blinked. Then it sunk in. Folly. The word Dario had seen on a videotape in Simon Snow's Aston Martin.

"For April's sake, I sure as hell hope not." Then Kendall swung her head around, the signature ponytail swaying with the movement. "Would you excuse me? I'd better see to Meg before she gets herself in trouble."

Duncan chatted in rapid Chinese. Salome wondered if he was explaining his family connection to Malabar Manor. Grace was now staring at him with uncharacteristic hostility but didn't switch to English to include Salome in the conversation.

Salome glanced around, her thoughts on a potential burglary right here at Tres Soeurs. She noticed the aged southern Democrat she'd last seen at Cookie's restaurant. He was popping strawberries and truffles into his large mouth. The same female aide who'd accompanied him to the auction stood alongside. Salome sipped her club soda and nearly choked as she saw the young woman surreptitiously drop several truffles into the pocket of her fashionable black jacket.

Then she heard Duncan say her last name followed by *"shui fong"* and a snicker.

At the same time, the music stopped and a bell began to ring. A man in a tuxedo standing on a chair bellowed, "Ladies and gentlemen. It's time for the unveiling. Please, if you'd follow me!"

"Ladies," Duncan said with a slight bow and slipped away.

"What did he just say about me?" Salome asked.

"It's nothing."

"Oh, come on, Grace," Salome said, slipping into a more informal mode.

Grace stiffened. "In Chinese Waterhouse translates to *shui fong*. It's also the colloquial name for Wo On Lok Triad. Moved from Hong Kong to Britain in 1984."

"Really? Does that make me an honorary member?"

"Don't even joke about it," Grace snapped. Though her voice was stern, in her eyes Salome saw a flicker of fear. "We must join the crowd now. Everyone's heading outside."

Grace grabbed Salome's hand and pulled her toward the nearest exit until a crowd clogging the French doors slowed their progress.

"I think Simon Snow was involved with the folly's

design," Salome mentioned, breathless at the thought of another burglary.

"Yes, he was. The details have been kept hush-hush, though. May and June's birthday gift to April. They even ordered her out of the house while the work was being done. She didn't go far though. Just over to their horse farm in Virginia. Didn't want to be too far from this man she's romancing."

"Who is he?"

"Maybe he'll be unveiled as well. I just hope he's not another of April's follies."

Chapter 17

ONCE everyone assembled in a semicircle around a structure hidden beneath a huge drop cloth, June Farquahar, the youngest sister of the birthday girl, addressed the group.

Grace had commandeered a place for them right in front using her elbows and voice, the latter sounding as if it came from a much larger person.

June, a blonde in her early fifties with a trim figure, swayed drunkenly as she declared, "We're so delighted all of you could share the happy occasion of our dear April's sixtieth birthday."

After a brief pause, June twittered, "Oh dear, I don't think I was supposed to mention the exact number, was I?"

A few snickers followed.

"There's some bad blood between them," Grace whispered. "Understandable, I suppose, when millions are concerned."

"So, without further ado, I present 'April's Folly'!"

On cue, floodlights were switched on, illuminating a

one-story red-and-white brick octagon with a castellated roof. Two narrow windows flanked the single door.

"April? Come out, darling, and officially accept your gift!"

There was a rustle like dried leaves in the wind as people looked around. Someone nearby said to a companion, "I haven't seen her all night. Have you?"

The companion answered with the shake of his head.

"Don't be shy, dear!"

Finally, June walked up to the door and started to open it. They could see her back tense and heard a rattling as she tried to open the door.

Looking a bit shamefaced, June turned around. "I'm afraid it's locked!" Under the scrutiny of the crowd, she tried each window, twice again unable to find a way in.

A man with a military bearing broke from the crowd and walked briskly up to June. Madame Wu informed Salome that he was June's husband, Barkely.

"Damn it, June!" Barkely hissed, loud enough for those crowded in front to hear. "Where's the god damn key?"

"Why not break a window?" someone called out.

So, with a tinkle of glass, Barkely did just that. He crawled through and a moment later opened the door from the inside.

Salome and Grace were among the first to enter the gloomy interior. Barkely, to his further consternation, couldn't find the light switch. June could be heard stumbling around, assuring her husband that the switch was "around here someplace."

A little light from the floods filtered through the door, and from the windows laid precise rectangles on the tile floor. Despite the gloom, people kept entering.

At the same moment Barkely's efforts finally met with success, there came a loud splash. The track lighting illuminated a fabulous mural covering the remaining five sections of the octagon. The muralist, presumably Simon Snow, had copied *La Grande Odalisque* by Ingres. The full-bodied nude figure gazed out over her shoulder wearing only three bracelets, her head turbaned and adorned with a jeweled pendant. For just a second or two, attention focused on the expanse of flesh reclining on a plush blue divan. Then reality, in the form of June, intervened. She sputtered and splashed in a rectangular crystal blue pool. Her scream pierced the eardrums of all those crowding the chamber. When the scream was repeated, the guests realized the *other* person in the pool was probably dead. The body swayed in the water as June thrashed about, yelling for her husband, and trying desperately to get out.

Finally she slopped over the lip onto the tiled floor. Her husband watched either in horror or fascination, not moving a muscle.

For a moment, the strange tableau seemed set in photographic fixer—the shocked guests, the immobile Barkely, June's terrified expression and awkward posture, and the body itself floating facedown, the once crisp white shirt and sharply creased black trousers now sodden.

Then, Salome saw a small door hanging open. It was located under the painted nude's right foot. Light glinted on something inside. When she saw the bottles, she realized what it was. A liquor cabinet!

Once Barkely finally moved, all the guests did, too, many retrieving cell phones to punch in 911 or, in some cases, the numbers of their media contacts.

As the water in the pool settled, Salome noticed the ribbons of blood snaking from the back of the dead man's head. Quickly assembling the pieces of this not-so-complicated puzzle, she reasoned that one of the waiters had come into the folly to burgle the safe. In all probability, he was the thief who'd stolen Kendall Wright's and Meg Moran's jewels and who somehow knew the combination to this safe but surely not its contents. Which brought up the question of who had bashed his head in?

Amid all the chatter and shouts a single word appeared in her brain: *Misdirection!*

Salome glanced down at her companion. Madame Wu's face was pale and she seemed to be having trouble breathing in the heavy, damp air. "Let's get you outside," she said.

Salome plowed through the milling crowd. More people from outside were trying to get in than people from the inside trying to get out. She collided with a man holding a camcorder who didn't even stop to apologize, just stormed on through.

Half dragging Grace toward some lawn furniture, Salome could already hear sirens in the near distance. She gratefully inhaled the fresh air. As they headed through the thick grass toward the main house, a number of waiters ran toward the folly to join the swarm.

"You stay here," Salome advised her mentor after sitting her down in a white wrought-iron lawn chair. "Take a few deep breaths." Then she put her own pashmina stole around Grace's shoulders to protect her from a chill and set her beaded clutch beside the chair.

Remembering where Grace had said April's bedroom was located, Salome ran back into the mansion, through the conservatory, and across the marble foyer. The house seemed to have been evacuated of both guests and servants alike. Even the woman who had been in the cloakroom was gone.

Salome dashed up a wide staircase, her footsteps muffled by the forest green carpeting. At the landing she turned and, hardly breaking stride, continued until she reached the third and top floor. Even with the sirens now blaring as the police breached the estate, she could hear a low moan. Of course her senses were on alert, and had been since she realized what was happening just moments ago. Still, she hoped she wasn't too late.

A pair of tall Directoire doors were open. She could just make out a body on the floor near the bottom portion of an enormous bed, the two posters the size of tree trunks. And bending over the body, back to the door, was a small figure dressed in black and wearing some sort of cap.

Without a thought, Salome ran into the room and tackled the figure. The person screamed in surprise and rage and the two of them rolled over onto the floor. Salome grabbed and kicked, her slit skirt allowing her legs freedom of movement. But she was no match for her agile opponent who was, fortunately, more interested in getting away than doing harm. Salome clutched at the cap and pulled it off. Long black hair immediately fell like a curtain over Salome's face. She started to grab a hank when the figure darted away. Stunned, Salome staggered to her feet, realizing she'd lost a shoe. The figure ran back to the body and swept up a large white plastic bag from the floor, then ran toward the study at the front of the vast room.

Kicking off her other shoe, Salome gave chase, following the swiftly moving figure now silhouetted against the ambient light from the outdoor display. Then the thief disappeared behind one of the tall Chinese screens Madame Wu had described. As Salome ran past the screen, she was suddenly stopped by a high kick to her head. Instantly time slowed and she seemed suspended in midair, her arms thrown wide. Then, just before she fell to the floor, she saw her attacker's face. It was the young

Chinese girl from Mah's shop on Wisconsin Avenue. She glanced at Salome to be certain she'd stopped her pursuit then leaped over a coffee table and disappeared through an open window into the trees.

Salome dropped to the floor, one of those dirty Persian carpets Grace had mentioned cushioning the impact.

Salome stared at the elaborate molding in the ceiling. Maybe a minute passed. Warm liquid trickled down both cheeks. She tasted metal and when she started to take a breath realized she couldn't breathe, at least through her nose. She rolled over and blood gushed from her mouth. Slowly she tried to push herself off the floor and at the same time heard someone enter the room.

"Oh my God! April, darling! Are you all right?"

Salome pulled herself across the carpet to the edge of the Chinese screen. She lifted her head and a pain like a blade of lightning shot from her nose to the back of her head. Her eyes watered. She pressed her lips shut to prevent any sound escaping, not wanting her presence to be known. Wiping her eyes, she peered out around the richly lacquered barrier. And at that moment would have traded her Healey for a camera.

Now she knew that the thief had been trying to remove a necklace from April McGann's neck. Salome's sudden intrusion had prevented it, but now the act was coming to a successful conclusion. The necklace came off and was dropped down the front of an expensive pair of trousers. In one swift movement, a pair of strong arms lifted the limp body of April McGann off the floor.

Out of the corner of her eye, Salome noticed the table holding April's collection of paperweights. With her remaining strength, Salome rose to her feet and grabbed the nearest one. Then, silently muttering a prayer, she hurled the crystal paperweight. It sailed the distance, all the way to just a foot or so before the open doorway.

And there it made contact, hitting the back of his head. He stopped. She could imagine the expression on his face. But he took a step forward. Blood poured from her nose and she was momentarily overcome by vertigo. As her legs started to give out, she uttered a little cry, for as she went down, so too did Duncan Mah.

"UNZIP HIS PANTS," SALOME ORDERED THE two police officers she'd found outside and lead upstairs to April's bedroom. On the way she'd related the details of her discovery of the thief and of Duncan Mah's entry into the room.

Mah had recovered his senses and was trying to raise himself off the floor, grimacing from the effort. The back of his white collar was soaked in blood. Hearing Salome's instruction to the cops, he managed a malefic stare that unleashed a whole quiver of poison arrows at her.

April McGann had also emerged from unconsciousness after being knocked senseless by the girl thief. She sat on the edge of the bed looking dazed.

"Believe me, that's where you'll find April's necklace," Salome continued, still queasy, a blood-soaked pillow in her hand, the one she'd grabbed off the bed on her way to find help. Her whole face felt numb. She hoped her nose wasn't broken.

Mah refused to undo his britches, the indignity apparently overpowering pain.

"Who is this crazy woman?" April finally managed, her tone imperious.

"Look, you need to get to the hospital," one of the officers said to Salome. He moved beside her and, taking her arm firmly, began to usher her out of the bedroom. "We'll take care of things here."

"My shoes—I lost them while chasing the thief!"

"Let's just get you downstairs. Someone will bring you your shoes."

Outside, the scene was one of semi-polite pandemonium. Many of the guests were indignant at being detained, believing that their name/position/financial status allowed *them* to determine when and where they would be questioned—if at all. Naturally enough, the First Lady was long gone, having been whisked away just moments after June screamed in the folly's pool. The others weren't so privileged.

"My friend needs attention, too," Salome said to the policeman as he led her toward one of the ambulances. "She's an elderly woman and I think she might be in shock."

"You know where she is?" he asked, frowning at the crowd.

"I'm pretty sure I do."

"Look, you go get her and I'll sign you off for an ambulance. Okay?"

"Officer, don't let Duncan Mah out of your sight!"

"Just make sure you get over to the precinct and give a statement ASAP. Something tells me that woman you claim was robbed isn't going to press charges."

Salome found Madame Wu in the same seat, her nephew standing nearby, his face pressed flat by boredom. Ladies in stages of distress and excitement occupied the remaining lawn furniture, protectively clutching their necklaces and other pieces of jewelry. Crime scene tape already fenced April's folly.

"Oh, my dear! What happened to you?" Grace gasped.

"I'll tell you later."

"That looks bad! If your nose is broken we probably won't be able to use you in the videos," Charles Wang prattled.

"Shut up, Charles!" Grace snapped and rose from her chair.

Charles immediately slid into the vacated seat, pouting like an adolescent.

"Come with me, Grace," Salome said and grabbed her clutch from the grass. As they moved away from Charles, she whispered, "We're getting out of here."

GRACE HAD A TEN-MILLIMETER FACETED CRYS-tal on a nine-inch red cord in her handbag. She pulled it out when Salome presented herself at the desk in the emergency room at Georgetown University Hospital. It was early yet—for emergency rooms—and only about a dozen people waited. Maybe it was the energy directed from Madame Wu and her swinging crystal, or maybe it was just the sight of all that blood on Salome's face and neck and on the pillow, which she didn't hesitate to wave around, but she was x-rayed (no breaks), stitched, and dismissed all in under an hour.

Grace looked exhausted. Even though Salome's house was only a few blocks away, she directed the cab driver to Grace's graceful old mansion off Dupont Circle first. The driver courteously helped Grace inside.

Once back home, Salome stripped off the blood-soaked gown and showered. While examining the unat-tractive stitches she recalled another day a little over a year ago when she was doing exactly the same thing, only that time the stitches were up on her forehead where a pale scar now disappeared into the hairline. Then, too, her involvement in a murder investigation resulted in a head injury. *Is this becoming a pattern?* she asked herself glumly.

*   *   *

BOTH JUDE AND HIS CAR WERE STILL GONE
the next morning when she left for the local precinct to
give her statement. She would have liked to discuss last
night's events with him but hoped that he and Cookie
had decided to stay the weekend in Virginia Beach.

The station house was a hive of activity, no doubt due
to the robbery/homicide at Tres Soeurs. She recognized
a number of people from last night's party, though their
expressions were presently less than congenial. Like Madame Wu the previous night, Salome discreetly carried a
small crystal on a nine-inch red ribbon. Emanating
strong, positive energy in a place where the negative pre-
vailed served her well. She was immediately escorted to
the desk of a clerk, her statement taken and before she
knew it, she was on her way home. Admittedly, the
black/purple eyes peering above the bandage across her
nose probably contributed to her speedy treatment.

Once home, Salome took Fiona's keys and let herself
into the back garden. She was determined to finish feng
shuiing so, carrying a cardboard box, she entered the
greenhouse to collect her plants that would spend the next
six months raising the ch'i in her landing library.

The air was warm and humid, but not unpleasant—at
least to someone who didn't mind the atmosphere of
greenhouses. Unfortunately, Salome was not one of those
people. No matter the placement, a greenhouse always
induced terror.

As she stepped on the soggy earth, moving toward her
plants, which sat on a shelf in the very back, her mind
filled with images of giant pods beginning to split, re-
leasing a bubbling slime. Her heart began to race and
breathing became increasingly difficult. Now she saw the
bodies, the featureless forms the pods were birthing.

What the shower scene in *Psycho* was to some, the
greenhouse scenes in *Invasion of the Body Snatchers*

were to Salome. Just a kid when she saw the original
movie made from Jack Finney's book, the frightful images and the concept that all friends and family members
were being replaced by aliens had burrowed deep into
her psyche, leaving the strongest and longest impression
of any movie she'd ever seen.

By the time she began placing the pots on in the box,
she was close to hyperventilating and her vision was blur-
ring. And when the hand reached out and grabbed her
ankle, the pots went flying and she screamed in bloody
terror.

Chapter 18

"JESUS Christ, Salome! It's only me," Fiona Cockburn stammered, half stunned by Salome's reaction.

Salome stood frozen amidst the overturned pots spilling their soil on the worktable and grassy floor. When she saw Fiona crawl out from under one of the tables she couldn't decide whether to hug or attack her.

"You scared me to death," she finally managed.

"Well, I'm sorry! I slipped on the ladder and when I reached out—"

"What ladder?"

"Under the table. It is soooo cool. You want to see?"

"Just give me a minute to recover."

A moment later they were in a narrow tunnel heading south. The floor was littered with candy wrappers, empty soda cans, bags of chips, spent candles, boxes of kitchen matches, newspapers, stacks of yellow legal pads, pens, a bedroll, and a suitcase.

"You've been living down here?" Salome asked incredulously.

"Yeah. Spend the day down here and go out at night.

Actually, I've gotten a lot of writing done. But, you probably want to know why.

"While you were off feng shuiing the Midwest, I continued to follow Duncan Mah around. One night I went to the carriage house to get my car and the next thing I woke up on the ground. My money and camera had been stolen. But I knew who was behind it. It was supposed to look like some junkie had robbed me but a junkie would have taken the purse and not hung around to empty my wallet. Anyway, I knew it was time to boogie.

"Fortunately, I'd exchanged the exposed film for a new cartridge. I decided to take the film to your house but I didn't want it to be too easy to find in case he decided to take an interest in you and your house."

"So what is this place?"

"Remember that print of Malabar Close Isabelle left me?"

"You hung it above the mantel."

"Right. Well, on the back was a diagram of the tunnels Whitfield Malabar built. He'd planned an entire system that connected each house and went down to the Potomac but only managed two before he died: one to my house and one to the Richmans' place. His paramour lived in my house so they were able to meet with no one the wiser.

"I had no clue it existed. The greenhouse has been here forever and I'm sure the people who sold me the house didn't know about the tunnel, otherwise they'd have told me. But then again, maybe not.

"I took the print down intending to have it reframed. That's when I discovered the diagram. Anyway, I kept it down here with me—wouldn't want that diagram to get in the wrong hands!"

She switched on a flashlight and moved a few paces ahead. After a minute they came to the end, to a door in the wall. The print was propped nearby. "It opens into the wine cellar. The other side is made to look like the rest of the interior wall. The door opens into a full rack of wine."

"Wow," Salome muttered. "Did you go into the manor house?"

"Are you kidding? I'm not that crazy. I did manage to get the door open but I was afraid of breaking a bottle and attracting attention. Not that it mattered. To my knowledge, no one goes down there. I never heard anyone."

Fiona turned the flashlight on Salome. "Jesus. You look terrible! What the hell happened?"

"We can talk over breakfast. I haven't eaten yet and I'm starved."

They started back toward the ladder, Fiona lighting the way.

"What did you do about going to the bathroom?"

"Shit in a flowerpot. Is that bad feng shui?"

Salome laughed then abruptly stopped as a pain caromed inside her skull. Carefully she said, "I don't suppose it is. You can hide out in my house until you're comfortable in your own."

"Is it safe?" Fiona asked as they gathered Salome's plants and placed them in the box.

"Of course. Duncan Mah's in jail." Then she felt a little frisson of uncertainty. "At least I *think* he is."

BUT DUNCAN MAH WASN'T IN JAIL. ON THE midday news, April McGann spoke briefly to reporters about the previous night's ordeal. The necklace wasn't even mentioned though she said she felt certain the police would catch the jewel thief.

Fiona, now clean and scrubbed, sat with Salome in the

blue club chairs watching the broadcast. Earlier, while preparing breakfast, Salome poured out the details of all that had been happening beginning with her adventures at Tres Soeurs. Fiona had been keeping current through newspapers and a radio using headphones so no sound would give away her hiding place.

"I don't believe it! Duncan must have convinced McGann that he picked up her necklace after she'd been attacked. But why wouldn't she question the fact that he stuck it down the front of his pants? Anyone else would have dropped it in their pocket. Of course it would be more noticeable in his pocket," Salome said, her anger rising. "Damn uncomfortable, though."

"God, Salome. What if he decides to file charges against *you* for assault?"

Salome moaned; the thought had never crossed her mind. But a moment later, after April's astonishing declaration, another one did.

"Since you're all here," April announced suddenly and incongruously beaming. "I'll take this opportunity to announce my engagement to Mr. Duncan Mah."

Salome doubted she would be called on to feng shui Tres Soeurs anytime soon. Certainly not after beaning April McGann's fiancé.

OVER THE NEXT FEW DAYS, EVENTS BEGAN to congeal and set.

The girl thief and April McGann's plastic bag of jewels vanished completely. Despite Salome's statement that she'd recognized the girl, that she'd seen her at Mah's Chinese Arts and Antiquities, Betty Wong, the shop's manager, denied the girl's existence. When Salome heard this, she went to the shop to confront Wong only to find a new manager. All he would tell her was that Betty

Wong had been a visiting relative and had returned to China.

The identity of the dead waiter was never discovered; most likely he was an illegal alien, one of Mah's expendable minions. The caterer had never seen him and denied that the young man had been on his payroll. Apparently, he simply dressed the part and joined the party, and had been given a key to the folly. After being hit on the head with a liquor bottle, like Snow, his neck had been broken, the killer most likely the girl thief. A fitting death since it was later determined that he had killed Simon Snow.

The newspapers printed a police artist's drawing of his face. Carl the gardener immediately came forward and identified him as the person he'd seen driving the florist's van the day of Snow's murder. Further, the couple that witnessed the hit and run that nearly killed Jett Malieu said they recognized the dead waiter as the driver of the van.

Finally, a female film student bought two cartons of used videotapes at the Thieves Market, where Cookie had discovered Gabe's furniture for sale. She played a few of the tapes featuring the elaborate interiors of pricey residences, and would have taped over them but came across two that had footage of white cards on which were written a series of numbers, the cards placed in rooms in which murals had been painted. She immediately turned the tapes over to the police, feeling they might be related to the Simon Snow murder case. She was right, of course.

When questioned by police, the vendor who sold her the tapes said he found them in a dumpster he'd been scavenging in Alexandria. Prints taken from the tapes matched those of the dead waiter. And the prints taken from the porn tape and the linguist staff, among those previously unidentified, matched his as well.

*   *   *

JUDAH SPENT A NUMBER OF HOURS EACH
day camping out beside Jett Malieu's bed waiting for a
confession. But Jett stuck to the story that he'd bought
his mother and siblings a nice little place in North Car-
olina with money he'd saved from modeling.

"He's not going to change his story, Jude," Salome
said one evening over dinner. "His loyalty is to whomever provided the money that enabled his family to move.
Sure, Snow's killer's been determined and the heat's off
Jett. At least as far as the police are concerned. But
doesn't he realize that the person who paid him probably
wants him dead now? That person, of course, being Duncan Mah."

Finally Jude had come around to her way of thinking
and agreed that Duncan Mah was behind the recent robberies and homicides in Georgetown. Unfortunately, they
didn't have proof. And Jett wasn't talking. Possibly Chimene could have extracted the truth from him but she
was no longer interested in Jett—which suited Jude just
fine.

The family trip to Virginia Beach and back did not, as
Salome had hoped, result in reconciliation. Cookie wasn't
ready to take her husband back. Could be, Salome reasoned, Cookie simply wanted to see him on his feet and
if not happy, at least adjusted to "civilian" life.

The trip did result in a change in Chimene, one so
drastic that pod people and body snatchers came to Salome's mind. After returning to the District, Chimene
gave her landlord a month's notice, sold her sporty Miata,
and reacquainted herself with public transportation. She
would be moving into her mother's town house just south
of the Library of Congress. She also lined up a summer
job with an architectural firm. Summer weekends would

be spent at the battered women's shelter painting both the interior and exterior. She sent Salome a handwritten apology that sounded as if her mother had been standing over her shoulder dictating the message. No matter, Salome thought. At least Chimene was taking an active part in her own rehabilitation.

One afternoon Jude received a call from Meg Moran. They spoke on the phone for nearly an hour. After hanging up, Jude dispatched Salome to Washington's Reagan National Airport. She went to a gate where people were waiting for a flight to Miami. As soon as she spotted Meg and Meg spotted her, Salome did as instructed and, finding the nearest women's room, entered a stall. She sat on the toilet and waited. After a moment, a manila envelope appeared beside her right foot. Salome collected the envelope and returned to her house.

WHEN THEY WERE BOTH SEATED IN THE basement office, Jude opened the envelope and pulled out a stack of black-and-white eight-by-ten glossies.

"Jeez Louise," Salome muttered. The photographs had been taken while Meg was in bed with the now-dead Chinese waiter.

Jude sat back and related the details as told to him by Meg. After the police left her house the night of the burglary, she'd gone over to Duncan Mah's. They were lovers and she'd gone to him for comfort. However, she couldn't recall any details between having a drink with him in his living room and waking up in her own bed later that morning.

"She was drugged, of course," Jude said and the photographs taken to blackmail her. "She found them in her foyer a few hours after April McGann announced her engagement to Duncan Mah. She swears she's never seen the Chinese guy in the pictures. And Kendall knew about her affair with Duncan Mah. In fact, the three of them went out for drinks together a few times. She figures Mah got ahold of the keys to their row houses and made impressions during one of their evenings out. Meg entertained him in her bath."

"God. What a betrayal!"

Jude opened a drawer and pulled out another manila envelope. "This was delivered by messenger while you were at the airport."

This time he pulled out thick stacks of bills and dropped them on the table. "Five-thousand-dollar retainer. She wants Duncan Mah's head on a platter. So, my dear, it appears I'm in business again. And soon enough, you'll have your house to yourself again."

Then another piece of information came in over the grapevine, actually, through Elle. When April McGann arrived in Bermuda, her fiancé was not at the airport to meet her as he said he would be. She waited five days but still Duncan Mah didn't show. Nor had she been able to determine his whereabouts. His Jaguar was discovered in long-term parking at Dulles Airport, and soon after, it was determined that the car had been leased. But Duncan Mah, like the girl thief, seemed to have vanished. The police searched the manor house but nothing was found that might be a clue to his whereabouts.

One day, over lunch at The Tombs, Jude, Gabe, and Salome did what most people in the metro area were doing: speculating.

"According to my source," Salome began but wouldn't mention Madame Wu by name, "Mah was probably a *sh'e tau,* a triad functionary known as a snakehead. They're responsible for illegal Chinese immigrants. However, when he inherited Malabar Close, he saw it as a chance to establish his own network, his own little fiefdom. He brought a crew with him, a few immigrants having to pay off their travel expenses by being more or less slaves, and trained them as thieves and assassins. And they were probably chosen for having some skill in the martial arts."

"I bet he'll pop up again," Gabe said. "He's not likely to forget you anytime soon, Mei. From now on, you better watch your back." Then he looked off wistfully, "Sort of a Professor Moriarty to your Sherlock."

"Oh please!"

Jude added, "Don't forget Jett. But who knows, maybe his silence will protect him. Still, I don't think Mah'll come back to the District anytime soon. He'll start over somewhere else—and it's my job to track him down."

The following morning Fiona came over. It was just after nine o'clock and Jude was packing. Gabe would be arriving around noon to help move Jude out and into his new apartment with home office off Thomas Circle. As yet, no one had told Gabe where his old furniture ended up. Not wanting to interfere with his new marriage, Salome kept quiet. Jude, she figured, wasn't about to jeopardize a relationship with Elle, who had proved to be an excellent source. Maybe Gabe would find out on his own; a visit to his mother-in-law's house would do the trick.

"There's someone you have to meet. *Now.*"

"Now? I'm still in my robe."

"It won't take long."

A moment later, Fiona introduced Salome to Daniel Hathaway, the attorney who had been involved with settling Isabelle Malabar's estate and provided Fiona with the print of Malabar Close and the "sketchy" information about Duncan Mah.

When they were comfortably seated, Hathaway dropped his bomb.

"Duncan Mah is dead."

Momentarily stunned, Salome didn't know whether she should cheer or respond with subdued respect for the dead. "Well," she mumbled. Then with considerably more force she asked, "How soon can the fence be removed?"

Daniel Hathaway, his face pale, gave her a steely look. "If you'd let me finish . . . his body was found by hikers in a wooded area near San Francisco."

Salome glanced at Fiona. "That's where you said he was from, right? So he must have gone back—"

"Hold on, Salome! Let the man finish!" Fiona squeezed her arm.

"Thing is, Ms. Waterhouse, Duncan Mah's been dead since November."

Silence filled the room. Salome frowned, and then blinked, then unsure that she'd heard properly, blurted, "What did you say?"

"He's been dead since November. The person who moved into the manor house was not Duncan Mah. Around the time Duncan Mah was preparing to come to Washington, he was murdered and his identity taken by your neighbor, an imposter."

Salome shivered. That he could so easily slip into a dead man's skin made him seem even more evil, more dangerous. "So who is he?"

"At the moment, we're doing our best to find out." Hathaway sighed. "I don't have proof yet, but most likely, he is—or was—a member of a San Francisco triad. The San Francisco police have talked to certain members of the Chinese community. But they—the Chinese—deny any knowledge of this guy. Pretty much what you'd expect."

"Tell Salome your theory, Daniel," Fiona prompted.

"Personally, I think he's a rogue. He was probably gaining status in one of the San Francisco triads but wanted more. He heard about Duncan Mah's good fortune and saw it as an opportunity to establish his own base of operations. Wouldn't be much of a problem here in D.C. where there's minimal illegal activity among the Chinese."

Hathaway's theory buttressed that of Madame Wu. Salome said nothing but was beginning to believe her mentor knew far more than she was willing to tell. She recalled the conversation between Mah and Grace the night of the party, particularly Grace's fear and his arrogance.

"Anyway, he must have found out about Duncan Mah's body being found and quickly departed our fair shores."

"Can you trace him through the store on Wisconsin? And what about the other stores you said he owned in San Francisco, Montreal, and New York."

"A money trail is being followed, Fiona." Hathaway snorted as if Fiona had just accused him of not checking out every possibility. No doubt his sensibilities were tender. And he seemed to be a decent man.

"God. April McGann doesn't know how lucky she is!"

Hathaway checked his watch. "I need to be going. But I thought you should know as soon as possible."

"Thing is, Mah—the imposter—is too good-looking not to be noticed," Fiona said as they walked to her front door. "He won't be able to hide for long."

"Fiona. He's a con man! He knows exactly how to alter his appearance. Hell, he could bump into you and you wouldn't recognize him. All he has to do is change his hairstyle, the way he walks and dresses. In reality, he's probably nondescript-looking; someone who can easily blend into a crowd whenever he wants to."

Fiona looked both disappointed and unconvinced. She opened the door. "He was gorgeous."

As they stepped outside, Salome thought of the Richmans and Ruby Nelson. She had a feeling Ruby was going to be stuck with the bill for her cruise. And the Richmans, well, they'd be disappointed that their house hadn't really sold for double the price.

"What's going to happen to the manor house now?" Salome asked.

"Most likely put on the market. The Malabar family line ended with Duncan Mah."

"Look, I'm serious about that fence being removed." He frowned.

"It's important!"

"I'll see what I can do," he said and hurried off.

It was a lovely morning, the Close bathed in soft light, the air sweet with spring's own fragrance.

Fiona pointed to the side of Salome's house. "What the hell's that?"

"Ah!" Salome smiled. "A Bagua mirror. I hung it to send the poison arrows right back at Mah. It'll stay until the fence is gone."

Fiona put her hand to her chest and said breathlessly, "Bloody hell, Salome! It worked! Shot Mah right out of the Close."

"He should never have destroyed that rose garden."

AROUND ONE O'CLOCK SALOME AND JUDE gave each other a good-bye hug. Both Jude and Gabe had responded to the news about Duncan Mah with the same shock as she had. Gabe, of course, welcomed it as material for a new mystery. He seemed to perversely enjoy reminding Salome again that as long as Duncan Mah's imposter was at large, she'd better watch her back. As if she'd forgotten.

Finally, as the truck pulled away, she called out, "Remember, Jude, keep the toilet seat and lid down!"

Once they disappeared around the corner, she stood for a moment looking around the Close. There was one way to be certain the rose garden would be restored—and with it, the good ch'i. She could buy the manor house.

After a few minutes of deep thought, her eyes rested on the carriage house. She smiled. It was time to get her car back. Salome pulled the cell phone out of her pocket and punched in Dario's number.

While walking back into the house, she considered which toothbrush to pack.

Epilogue

☯

COMPARING Simon Snow's and Dwayne Twomey's houses, the murder houses, as she referred to them in her computer files, Salome found one common factor: the main entrances. From the buckled sidewalk to the dirty front door, Twomey's entrance problems were extensive. The approach to Snow's house, on the other hand, was pristine, beautiful, and displayed no problems attracting beneficial ch'i. However, the dark and shadowy recessed area around the door prevented the good ch'i from passing inside. It was a perfect breeding ground for powerfully destructive sha, primarily because of the lack of light. Had Salome been asked, she would have suggested installing bright lights beside the door, or, even better, tearing out the area altogether.

The other indicator of peril at Snow's residence was the position of the desk. With his back to the door, he left himself vulnerable in the extreme. So, she concluded, the primary factors working against Snow were his dark entrance and the position of his desk.

In the Twomey house the two things that pointed to

destruction and created very bad ch'i were unrelated to the overall neglect of the exterior and general poverty of the neighborhood. Both indicated severe personality disorders, which Salome discussed in a long email to Kayla Rudd.

Since the file of news clippings from the *Willard Beacon* had been in the stolen briefcase, Salome asked Willow to fax replacements. Like her sister, Willow possessed a highly curious nature and expanded the request. She included stories from the *Houston Post* and smaller alternative newspapers in the area. This increased Salome's information base enormously, especially concerning the two victims. Kayla had done little more than report names, ages, and professions. Willow had gone even further and tracked down a couple of Dwayne Twomey's former tenants who underscored some of Salome's feng shui findings. Then Jude did some checking around and further filled out the lives of Dwayne Twomey and the two murder victims.

TO: Kayla
RE: MURDER HOUSE

Dear Kayla,
If you'll pull out the copy of the Bagua I faxed yesterday, it'll be easy for you to follow what the house reveals about Dwayne Twomey. But first off, some tips about selling the house:

1. Paint it yellow. For some reason yellow houses sell faster than others.

2. A cracked walkway leading toward the front door is a real no-no. Tear it out and substitute nine stepping-stones laid out in

a meandering pattern from the sidewalk to the front porch.

3. Place two pots of colorful aromatic flowers on the porch just above the steps on either side.

4. Get rid of the newspapers and junk mail on the table in the foyer. Put out a vase of fresh-cut flowers. Replace the burned-out bulb in the overhead light.

5. On the day you plan to show the house, bake bread in the downstairs kitchen. One of those ready-to-bake loaves from the freezer section in the grocery store will do the trick. What you want is the enticing, homey aroma. If you bake it downstairs, the scent will rise to the upstairs apartment.

That should do for starters. I realize that those interested in buying will know the house is a "fixer upper" and that painting the house is an expense Rudd Realty—or, I should say, Dwayne—may not want to incur. However, new paint can add a substantial amount to the selling price.

The Feng Shui of the Twomey House

One of the most disturbing aspects of the Twomey residence is revealed immediately upon entering the house. You told me Dwayne remodeled a couple of years ago and it was he who installed the two staircases curving up either side of the entry. Now, while he may see this as elegance, this feature strongly suggests a split personality. We already noted that any good ch'i entering the house rushes down the hall and out the back, which means that anyone living in the house has few opportunities in life. Too, that means there's nothing to balance the negative force of the split staircase.

Now let's move to the entrance of his apartment. What we see first are those mirrored tiles in the hall. While he probably got a good deal on them (as they are used downstairs as well) they indicate fragmentation wherever you find them. So, as soon as we enter the apartment, we find this extreme imbalance in the career gua. Mirrors are very powerful and need to be used carefully. Mirrored tiles should be avoided altogether.

Let's move to another revealing area of his apartment, the relationship gua, where we find the kitchen. If Dwayne has a weight problem, it's no coincidence. He has an intimate relationship with his refrigerator, the most costly and well-maintained object in the entire house. Further, the interior gleams and smells fresh and reveals that he has expensive taste for a person who depends on odd jobs for support: gourmet mustards, chutney, and cheeses; not a bottle of ketchup or a slice of Velveeta in sight. What do we find in the freezer compartment? Expensive cuts of beef and pork, all labeled and dated. He trusts the refrigerator to protect the object of his affection—food.

His bedroom supplies other clues about this man. Looking at the Bagua, we see his bed is in the children/creativity gua, the door (in helpful people)

252 · Denise Osborne

opening onto the bed's left side. This is not a good
placement as the energy entering the room bom-
bards the bed first thing. If he is not a light sleeper,
I'd say he's a restless one. Most revealing though
is the highboy opposite the bed in the family/health
gua. Notice the photographs. All are of his parents.
In the pictures themselves, neither parent is shown
to be more dominant. Both are either sitting or
standing side-by-side. In the pictures in which they
are looking at each other, they are smiling. In those
where their attention is directly ahead, on the un-
seen photographer, they appear more somber. Now
consider how high above the bed those photographs
are placed.

Every night before he goes to sleep, Dwayne sees
his parents looking down on him. And I don't believe the association here is of security or protection. They are literally *looking down* on their son,
passing judgment. Dwayne's parents appear to
have been close, a true unit, but who made Dwayne
feel like an outsider, someone who took away from
rather than enhanced their happiness. Both of them
stood together against him, leaving him without
any support. As a child, he probably worked hard
to gain the approval of not just one but both his
parents. It's doubtful he ever succeeded.

Dwayne has the power now, and has put things
right, at least in his own way. We see this from the
position of his bed *above* the apartment below.
What is there directly beneath his bed? The bed of
the tenant. Now then, note, too, that these two bedrooms are in the family/health gua of the house. I
don't think it's any coincidence that the two vic-

tims both stayed in that particular room downstairs.
They were not strangers to Dwayne, after all. As it
turned out, they were, in a sense, family. Here, I'll
add to your information about Carl Florence, Angela Gray, and, of course, Dwayne.

Did you notice those novels in Spanish in the fame/
reputation gua of Dwayne's living room? Well, he
was a Spanish speaker, as one would expect of
someone who had spent several years in Mexico.
Carl Florence, the musician and second murder victim, sang Spanish ballads at that bar where the kids
hang out. Angela Gray spoke Spanish to Hispanic
customers at the restaurant. A couple years before
Dwayne moved to Willard, he and Carl and Angela
robbed banks in Mexico. To shorten the story (for
more details you can exercise your investigative
skills), Carl and Angela were eventually caught and
did time. Dwayne disappeared with what amounted
to about a quarter of a million dollars. Eventually,
he made his way home to Willard, to his parents'
house, probably figuring it was a good place to hole
up. Now, I ask you, why would he go to Mexico,
where the Federales were looking for him, on a
vacation with his parents? But we'll get back to
that.

When they finally got out of jail, Angela and Carl
went looking for Dwayne. The trail led to Willard.
They each got jobs. Certainly their appearances had
changed. Angela had been barely out of high
school when she hooked up with the two guys, both
men in their early twenties. There is the possibility
Dwayne recognized them when they came to see
about a room. But he must have kept that to himself

otherwise it's not likely they would have stayed in
the house if they knew he knew who they were.
And from newspaper accounts I've read, they were
each tenants for about two weeks before they were
murdered. Other tenants of Dwayne said there's no
way they would have stayed in the room on the left
and that that was the one he always offered first.
The bricked-up fireplace and partition half covered
with those tiles put most people off. So why would
Angela and then Carl agree to stay in that very
room? My guess is they were looking for the
money and that bricked-up fireplace seemed a
likely place for it to be hidden. I recall noticing
two areas where the grout appeared newer. Chances
are they each attempted to remove the bricks and
when Dwayne discovered this he killed first Angela
and then Carl. Initially, I thought that might be
where he put the bodies of his parents but I've
since changed my mind. Those trees in the back
were still standing when they died. You said he
didn't remodel until a couple years ago. He bricked
up the fireplace then, when he no longer needed it,
having moved upstairs.

Possibly my suggestions for sprucing up the Twomey
house won't matter in the least if you find what I think
you will when you suggest to Clyde that he get a court
order to dig up the tomato garden. Because of all
those trees scattered around back, that patch was the
only place where he could dig deep enough without
being hampered by root systems. And he had no
worries about the bodies appearing after a heavy
rain. My brother-in-law saw to that when he diverted 'Dillo Creek. I think you'll find that Ruth
and J. T. Twomey didn't disappear in Mexico, but

are located in the relationship gua of the overall property.

He's probably been changing the money over time from pesos to dollars, a little here a little there, never in the same place. He might even have a Hispanic friend he pays to do the chore for him at the big banks in Houston. In the meantime, he has to keep it someplace. My feeling would be in the kitchen.

Finally, just to underscore my findings of a split personality, repeat his surname slowly.

Next time I visit Willow, I'll give you a call. Then again, maybe you'd prefer that I don't. Like I say to my clients, you can use my suggestions or not. I'm just the messenger, my medium being feng shui.

Blessings,
Salome Waterhouse

P.S. For the sake of your finances, I hope everyone's keeping the seat and lid of the toilet down! Remember, money is the magic word.

(Reply from Kayla Rudd)
Let me put it this way, since he moved to Willard, Dwayne's performed a public service by helping out his neighbors. I can't imagine what would have happened to those poor souls if Dwayne hadn't been around. How he conducts his personal life is nobody's business.

And, you're right. Don't call next time you come to Willard.

Kayla Rudd

P.S. The toilet seat and lid remain up. We're patriotic Americans and not about to change!

Several nights later, Willow called.

"What's up?"

"Police found two bodies under Dwayne Twomey's tomato plants."

"My goodness."

"Seems that they're Twomey's parents. Not only that, they found gobs of pesos hidden in the wall behind Dwayne's refrigerator."

"Was he arrested?"

"Oh yeah. And they're reopening the investigation of the two murders. Looks like Dwayne's not so innocent after all. It's sad. He was kind of like a local Robin Hood. When some of the old folks didn't have the money for food or medicine, he'd take care of it."

"How'd this come about?"

"Kayla's assistant at the *Beacon* read a recent email Kayla neglected to delete before she and Clyde left for a fishing trip in Colorado. Funny how things happen, isn't it, Mei? Something tells me Clyde's going to be out of work when he gets back.

"I'll keep all the newspaper accounts for you so you can fill out your case history."

"Thanks, Willow. Your efforts as much as anyone's helped determine facts that Kayla either overlooked or just omitted. Judah's database came up with the criminal backgrounds—information I find hard to believe Clyde Rudd couldn't find."

"Maintaining status quo, that's Clyde's dictum." Willow paused, then said, "You know, this project of yours could turn into something big. Why not write a book?"

Salome hadn't thought about a book. But why not? Of course it was early days yet, but with enough cases she could point to common factors, which, by using feng shui, could possibly *prevent* crime.

"There's no shortage of murders, Mei."

"Unfortunately."

"Or, for that matter, murder houses."